Praise for N.J. Walters's *Isaiah's Haven*

"The plot is an engrossing one, with hot love scenes and suspenseful action packed moments also. This is one of the best werewolf romances I have read this year."
~ *The Romance Studio*

"I love N.J. Walters' wolves. I fell in love with them in the first book of this series, *Alexandra's Legacy*, and *Isaiah's Haven* gave me another marvelous reading experience...A fantastic book for shifter fans -- do yourself a favor and grab a copy of your own."
~ *Long and Short Romance Reviews*

"...fast paced, action packed look into the world of werewolves and the hunters who seek to destroy them."
~ *Literary Nymphs Reviews*

Look for these titles by
N.J. Walters

Now Available:

The Jamesville Series
Discovering Dani
The Way Home
The Return of Patrick O'Rourke
The Seduction of Shamus O'Rourke
A Legal Affair
By the Book
Past Promises

The Legacy Series
Alexandra's Legacy
Isaiah's Haven
Legacy Found

Spells, Secrets and Seductions Series
A Touch of Magick

Isaiah's Haven

N.J. Walters

Samhain Publishing, Ltd.
577 Mulberry Street, Suite 1520
Macon, GA 31201
www.samhainpublishing.com

Isaiah's Haven
Copyright © 2011 by N.J. Walters
Print ISBN: 978-1-60928-175-5
Digital ISBN: 978-1-60928-148-9

Editing by Heidi Moore
Cover by Scott Carpenter

This book is a work of fiction. The names, characters, places, and incidents are products of the writer's imagination or have been used fictitiously and are not to be construed as real. Any resemblance to persons, living or dead, actual events, locale or organizations is entirely coincidental.

All Rights Are Reserved. No part of this book may be used or reproduced in any manner whatsoever without written permission, except in the case of brief quotations embodied in critical articles and reviews.

First Samhain Publishing, Ltd. electronic publication: August 2010
First Samhain Publishing, Ltd. print publication: July 2011

Dedication

This book is for all the readers who loved the Striker family as much as I do and asked for more. Thank you for embracing the Legacy series.

To my husband, who is my inspiration, I can't begin to tell you how much your love and support mean to me.

And thank you to my amazing editor for all your hard work and enthusiasm. You're one of a kind, Heidi.

Prologue

Meredith Cross closed her eyes and let the slow, sultry music swirl around her. It enveloped her like a lover, making her feel warm and safe. She opened her eyes and looked around Haven, the bar she owned and operated with her family. She'd done something good here. *They'd* done something good here.

She glanced toward the crowded bar area and smiled as her two sons—Michael and Benjamin—charmed the female patrons and kept the male ones under control as they doled out drinks. They both were big and strong and loyal. Sons any mother would be proud to call her own.

"Everything okay?"

Meredith turned and smiled at Hank. He was one of her four adopted children. They were her family, not by blood, but by choice. She loved them as fiercely as she did her biological children. Hank was built like a tank and kept his blond hair in a buzz cut. He'd been a soldier and looked the part. He was one tough sonofabitch, which made him an excellent bouncer and bartender. He was also her youngest son and, in many ways, a sensitive soul. "I'm fine."

He stared at her with his pale blue eyes. Most people would have been intimidated by his laser gaze. But not her. Reaching out, she patted his arm in a familiar caress. "Really."

He nodded, not looking convinced, but taking her at her

word. He returned to his post at the door, his large body moving gracefully for such a big man.

Meredith studied the room with its dark oak bar and cozy seating arrangement. The minuscule stage at the far end currently held a jazz quartet. Haven was known for its jazz, blues and folk music. They were an eclectic club and they liked it that way.

A door next to the bar area swung open and Neema strode out carrying a large tray filled with onion rings, fries, nachos and other pub snacks. The food wasn't fancy at Haven, but it was exceptionally good. A group of young men flirted with her adopted daughter as she served up their order. With her café au lait skin, short, curly black hair and expressive brown eyes, Neema attracted more than her share of male attention. Not that she noticed.

This was Meredith's home. She lived in an apartment upstairs. In fact, all of them lived in apartments above the bar. It was why she'd bought the building about twenty-five years ago when real estate prices had been cheap. She'd wanted a home for her family. It might have taken another dozen years or so of running before they'd settled here, but she'd always known the building and the city was waiting for them.

She rubbed the back of her neck, trying to dispel the restless feeling that had been haunting her these past few days. A sense of dread had been creeping up on her at odd moments. As hard as she tried, she couldn't rid herself of the sense that something was coming. And soon.

Shaking herself, she made her way over to the band just as they were finishing up a song. She knew them well and occasionally sang with them. Tonight was one of those nights. She wanted to sing, to lose herself in the music.

Whatever was coming, she could do nothing to change it.

All she could do was wait and protect her family as she'd always done.

The band began to play one of her favorite songs without her even having to ask. She let the familiar notes surround her and then she opened her mouth to sing.

Isaiah strode through the woods just beyond the family compound in Wolf Creek, North Carolina. This far out there were no artificial lights to be seen. The sky was awash with stars, the moon a silver sliver in the indigo sky.

He liked being alone. Disliked feeling hemmed in, whether it was physically or emotionally. So why had he agreed to travel to Chicago?

He paused by a large oak and calmly began to strip off his clothing. As he removed each piece, he folded it and tucked it safely beneath the tree. Not that there was much. He was only wearing a T-shirt, jeans, socks and sneakers. With each garment he removed, a layer of civilization was stripped away. Not that he was very civilized on the best of days.

Naked, he raised his arms above his head and let the cool night air surround him, caress his skin. With his metabolism, he was barely aware of the cold. It felt good. Refreshing.

This was what he loved more than anything. Being alone in the woods, unfettered. Why then was he headed to the city as a favor to his brother and sister-in-law?

"Because family comes first," he muttered. That was his Achilles heel. He might have abdicated his responsibilities to the pack, but he would never relinquish them with regards to his family. His four younger brothers and his new sister-in-law, Alexandra, were all that were important to him.

Shoving away all his misgivings about his upcoming trip, he threw himself into the change, embracing the other side of himself. His bones cracked as he fell forward on his hands. Bones lengthened. Fur grew thick, covering his skin in a soft, rich pelt in various shades of brown with patches of black.

When it was over, he stood on all fours, an enormous wolf, king of the forest. He tilted back his head and howled. A warning to all others in the area. This was his time and his swath of woods. He wanted no company.

His keen sense of smell scented only small game and the pungent smell of half-rotting leaves mixed with fresh pine. A fox scurried away off to his left. An owl hooted in the distance. The familiar feeling of joy filled him and he trotted off into the underbrush, gaining speed as he went.

Here he could let the human side of himself slip away, be buried under the instincts of the wolf. It was never truly gone, but in these moments he could simply be.

He jumped over a downed log and went under another, his lean, muscled body moving easily through the darkness. A lethal shadow. Running. Always running.

From who or what, he was never quite sure.

The restlessness that had plagued him most of his life had gotten worse since his brother had taken a mate. Life in the pack had changed. There had been death and betrayal and bloodshed. When the dust had settled a new pack alpha had emerged and his brother had claimed his mate.

Thoughts of Alex and his brother together made him smile when little else did these days. She was more than a match for Joshua. He was glad his brother was happy, but it had simply made the cavern of dissatisfaction growing within him even larger.

The wolf grew restless, so he suppressed all thoughts of the future and threw himself into the run. He was here at the moment, free and wild, and that was all that mattered.

Yet even here he couldn't quite shake the feeling something was coming. There was change on the wind. Whether it was good or bad, only time would tell.

Chapter One

Isaiah Striker prowled restlessly down the busy street. Cars and trucks drove by and the "L" rumbled off in the distance. People talked or yelled, depending on their purpose. The city was never quiet. That's what he hated the most. All the noise. It was enough to drive a man, or in this case a werewolf, mad.

His thoughts wandered as his long legs ate up the sidewalk. He noted the way women watched him with a combination of lust and fear in their eyes or the way men stared warily as he walked by. He was a big man, more feral than civilized. Humans might be far removed from the wilds of their ancestors, but their survival instincts were still there. When they sensed a predator in their midst they had brains enough to get out of the way.

Even now, he still wasn't quite certain how he'd ended up in Chicago. He'd needed to get away from his home in the hills of North Carolina, but being trapped in a crowded city wasn't exactly what he'd had in mind. As a wolf, he needed open space in which to run free. As a man, he wanted to be alone.

He cursed under his breath as he tried to ignore the stench of human body odor and garbage tinged with that of drugs, alcohol and perfume. His preternatural sense of smell was making the experience quite unpleasant. Occasionally, he'd catch a whiff of something quite wonderful wafting out from a restaurant as he passed by. His stomach growled in protest.

It had been hours since he'd eaten. He'd come to Chicago at his brother's request. One corner of his mouth turned up in a ghost of a smile. Who'd have thought his brother, Joshua, would be the first of them to be mated. As the eldest, Isaiah had grown up assuming it would be him. But that hadn't happened and wasn't likely to any time soon.

Female werewolves were scarce. The past hundred years had not been kind to their species. Children were far and few between and what children were born were mostly male. Add that to the infighting between packs and the paranormal bounty hunters who pursued them relentlessly and it was no wonder their kind was on the brink of extinction.

Which led him back to the reason why he was here—Alexandra, his new sister-in-law. She was a half-breed who'd been discovered and hunted as a potential mate by some, while others had sought to destroy her.

He rolled his shoulders and fisted his hands at his sides at the mere thought of anyone harming her. In the short time she'd been mated to his brother, he'd come to respect and like her.

She and her father, James LeVeau Riley, had left Chicago quickly. Isaiah was here to tie up loose ends and have their belongings shipped to the Wolf Creek pack compound back home. So far, all he'd been doing was watching the garage they'd called home to make certain no hunters or other wolf packs were still sniffing around. When he was certain all was clear, he'd make contact and start the process of moving their stuff to Wolf Creek. Another day or so. Maximum.

Once this responsibility was dealt with, he promised himself he'd take off on his own for a while. He'd been feeling even edgier than usual lately, not at home in his own skin. And he didn't like the sensation at all. He almost wished someone would pick a fight with him. It would be a good way to blow off some steam.

But a brawl with a human wouldn't be fair. He was many times stronger and faster than any normal male. It would also draw attention, which was the last thing he wanted.

His phone rang and he sighed as he reached into his pocket. "Yeah?" he answered, knowing who it was without even checking the display.

"How are things going?"

Isaiah stifled a sigh. His brother was turning into an old woman, worrying and nagging him. The thought made him grin. No one but him would dare think of Joshua in that way.

Joshua was Striker of the Wolf Creek pack. He was the enforcer, the judge, jury and, when necessary, the executioner. He was tough and ruthless. He did whatever had to be done to protect the pack.

The job should have been Isaiah's but he'd refused to accept it when their father had been killed. He owed his brother for taking over the responsibility he hadn't been able to. Besides which, he knew his brother loved him and worried about him so he bit back his acidic retort. "I'm fine."

There was a long silence on the other end of the line before Joshua finally spoke. "I know that's not true, but I appreciate you taking care of this for me. The pack is still in an uproar over everything that's happened and I can't be away right now."

"I'll handle it."

He heard a female voice in the background and Joshua added, "Alex adds her thanks too."

"It's no problem." He glanced around as the fine hairs on the back of his neck rose. Someone was watching him.

"You seen Damek yet?"

"I'm on my way there now. I'll call you tomorrow." He ended the call, slipped the phone into the back pocket of his jeans and continued down the street.

Isaiah glanced casually over his shoulder, scanning the area behind him. Moving quickly, he darted across the busy road, ignoring the blare of horns and the shouts that followed him. Thankfully, he was in the downtown area and it was busy. He kept walking, opening all of his senses as he tried to figure out where his pursuer was, which was impossible given the crowds.

The feeling faded after a while, leaving him to wonder if he was simply being paranoid. No one but his immediate family and his alpha knew where he was.

It was time to take care of some business. He headed toward the Fulton River District, following Joshua's directions. The area was a contradiction. Empty warehouses sat alongside million-dollar condos. It was easy to see that development was thriving in this section of the city.

His destination was one of the warehouses. He turned down a dimly lit alleyway. It wasn't late, but darkness was quickly descending on the city and its citizens were already seeking the mind-numbing distractions of booze, drugs and music that could be found in a multitude of clubs in the area. There was something for everyone from posh to seedy dive.

None of it interested him. He hated being surrounded by people. Closed inside a building. Still, duty called.

Isaiah ignored the short lineup and went straight to the closed iron door. He raised his fist and pounded on the thick panel.

The door opened and a bouncer eyed him with suspicion. The guy was about six-foot-eight and wore leather from head to toe. His bald head and scowling face were meant to intimidate.

Isaiah didn't give a shit. He wanted to complete his business and get out of here. "Damek."

The bouncer raised an eyebrow in question. "And you are?"

"Striker. Isaiah Striker."

The big guy sighed and rubbed his hand over his bald skull. "Another one, huh. I met your brother a while back. Come on in and wait."

No one in the line protested as Isaiah followed the bouncer inside. The heavy door slammed shut behind them and he had the sensation of being entombed. Not too far fetched, considering the club was owned by a vampire.

The music pounded around him, vibrating through the floor and into his body. A blast of heat hit him as he stepped down several steps and headed to the bar. Thankfully, it wasn't too crowded yet. But there were still way too many people for Isaiah's liking.

He pushed past the mass of writhing bodies on the dance floor, ignoring the way the men and women groped at one another. The club was aptly named Inhibitions, as anyone who entered seemed to lose theirs.

Isaiah leaned against the bar. The bartender eyed him but a word from the bouncer and he was left alone. Not that there was any peace or quiet to be found. The music, if you could call it that, was loud and obnoxious with little melody. It was pulse-pounding, fuck-me music, designed to whip all the patrons into a frenzy.

From the looks of things, it was working. He counted no less than four couples having sex, while about a half-dozen more were in various stages of undress. Two women trolled across the floor toward him. Both of them wore what he supposed passed for dresses, but looked more like shrunken Tshirts. The necklines dropped almost to their nipples and the hemlines covered their crotches. Barely.

"Hey, looking for some fun?" One of the ladies pushed up next to him, straddling one of his thighs and grinding her pussy against it. Her perfume filled his nostrils, making it hard for him to breathe. He set her aside.

"No."

"Ah, come on." The other woman pouted. She lifted his hand and placed it on one of her incredibly huge breasts. "I can do things to you that will blow your mind."

"I'm sure you can," he agreed, as he looked over her head, desperate to be away from this place.

The first woman, not to be outdone, grabbed his cock through his jeans and squeezed. "You're a big one, aren't you? Plenty to go around."

Isaiah had had enough. He gently disengaged from both women and headed to the short corridor beyond the bar with their soft complaints trailing behind him. He was done with waiting.

The bouncer met him just beyond the door to Damek's office and held it open. Isaiah stalked into the room, grateful when the door shut, closing out some of the grating noise and overwhelming smells.

"How the hell do you live here?" His preternatural senses told him the vampire was with him. Power pulsed all around him, potent and strong.

Laughter rose from the corner of the room and Damek strode forward—tall, dark-eyed and pale-skinned. "You get used to it. It does have benefits."

"If you say so," he muttered. Of course, Damek needed blood to survive. It was smart to keep your food source close.

Joshua had told him Damek was rumored to be almost a thousand years old. Isaiah had no idea if it was true and, at the moment, couldn't care less. He wanted out of here.

"It's good to see you again, my friend." Damek waved to the chair opposite his desk. "Sit."

They weren't friends and he wasn't sitting. They occasionally did favors for one another, but that was as far as it went. Werewolves and vampires were naturally suspicious around one another. But the survival of their respective species had pushed aside the natural boundaries that had kept them apart since the beginning of time.

The paranormal bounty hunters had given them a common foe, one that had made them reach out to one another in a way they wouldn't naturally do.

"I'll stand, if you don't mind." He wasn't exactly polite, but he didn't want to antagonize either.

"Very well. What can I do for you?"

Isaiah kept his hands loose by his sides and did his best to keep his guard up and his mind blank. He had no idea if Damek could read his mind or not. Keeping apart for so long meant neither species knew as much as they should about the other. It kept them all on edge.

Isaiah figured Damek probably enjoyed that.

"Just a courtesy call to let you know I was in the city." Damek was head vampire in Chicago. Isaiah didn't want problems with the local paranormals while he was here.

"Ah, I take it you're here to see to James LeVeau's belongings and, of course, those of his exceptionally beautiful daughter."

Isaiah growled. "Careful, vampire. That's my sister-in-law you're talking about."

Damek laughed. "So Joshua is as smart as I thought him. Good."

"I'm outta here." Isaiah made for the door, but stopped as power surged around him. He turned and glanced over his shoulder.

Damek shook his head. "You Strikers, you're so arrogant."

"And you're not," he countered.

The vampire smiled, this time showing his teeth. "Enjoy your stay in Chicago." Damek seemed to merge with the shadows, disappearing even from Isaiah's preternatural sight.

He didn't linger, but walked straight through the bar and out the door. Power clung to the place. No one knew if Damek was good or evil, but the sonofabitch sure was powerful. Not an enemy he'd want. The bastard would be relentless. You had to respect that.

The night air helped to cleanse the stench of the club from his skin, but nothing soothed the restlessness tugging at him.

He kept heading northward, ambling aimlessly and eventually hitting Wicker Park. He knew he should be going in the opposite direction, back to Riley's Garage on the South Side. But he didn't want to go back, not yet. He knew he wouldn't sleep so he might as well walk and enjoy the sights.

The city itself was vibrant and alive, filled with many different ethnic groups and economic levels. He'd seen homeless people and folks in limousines, those decked out in jeans and others in diamonds. The food and the nightlife were just as diverse. Maybe that's what he needed. Some good food and some decent music.

He wandered past a bar and a woman's voice drifted out on the cool October breeze. He froze, coming to a complete stop in the middle of the sidewalk. A guy bumped into him from behind and started to curse him, but one look at Isaiah's face and he quickly moved on.

Isaiah felt his entire body clench with need as the woman's low, sultry voice wrapped around him. Turning slowly, he stared at the outside of the small club. Haven, it was called. It was a typical older, three-story brick building with a business on the bottom and what looked to be apartments above it.

A sense of urgency filled him. An air of expectation swirled around him. Somehow he knew if he went inside this bar his life would be changed forever.

All the more reason to keep walking.

He whirled on one heel and strode in the opposite direction. About twenty feet away, he stopped.

"Fuck!"

The wolf inside him was howling, practically clawing at his skin to be free. His lungs couldn't take in enough air even though his chest was heaving. He raked his fingers through his hair and swore again.

His instincts would not be denied. Spinning around, he stalked back to the bar. He paused on the doorstep, took a deep breath and crossed over the threshold.

The bouncer on the door nodded at him as he passed. The guy was about six-one and built, his shoulders practically filling the doorway. His blond hair was buzzed off in a crew cut and his pale blue eyes missed nothing as he watched the door and the crowd within.

The light was dim, but that was no problem for Isaiah. With his preternatural sense of sight he could see easily. The smell of liquor and warm bodies mixed with the spice of sexual arousal, creating a heady perfume. He could also smell food, and it reminded him once again that he hadn't eaten in hours. His fast metabolism required him to eat several times more than a human male and he was running on empty.

He found an empty table for two in the far corner and sat with his back to the wall as he scoped out the place. The woman was no longer singing. No matter. He'd find her before he left here.

The place was crowded for a Thursday night. He could see only one other free table. Several couples were dancing to a bluesy number being played by a four-piece band that managed to fit on a tiny stage at the far end of the place. The bar dominated one wall with plenty of seating surrounding it. The bartender was a big guy who looked up when Isaiah's eyes landed on him. Their gazes met and held, neither of them backing down. The guy finally looked away when a woman walked up beside him and placed her hand on his arm.

And holy shit, what a woman. Isaiah was ninety years old. Still relatively young given his five-hundred-year lifespan. But in all those years, he'd never seen a woman like this one.

Even from a distance, he could tell she was tall. Long black hair fell like silk over one of her shoulders and didn't stop until it hit her waist. Her features were more striking than beautiful. Exotic. Strong. Her full lips were painted a deep red that all but begged a man to kiss them.

Isaiah's cock swelled in agreement, pushing against the zipper of his jeans. He hadn't been aroused this quickly since he's been a young male just coming into maturity.

"What can I get you?" He resented the perky female voice that shouted near his ear. He didn't want to stop staring at the woman standing behind the bar. It wasn't easy, but he managed to drag his eyes to the waitress standing by his table, tray tucked under her arm as she waited for his order. She was probably in her early twenties with tousled blonde curls and an open, friendly smile.

"Beer. Whatever's on tap." It didn't matter to him what it

was. His metabolism ensured he couldn't get drunk on it no matter how much he drank.

"Sure. Anything else?"

He was about to say no when his stomach growled again. "Is the kitchen still open?"

"Absolutely." She handed him a small menu even as she listed off several items. He ordered two double cheeseburgers and fries to take the edge off his hunger. She nodded and gave him another smile. "No problem. I'll be right back with your beer."

Isaiah reached out and snagged her wrist before she could get two steps. The waitress raised her eyebrow in question. He tugged her closer so he wouldn't have to shout. "Who is the woman behind the bar?"

The waitress glanced over toward the bar and then back at Isaiah. "That's Meredith. Meredith Cross. She owns the place."

Meredith. He let her name roll over his tongue as the waitress slipped away. He liked the sound of it.

A few minutes later, the waitress returned with his beer. He nodded and slipped her the money for his order and a generous tip. "What's your name?"

"Tammy."

"Thanks, Tammy. Keep the change."

Her eyes widened and she smiled. "Thanks."

Isaiah picked up the glass, rubbing his thumb over the condensation forming on the side. He sipped as he let his gaze wander around the small club. Meredith left the bar and disappeared into the back. His gut tensed, but he relaxed when she returned a few minutes later. She chatted to customers in an easy manner as she worked her way across the floor.

The whole place had a laid-back vibe that slowly eased the

tension out of him. Tammy returned with his food and set it on the table. Isaiah devoured all of it, even the pickles, which he really wasn't fond of, but he was too hungry to care. He was surprised by how good the burger tasted. When he was done, he pushed the empty plate aside and ordered another beer.

Meredith ran a smooth operation. Everyone did their job and well. He sat back in his chair and continued to watch her and everyone around her. The big guy behind the bar wasn't the only bruiser who worked for her. He noted another man working the far end of the bar. About six-four, he looked enough like the first bartender to be his brother.

A tall man with brown hair came from out back to ask Meredith something. She went up on her toes and kissed his cheek before he returned to wherever he'd come from.

Jealousy reared deep within him, dark and ugly. Why was she surrounded by all these men? On the one hand, he was glad she was well-protected. On the other, he felt like she belonged to him, was his to protect.

Which was crazy. He couldn't protect anyone. Hadn't he proven that when his sister had been kidnapped by paranormal bounty hunters thirty-five years ago? She'd only been fifteen, not yet a woman when they'd taken her. He'd been going for a run in the woods and she'd wanted to come with him. He hadn't wanted his baby sister tagging along with him so he'd told her no and taken off, not realizing until much later she'd tried to follow him.

He'd returned home later that day to find his sister missing, his mother shattered and his father and brothers all out hunting for her. What they'd discovered was grim. There had been no mistaking the stench of bounty hunters in the woods.

Isaiah had held himself responsible and made it his

mission in life to kill as many hunters as possible. He'd never found a trace of his sister though he'd searched for years. Eventually, the family had accepted that she'd been killed. They'd never been the same.

When the time had come for him to assume the mantle of Striker for his pack, he'd known he couldn't do it. He'd failed the one person who'd needed him the most—his sister. His loyalty was to her memory. He couldn't trust himself to put the welfare of the pack over that of his own family. He had four brothers left and now a sister-in-law. And he'd kill anyone who threatened them no matter what, even if that meant killing another member of his own pack.

Ever since the life-changing incident with his sister, Isaiah had felt apart from all of them, as though he no longer quite belonged. For a werewolf, the pack was everything. He felt more like an outcast, a loner, as time went on.

He shook off his bitter memories and took another sip of the now warm beer. He should leave and head back to watch the garage. In a day or two, he could start loading up the truck and head home.

The thought of being able to deliver Alex's stuff and then take off by himself for however long he wanted should have made him feel better. It didn't. He'd been alone for most of his life and liked it that way. He enjoyed his own company and didn't need anyone. But for the first time, he felt...lonely.

He shoved back his chair and got to his feet. This was stupid. He didn't know what the hell was wrong with him, but he didn't like it. It was time to leave this place and these strangers, including the alluring woman.

As though he'd conjured her from his thoughts, Meredith stepped up onto the stage. The dress she was wearing fell to her calves and shimmered in the spotlights. Two thin straps held up the top and the fabric molded two very fine breasts. The neckline dipped low, exposing quite a bit of cleavage. She was slender but curved in all the right places. Isaiah's fingers itched to dip into that neckline and tease the curves of her breasts.

The band stopped playing and the crowd clapped. She held up her hands and laughed. He felt that laugh all the way to the tips of his toes. Every muscle in his body tensed and his balls grew heavy.

"If you don't mind indulging me, I think I'll sing another song for you this evening."

The crowd went wild, hooting and stomping. From their reaction, Isaiah guessed this must be a normal occurrence. Meredith glanced at the band and nodded. They began to play a song he recognized. Then she opened her mouth and sang.

He sank back down onto his chair, mesmerized. It was the voice that had drawn him to the club in the first place. As if she was stroking him physically, his body responded to every note she sang. He didn't care about the words of the song, which were about a woman who wanted someone to watch over her. Although it was no hardship at all to watch her sing, all he cared about was the way her voice made him feel.

Aroused? Without a doubt. His cock was as hard as a steel post. He ached with wanting her. It was all too easy to imagine stripping off the form-fitting sparking blue dress she was wearing and kissing and licking every inch of her creamy skin.

Her long hair streamed down her back like a dark waterfall. He wanted that hair skimming over his naked body, her fingers wrapped around his engorged cock as she stroked him.

His large body shuddered as her voice continued to seduce him. Once he had her naked, he'd spread her legs wide and feast on her pussy until she screamed his name in pleasure. Then he'd fuck her until neither of them could remember their own name.

Sweat beaded on his forehead and trickled down his back. This was crazy, but there was no denying the pull he felt for this woman. He hadn't even met her, and he was already fantasizing about having her in his bed or against a wall or anywhere he could get her. He didn't care where it was just as long as he had her.

For all he knew, she belonged to one of the men who worked here. A low growl of warning slipped from him. He'd rip out the throat of any other man who touched her.

That thought stopped him cold. He'd never felt possessive about a female in his life, let alone a human. It just wasn't right. She might be beautiful, but no matter how much sex he had with her, she wouldn't be able to still the relentless need pounding within him. Only a female werewolf could do that. And only the one meant for him could truly ease the edginess that seemed to be a permanent part of him.

He'd given up looking for such a female years ago.

Her song ended and Meredith smiled as the crowd applauded. Then she announced the last call for the bar. Isaiah glanced at his watch. It was later than he'd realized. The crowd began to thin out as people finished their drinks and left.

Isaiah sipped the last of his beer until the glass was empty. He didn't want to leave, which was starting to piss him off. He forced himself to stand, but instead of heading for the doorway, he headed toward her. Meredith. He couldn't leave. Not without speaking to her.

As if she sensed his attention, her head jerked up and she stared at him. Her eyes widened the closer he got. He knew he was big and probably looked quite menacing right now. Arousal was riding him hard and it was all he could do to control his primal nature, his need to toss her over his shoulder and drag her off into the night with him.

Her eyes were a stormy blue. That's the first thing he noticed about her when he stopped in front of her. He took a deep breath and stilled. He could smell the light scent of her perfume, something sweet and sultry. It was mixed with the smells of the bar and tinged with fear. But beneath it all was something spicy. He could almost taste it on his tongue. It caused his already erect dick to get even harder.

He stared down at her in amazement. "You're a werewolf."

Chapter Two

Meredith stared at the gigantic stranger as a combination of fear and arousal streaked through her. She'd noticed him the minute he'd walked into her place and had steered clear of him. Any man who made her uneasy was to be avoided at all costs.

Michael and Benjamin had noticed him too and had warned her away from him. As much as she loved both of her sons, they could be as overbearing as any male at times. But she knew their concern came from their love for her, so she forgave them when they overstepped their bounds. She was an adult after all.

She had to tilt her head back to look at the male, which in itself was amazing. She was five-eleven and was wearing three-inch heels, and he was still about four inches taller than her.

And wide. He had shoulders a mile wide. His shaggy mahogany brown hair fell wild around his shoulders, giving him an untamed look. His eyes, which were devouring her, were deep brown, almost black, the color of bittersweet chocolate.

He'd never be called handsome. His features were too rugged for that. He was compelling and sensual. He exuded a latent male sexuality without even trying. He'd garnered quite a few looks from the women here tonight, but he'd ignored all of them. She knew because she'd been watching him.

He made her breasts tingle and swell. Just looking at him

made her cream her panties. This was a man who looked like he just might satisfy her in bed.

He was also a threat to her and her family. No one could know they were werewolves. That was how they'd survived all these years. They blended with the human population, not making waves and taking care of any problems that arose. She sensed this man was a huge problem.

She forced herself to laugh. "I think you've had one too many to drink tonight." As if on cue, her sons flanked her.

The stranger's eyes flickered to both men and then back to her again. Behind him, she watched Hank usher out the last of the patrons and the few humans on staff and close the door. Whatever happened, it was only family here now.

"It's time for you to leave." Michael stepped forward. He was almost as tall as the stranger, but she sensed he was nowhere near as dangerous. She placed her hand on her son's arm to restrain him.

"My name is Isaiah." He held out his hand to her. "Isaiah Striker."

The name was strong and suited him. She nodded, but didn't dare touch his hand. His mere presence was arousing enough. She didn't know what would happen if she touched him. It was embarrassing enough for her to know her sons were standing so close they could smell her arousal. Sometime she damned their preternatural senses.

She had no reason to be embarrassed. They were werewolves and their natures were primal and basic at times in spite of their humanity. She was coming into heat soon. It happened once a year and she knew the signs. These past few nights, she'd felt the familiar tension spiraling through her body and cursed it.

And though it was much more manageable than it had

been when she was younger, she still felt the urge to mate with a male. And the one standing in front of her was a prime specimen who would attract any female, werewolf or human. Thankfully, the days of her having to permanently mate with one was long over. These days she usually locked herself in her apartment and took care of the problem herself with her handy vibrator until it passed.

He lowered his hand back to his side, but his eyes never left her face.

"Is there a problem?" Hank strode up to stand just to the side of the stranger.

"No problem. This gentleman was just leaving." She pleaded with Isaiah with her eyes. If he insisted on repeating his claim of her being a werewolf, he wouldn't get out of here alive. There was only one of him and three male werewolves. Was he a hunter or just a human who believed in such things?

She took a deep breath. She needed to be calm. What she got was a blast of pheromones and a jolt of arousal. A spicy scent filled her nose and made her sex clench with need. She almost moaned aloud as a shiver of need wracked her body and her nipples tightened. How had she missed this? He was a werewolf.

Impossible. She blinked in astonishment. In all the years they'd been here this had never happened. Male werewolves tended to stay away from the city, not liking the crowds or the closed-in space. It was one of the main reasons why she lived here with her sons and her adopted family.

Oh God! Hank. He was only a half-breed and many full-blooded werewolves were as bad as the bounty hunters wanting them dead. Teague, Neema and Kevin were all half-breeds as well. Their safety depended on her keeping control of this situation at all costs. She straightened her shoulders. If he thought to threaten her family, he was mistaken.

"You need to leave," she repeated. "Now."

He shook his head, the corners of his mouth turning up ever so slightly. It made him look sexier, if that was even possible.

Hank reached out to grab Isaiah's arm.

"You don't want to do that, pup," Isaiah warned.

Hank froze with his hand in the air. Benjamin growled low in his chest. Kevin came out from the back office, adding to the growing tension. "What's going on?"

Isaiah was still trying to process the fact that the woman he lusted after was a female werewolf, and a beautiful one at that. She was also coming into heat. There was no mistaking that enticing spicy perfume. No wonder he was attracted to her.

What was even more surprising was that she wasn't the only werewolf here. They all were. The odor from all the human patrons, the liquor and the food had masked their scent. Now that they were the only ones left, there was no disguising it.

It was crazy to see a group of werewolves living in a city surrounded by the myriad sights and sounds which assailed their senses daily. Bounty hunters frequented the cities for supplies and new recruits. Not to mention that vampires, witches and demons preferred to live in the city. And while the different species weren't exactly at war, they weren't sending each other Christmas cards either.

Around him several of the males began to growl. As if drawn by the tension, a lean red-haired male pushed through the kitchen door, wiping his hand on a white towel as he came. The sleeveless shirt he was wearing displayed an array of tattoos running up and down his muscular arms. With the trio of gold hoops in both ears and his eyebrow piercing, he looked like trouble. He was followed by the slender, curly-haired female Isaiah had seen waiting tables earlier in the evening.

Meredith held up her hand. "Enough."

Several of the males shot her a glare, but subsided. Isaiah was surprised at how all the males deferred to her. She was obviously the alpha female of this little pack. But where was the alpha male?

The thought of another male having the right to put his hands on her made Isaiah see red. A low, menacing growl came from deep in his chest. The younger woman took a step toward the red-haired male. He wrapped his arm around her protectively.

The tension in the room grew until it was so thick it was almost impossible to breathe. He didn't give a shit. He wasn't leaving. Not until he talked to Meredith.

The woman in question stepped forward and placed her hands on her hips. She exuded confidence, which was sexy as hell and turned him on even more. "Don't think you can come in here and threaten my family, wolf." She spat the last as though it were a bad word.

Having her so near, he could see the smoothness of her skin and smell her delicious scent. Unable to resist, he lowered his head and sniffed the curve of her neck. She smelled like something rare and exotic, a combination of musk, cinnamon and heat that was intoxicating. She shivered and started to lean toward him. He wanted to howl with pleasure. But it ended far too soon for his liking when someone pulled her away.

Isaiah jerked his head up to see who had ruined the moment between him and Meredith. It was one of the younger men. He started toward him, the promise of retaliation stamped on his face, only to have Meredith step in front of him again.

"He's my son."

That brought Isaiah up cold. If there was one thing he could understand, it was wanting to protect family. He addressed the younger man directly, looking over Meredith's head. "I mean her no harm."

"What about the rest of them? Why are you here? Who sent you?"

Meredith was still in front of him demanding answers.

He sighed and rolled his head to work out some of the kinks in his neck. "No one sent me. I didn't come here to find any of you. I was just wandering the streets, heard a woman singing and came in."

"I don't believe you," said the man Meredith had called her son.

"Michael," she warned, and he subsided, but not without first giving Isaiah a look that promised death if he made a move toward his mother. Isaiah could respect that.

"There's nothing for you here. You need to leave." Isaiah understood her wanting to protect the pack, but he was curious why Meredith was in such a hurry to get rid of him when he obviously meant no harm.

"I'm not sure we should let him leave." The bouncer from the door spoke up. "What if he's working with the hunters?"

The menacing growl that came from Isaiah was impossible to suppress. "I kill hunters, pup, and anyone who works with them."

"So you say," the other male who'd worked behind the bar countered.

"Are you questioning my word?" He'd never had anyone do such a thing. He was a Striker. Their loyalty and honesty was above reproach.

"Enough." Meredith tapped the toe of her high-heeled shoe on the wooden floor. It drew his gaze down over her long, shapely legs and back up again. "No one is going to hurt anyone. And you're leaving."

It was time to regroup. Things were too volatile with so many males in the mix. They were on a short leash at the moment, but Isaiah had no doubt all the males would swing into action in the blink of an eye if they thought it was necessary. He didn't want to be put in a position of having to hurt them. That certainly wouldn't go over well with Meredith. The last thing he wanted was to antagonize her any more than he already had.

"I want to talk to you. Two minutes," he added before she could protest. "Alone."

Predictably enough, the males protested, but in the end Meredith was alpha and the rest of them headed toward to the kitchen.

"I'll only be on the other side of the door," Michael warned.

Isaiah inclined his head in understanding.

Meredith waited until they were all gone before turning back to him. "We're alone. What do you want?"

He shifted until they were so close they were almost touching. He could feel the heat from her skin, see the way her pupils dilated and the pulse in her neck beat faster. There was a slight hitch in her breathing as he invaded her space.

They weren't touching, not quite. He raised his hand and lightly brushed the curve of her cheek with the back of his knuckles. She sucked in a breath and the movement had her breasts touching his chest. Even through the layers of their clothing, he could feel the hard tips of her nipples.

Need roared through him. Raw desire pumped through his veins. He wanted Meredith more than he'd wanted anything in his life, as though she was somehow necessary to him.

He leaned down, his lips practically caressing hers as he answered her question. "You, Meredith. I want you."

He didn't give her time to answer, but closed the miniscule distance between them and pressed his lips to hers. They were soft and lush and he groaned as the power of that small caress blasted through him. Every muscle in his body tensed as he rubbed his lips against hers, willing her to part them and let him in.

Then she did. It was slight, but she did move them. He snaked his tongue into her mouth and groaned. She tasted like fine wine and long, hot nights. He explored, learning what turned her on, what made her moan.

She went up on her toes to get closer and he wrapped one arm around her slender waist, holding her firmly against his body. Her breasts pillowed against his chest and her pelvis was aligned with his. His cock pressed against her mound and belly. Heat rolled off him in waves as need raked at his very being.

He had to have her.

Cupping the back of her head with one large hand, he tilted it so he could deepen their kiss. But she was an alpha and not about to be led by anyone. She clutched at his hair, yanking him even closer. The slight sting of his scalp was tangible evidence that she wanted him as much as he wanted her. Their teeth clinked and he tasted blood. It was warm and spicy and fired his lust.

He devoured her, plunging his tongue into the warm cavern of her mouth, staking his claim. He would have her. Had to have her.

More. He needed more of her. Tearing his mouth from hers, he nipped at her jaw and left biting kisses down the slender column of her neck. Her breasts beckoned, firm and full. As he'd longed to do all night, he traced a finger over the lush curve and dipped into her cleavage. "You're not wearing a bra, are you?"

She shook her head, a long lock of her hair feathering against his face. He savored the touch of her silky hair even as he slipped his finger beneath the fabric of her dress.

She held her breath as he fingered a bare nipple.

Madness. It was pure madness. She'd blame the fact that she was almost in heat, except she'd never reacted to a male like this before. Not even her mate.

An alarm bell went off in the back of her brain, but it was drowned out as Isaiah touched his finger against her straining nipple. Heat flashed from her breast to her sex and she knew her panties were wet. There was no way he wouldn't be able to smell her growing arousal.

But he was aroused too. The large bulge of his erection pressed against her in a provocative way. He was more than big enough to help ease the seemingly never-ending ache inside her. Sex with him would be mind-blowing. It would be primal and hot. He'd have the stamina to keep up with her, to give it to her long and hard.

She whimpered as a second finger joined the first and he tugged gently on her nipple. The large hand at her back moved lower until it cupped her ass, tilting her hips so her mound was positioned directly against his hard cock.

It felt so incredibly good as she rubbed herself against him, stimulating her clit through their clothing. Breathing was getting harder by the second, but she didn't care. She ground her sex against his erection, drawing a groan from him.

He tugged the material of her dress over her breast, exposing it to his view. "Beautiful," he breathed before he covered the tip with his mouth and sucked. Hard. Her pussy clenched. She felt empty. Needy.

She stroked his broad shoulders, the thick column of his neck and his chest. His skin was darker than hers, tanned a golden brown. His shirt frustrated her and she reached for the buttons. She was in a frenzy of need to have him.

A crash from the kitchen was as good as a bucket of cold water being thrown over her. What the hell was she doing?

She jerked away from Isaiah and stared at him, her chest heaving as she sucked in much needed air. He looked feral, an aroused male deprived of the female he wanted. His pupils were dilated, his nostrils flared with each breath. His lips were pursed together and his hands were fisted at his sides.

His erection pulsed against the front of his jeans and a sheen of sweat covered his skin. And he was staring at her chest.

Meredith looked down and gasped. Her breast was still exposed. She jerked the material back into place and took a step back, wobbling on her high heels. He reached out to steady her, but she took another step away. No telling what might happen if she let him touch her again.

"You need to leave." Before she did something stupid like throw herself at him. She couldn't believe she'd acted so wantonly with someone who was practically a stranger.

He nodded, but made no move to leave.

"They won't wait much longer." She indicated the kitchen door and he nodded his understanding.

"This isn't finished." His low, gritty voice, thick with passion, caressed her skin. She tried to ignore the way her breasts swelled and rubbed against the fabric of her dress.

She shook her head. "This is done. You need to leave and

not come back." On that, she was firm. Her family came before anyone, before anything else. It didn't matter that she felt such a magnetic pull to this male. She knew nothing about him. He had no idea that four members of her pack were half-breeds, and she wasn't willing to risk their safety just because she wanted to tear up the sheets with him.

Isaiah straightened his shirt and studied her. A slow smile turned up the corners of his lips. Her mouth went dry. He was handsome in a rugged way, but when he smiled he was irresistible. He reached out to touch her, but she tilted her head out of reach.

He chuckled. It was a rusty sound and seemed to surprise even him. "It's not over, Meredith. It's just getting started."

A promise or a threat, she couldn't be sure, but she suspected it was a bit of both. He turned and sauntered toward the door and let himself out. When the door shut behind him, the tension in the room escaped, much like the air leaving a balloon.

She put her hand to her lips, still able to feel his against them. Her skin felt extra sensitive and her body ached.

The door behind her pushed open. Meredith straightened and combed her fingers through her hair. Taking a deep, fortifying breath, she turned to face her family.

All the males were scowling and Neema looked frightened.

They were all waiting for her to speak. Although her body cried out for Isaiah, the safety of her family came first. "We may have a problem."

Steve Macmillan shoved open the door of an all-night diner and stepped inside, letting the door slam shut behind him. The waitress behind the counter glanced his way and then went back to filling the napkin dispensers she had lined up on the counter like good little soldiers.

One corner of his mouth crooked upward. He liked the thought of having as many soldiers at his disposal as she had napkin dispensers, but one made do with what one had.

What he had, for the foreseeable future, were the four men sitting at a corner table. Jones raised his head and nodded as Steve started toward them. "Coffee," he barked at the waitress as he passed the counter.

She sighed, dropped the metal dispenser down on the counter and shuffled over to grab her coffee pot and a fresh cup. By the time Steve seated himself at the table, she was there beside him. Placing the cup in front of him, she filled it and then topped up the rest of the men's half-empty mugs.

He put her age at about forty even though she looked older. Years of working a job like this had taken a toll on her body. Her hair was blonde with slightly graying roots. She'd probably been pretty once, but now she was no more than a pale shell of the young woman she'd been. She was about twenty pounds overweight and wore no wedding ring.

But she was quick and quiet and shuffled back behind the counter. He liked that in a woman. In the dark, he wouldn't care if she had a few too many wrinkles. She had a great rack and a plump ass. All features he liked.

Maybe he'd meet her after work and let her take him home for a quick fuck.

"Boss." Jones's voice pulled him away from his meanderings. He ignored his hardened dick and got down to the work at hand.

Steve let his eyes wander around the small group. He knew Warren and Collins, and had worked with both men before. They were dependable, but better than that, they were loyal. They followed orders without question and would die in the name of the cause.

Which was good, because he had no intention of dying. His job was to find the bitch who'd killed his father. He'd been living and working out west when he'd gotten the news. His father, who'd been running the east coast hunters for the past five years, had been murdered by the female werebitch he'd kept as a pet. Steve hadn't seen the female in years, but he'd find her and kill her if it was the last thing he did. So he'd come back east to take over his father's position and look for his prey.

Steve had been raised to enter the family business—bounty hunting. And not just any kind of bounty hunting. No, his family were legendary werewolf hunters.

Most of the human population had no idea that paranormal creatures wandered among them. Steve had no pity for them. Cattle, all of them. Living according to the laws of some government that had long outlived its usefulness. No, he and his comrades believed in the freedom to live as they wanted, and that meant killing werewolves.

He'd grown up in the wilds of Washington State where his father had been stationed at the time. His father had taught him to hunt and fish. How to survive and how to hunt and kill werewolves. He'd also taught him to value his friends, but to watch his back.

He didn't know the fourth man at their table at all. "Who are you?"

"Quinn." The big, light-haired man leaned back in his chair like he didn't have a care in the world. Cocky sonofabitch. Steve respected that.

"Quinn came highly recommended from the Southeast faction," Jones added.

Bounty hunters were an independent lot, but they maintained loose communications. All the better to capture their prey. He'd check on Quinn himself. He didn't trust anyone, especially not a fucking new guy.

"Why am I here?" He wanted this meeting over. He was in the mood to get laid and he planned to let the waitress fill his needs, generous soul that he was. He looked over at her, already feeling her large tits cradling his cock as he fucked her mouth. It was a great way to get off, keep a woman quiet and not have to worry about wearing a rubber.

"I caught a glimpse of a guy watching Riley's Garage. He moved like one of *them*."

His gaze jerked back to Warren. No need to ask who he meant by one of *them*. "Who?"

"Don't know, but he definitely might be a werewolf."

"Go back and keep a watch." There had been a lot of buzz around that garage about a month ago. Rumors of infighting among wolves and the death of several hunters had been big news. Those bastards were short of women, so some group would take in his father's murderer. It was a place to start.

He stood. "We're done. Keep me informed." Sauntering over to the counter, he smiled at the waitress.

Chapter Three

Meredith stared at the six pairs of eyes staring at her, watching her with varying degrees of anger, distress and fear.

"We shouldn't have let him go." That was about the tenth time Hank had made that proclamation since Isaiah had left and it was beginning to wear on her.

"I agree with Hank," Michael added.

"What should we have done? Kill him?" She threw up her hands in frustration. "That would make us no better than the hunters." They walked a fine line between protecting themselves and turning into the things they most dreaded—cold-blooded killers.

They'd killed before. All of them, with the exception of Neema, had been forced to take another life in order to protect themselves. Hunters had come before and would again. There had been two other werewolves in the early years who'd wanted to destroy Neema and Kevin. Thankfully, she'd found the half-breed children first and with her sons' help had been able to protect them.

"It's not like that, Mom," Benjamin soothed. Her youngest was tough, but was more reasonable than her eldest.

"Then what is it like?" She took in all of them with a single, dark gaze. Teague sat with Neema in his lap, his arm wrapped protectively around her. Kevin stood off by himself looking thoughtful, as usual.

The other three—Hank, Michael and Benjamin—paced and sat and stood and paced some more.

Fatigue washed over her. It had been a long day and an even longer night. "He said he means us no harm and I believe him." She didn't know why she did, but she trusted her instincts. Given his immediate negative reaction to the mere mention of bounty hunters, she didn't think he would have anything to do with them.

But as much as she might think he was trustworthy, she couldn't risk their lives. Too often, some elitist werewolves would tip off other wolves or, even worse, hunters to the location of half-breeds so the hunters could do their dirty work for them.

That had happened when they'd been living in Vegas back in the nineties. It had been a close call. One that still gave her nightmares on occasion. She'd come close to losing Benjamin and Kevin that time. Thankfully, they'd managed to destroy the hunters. Which brought her back to the problem at hand.

"Still," Michael began to protest.

She held up her hand for silence. He shut his mouth, his jaw working as he swallowed his anger. "Still," she echoed. "We cannot take a chance. We'll start round-the-clock guard duty." She turned to Benjamin. "You take the first shift and wake Hank next. After that, Kevin, Michael and Teague can all take a turn. It will be easier in the day. All of us will need to be more aware than ever for the next few weeks until we're certain there is no threat from hunters or...others."

She couldn't bring herself to say his name aloud. Just the thought of him was enough to raise her blood pressure and send her hormones spiraling out of control.

The men looked slightly appeased and nodded. Good. It

wasn't always easy for her to maintain control of her small pack. She was alpha, but she was also female and the males were coming to an age where they wanted to test their boundaries and limitations. She worried about that constantly and struggled to balance all the wants and needs of her pack against their continued safety.

She lived in fear that someday one of them, or perhaps all of them, would leave. That would break her heart. She'd sacrificed so much, but she regretted not one moment of it. As long as her children were safe nothing else mattered. And they were all hers. Only two had been born of her body, but the other four were the children of her heart.

Michael strode to her side, went down on one knee before her and bowed his head. The formal pose was a tribute to her status as alpha. "It will be done." He stood and placed a soft kiss on her cheek. "You should rest. You look tired."

She touched her hand to his cheek and leaned in to kiss his forehead. Love swelled in her heart for her son. She had been on her own since he was a pup of seven, two years after Benjamin was born. She'd kept them both safe for the past thirty odd years, adding the others to the mix over the years.

They all came to her. One by one, they kissed her good night and offered their unwavering support. Hank came last, his head down. She tipped his face up until he was looking at her. "I'm proud of you, son. You've come a long way." And he had. He'd been with them only five years. He'd spent his teenage years on the street and several in the army before the changes in his body had sent him running from everyone and everything he'd ever known.

All her adopted children had been alone in the world, not knowing about their heritage until she'd found them. The fact that they'd managed to stay alive and sane was a miracle in itself.

Hank's pale blue eyes met hers and he nodded. She stroked his short hair, letting the bristles tickle her palm. That was one of the things he carried over from his time in the military. The discipline they'd taught him had enabled him to survive until he'd found them.

"I won't let you down," he promised, his words fierce.

"I know." She stood and gave his arm one final pat before heading to the back of the bar to the staircase that led to the apartments above. Benjamin was already on watch and would patrol the building inside and out until it was time for the others to take their turn.

Her steps were slow and measured as she made her way to her one-bedroom apartment. She'd given her sons the larger apartment on this floor, knowing they needed their privacy. She needed hers too. Now more than ever.

A sense of relief hit her as she closed the door behind her and set the lock. The warm, open space welcomed her. She'd decorated the place to her taste, had chosen every piece of furniture carefully. The plush brown sofa and chairs were welcoming after a long day. She'd whiled many an hour away curled up on that sofa reading, watching television or working on her laptop.

The kitchen and living space were separated by a counter. There were three stools there in case anyone dropped by to enjoy a coffee or a meal with her. She also had a little built-in eating nook beneath her kitchen window. It allowed her to enjoy a hot mug of tea and a good book while staring out at the city street below.

She didn't bother with a light as she went straight to her bedroom. She didn't need it. Not with her preternatural vision. But more than that, she knew this place like the back of her hand. She needed no light to know that her bedroom was painted a pale yellow with accents of green. Just being here soothed her, and right now she needed that.

Her shoes were hurting her feet after so many hours, so she kicked them off, sighing at the instant relief. She padded to her large closet, unzipping her dress as she went. Her nipples were still taut, her breasts swollen. The fabric rubbed against them as she pulled it off. She moaned, closing her eyes as heat ricocheted from her breasts to her sex.

It took every ounce of discipline she possessed to drape her dress on a hanger and put it with the other garments waiting to be taken to the drycleaners. The tiny pair of bikini panties she wore felt confining, so she yanked them off, stuffing them in the laundry hamper. They were still damp, a reminder of her arousal.

Naked, she padded to the bathroom. She needed a shower, but was too tired to take one. She settled for removing her makeup before stumbling to bed.

She pulled back the two thick comforters and climbed beneath. Sighing, she sank into the pillows, figuring she'd be asleep within two seconds. But sleep didn't come.

The bold green comforters she'd chosen for the room were restricting rather than cozy. She pushed them down to her waist, letting the colder air of the room hit her skin. It cooled her heated skin somewhat, but also caused her nipples to pucker even more.

Groaning, she rolled over on her side, keeping her thighs clamped together. She was horny. No doubt about it. While it was perfectly normal for a female of her kind, a purely biological reaction, it was worse than it had been in years.

Once a female werewolf mated, the craving subsided somewhat. But not much. Having two children had subdued it a bit more, as though nature was satisfied now that she'd procreated and ensured the survival of the species.

But it never went away. Continuing to control her life. Thankfully, it was only once a year. But for those couple of days, she usually locked herself in her room away from her family. In the early years, after her husband's death, she'd taken human lovers, one after another, to try to ease the physical ache. That hadn't lasted long. Not only did it not help much, but she hated having sex without the emotional attachment. It reminded her too much of her mating.

No, she wouldn't go there. Maxwell was dead and he'd given her two sons who were the joy of her life. For that alone she would forgive him for taking her unawares and forcing her to mate with him before she'd really had a chance to choose from the males of her pack.

Her chest ached and she rubbed her sternum. All her life she'd known she'd mate as soon as she came into heat for the first time. She hadn't minded it too much even though there was no male in her pack who had made her feel anything beyond mild interest.

What she had been looking forward to was being able to shift into her wolf for the first time. That happened for males when they reached maturity, but females had to mate first, the act of sex allowing them to be able to shift. She'd always thought that grossly unfair, but such was life.

Still, she'd understood her duty and had been ready to do it. Maxwell had caught her out in the woods when the first pangs of heat had finally taken her. He should have taken her back to their pack compound, to her parents. Instead, he'd thrown her to the ground, mounting her from behind and taking her. And she'd been so far gone, so needy, she'd accepted him. At least her body had.

While there had been some complaints, they'd died a quick death. Maxwell was the alpha's son and, as such, was too powerful for any to challenge.

"Go away, Max." She whispered her plea into the dark. She had no idea why she was even thinking of him. She rarely did these days and her sons never asked about him. They knew he was dead. Killed by hunters. They also knew why she'd chosen to take them and run from one end of the country to the other rather than stay with their pack.

She'd had one forced mating and wasn't ever going to allow another one. After Maxwell had been killed, her alpha had decreed that she needed to mate again. She'd kept her thoughts to herself and planned her getaway, taking her sons with her.

The early years had been tough. She gave a bitter laugh. That was putting it mildly. She'd had two young children, no marketable skills and a pack of werewolves on her tail. Not to mention bounty hunters.

What she'd had was a small nest egg of cash left to her by her maternal grandmother, which her husband hadn't known about. No one had. Her grammy had given it to her and bade her tell no one, not even her parents. It was that money that had allowed her to run and to buy the building they now lived in.

She'd bought it cheap in the mid-eighties, long before the area's revival. But it was only about twelve years ago that she'd felt safe enough to actually move to Chicago and take up residence here. The fear of her former pack had kept her running for years.

Those were memories best left buried. But Isaiah had dug them up and she knew why. She hadn't felt this attracted to a male. Ever. He threatened her peace of mind, everything she'd built. There was no way she'd subjugate herself to a male ever again.

She chewed on her lower lip as she stared out into the night. The blinds were open, letting in the lights of the city. She missed the forest sometimes, the ability to change at will and run free. But those days were gone. When nights got too bad, she'd run in one of the large city parks, alone or with several members of her pack.

Right now, she wanted to run. Wanted to feel the change taking her over. Her skin rippled as her wolf sensed her unease. She swallowed hard and forced herself to be calm. There was no way she could run. Not now. Not with the threat of Isaiah out there somewhere in the city.

Her sex throbbed at the mere thought of him. The sensitive lips were swollen and flushed with need. Her breasts ached. She wanted to touch herself, to relieve the sexual tension swelling inside her, but she didn't. It would leave her feeling worse than before.

The only time she gave into her sexual needs when she was in heat was when it was fully on her and there was no escape. To do so any sooner just made the problem worse.

She flumped over onto her back and started a mental list of supplies she had to order for the bar and the kitchen. Anything to try to take her mind off Isaiah and the heat consuming her body.

She wondered briefly where he was and what he was doing. Was he lying naked in bed, thinking of her?

Her skin flushed and the ache between her legs grew. She spread them wide, hoping the cool sheets would ease it. Knowing that it wouldn't.

Closing her eyes, she began counting sheep and praying for morning.

Isaiah stared up at the ceiling as the walls seemed to close in around him. He wanted to fling open the door, change into his wolf and run until the unending edginess gnawing at his guts left him.

There were parks in the area, but he wasn't certain which ones, if any, were safe. The last thing he wanted to do was start a rumor of a wolf in the area. That would bring every hunter within a five hundred mile radius running. And that was the very thing he didn't want to do.

Instead, he lay naked, his body coated with a layer of sweat, and replayed every second he'd spent with Meredith. He could still taste her erotic flavor on his tongue. Sweet, like honey.

He groaned as his cock pulsed. He wondered what she'd taste like between her legs. He longed to strip her naked and crawl between them to find out. Thick and rich, like the finest cream. He was positive that's what she'd taste like.

He rolled onto his side and stared out the second floor window. There was no balcony, so he'd left the drapes parted slightly, allowing him to see a sliver of the moon. It kept him from feeling quite so claustrophobic. The city was closing in on him more each passing minute, reminding him of how much he longed to run free. He felt fettered here. Chained in a way that was unnatural to his kind.

Funny, but he hadn't even noticed that when he'd been at Haven. He'd been too enthralled with Meredith and watching her every move. She'd driven all other thoughts from his head.

His phone rang. It had been doing that on and off for the past hour. He thought about ignoring it again, but figured if he didn't soon answer it, Joshua would be banging on his door before too long.

Reaching out, he snagged the disposable cell phone and

answered. "What?"

"Where the hell have you been? Why haven't you been answering your phone?"

His brother's demanding tone rankled and set him to growling. "You're not my damn alpha, Joshua. I don't answer to you."

Dead silence came across the line, but Isaiah refused to break it.

After a few tense moments, Joshua sighed. "I don't understand you at all lately, brother."

Isaiah rolled until he was sitting on the side of the mattress, the phone to his ear. The moon was practically invisible given all the lights of the city. But he knew it was up there, was able to see it due to his enhanced vision.

His shoulders bunched as the muscles tensed. He knew Joshua meant well, knew he owed his brother more than he could ever repay for taking over the position of Striker with their pack. Then there was the unavoidable fact that he loved him. Isaiah rolled his shoulders and tried to relax. It wasn't easy with his cock throbbing incessantly.

"I went out for a walk." He didn't give details, didn't want to discuss Meredith with anyone.

"I know the city is hard on you and I appreciate what you're doing for me, for us. It's been hard enough for Alex trying to settle in. I want her to have her own things around her. I know she misses having her own clothes and stuff."

Now he felt like a dick. Joshua was a good man with more than enough to handle at the moment without Isaiah adding to it. "Look, it's no problem. I just need a few more days to check things out." And to see Meredith again. Although that was his business and no one else's. "As soon as I'm sure things are clear over at the garage I'll make contact with Divine and load everything up." Divine was the human female who now owned the garage.

"I'll tell Alex it won't be long now."

"I'll call you when I have some news."

"One more thing," Joshua added before Isaiah could end the call.

"What?" His brother hesitated, raising his curiosity. "What do you need?"

"Alex has a short list of things she'd like you to pick up in the city while you're there."

Isaiah snorted. "Do I look like a personal shopper?" he groused even as he knew he'd do it. Their females were important to the future of the pack and, if his sister-in-law wanted him to buy her a few things, he'd damn well do it. He wouldn't enjoy it, but he'd do it.

He yanked open the drawer of the nightstand and found a sheet of motel stationary and a complimentary pen. Dragging them both out, he tucked the phone between his shoulder and his ear. "Shoot."

Joshua listed off a dozen items, mostly food related, including several pounds of specialty coffee. Isaiah grinned in spite of himself. Alex sure did love her coffee. "That it?" he asked when his brother finished speaking. "Sure I can't buy you some new underwear or a few pairs of socks for the rest of the boys?"

Joshua snorted. "I've never worn underwear a day in my life and neither have you."

"Thought maybe the little woman might want to civilize you," he taunted.

"The little woman likes being able to get to my equipment whenever she wants it."

Isaiah was reminded of his own hard-on and the fact that he was alone. Meredith was home in her bed. Alone. The fact that she'd kissed him back led him to assume she didn't have a mate. His stomach churned and he tensed again. She damn well better be alone.

"You still there?" Joshua asked.

"Yeah. I got everything. Tell Alex I'll make sure I get all of it."

"Thanks, bro. I really appreciate it."

"No problem. Talk to you in a few." He ended the call and tossed the cell phone and pen onto the nightstand. "Fuck," he swore as he drove the heels of his hands into his eye sockets. There was no way he was going to sleep tonight. Not with an erection the size of a steel spike.

Blowing out a breath, he rolled back, sprawling on top of the sheets. He wrapped his hand around his erection and thought about Meredith. It had been years since a woman had drawn his attention, had tempted him.

There was something about her that made her shine. Her confidence, certainly. Her voice. Damn, her voice could bring a man to his knees. It was throaty and low. Sensual. A bedroom voice. One that bespoke of silk sheets and hot sex.

Then there was her body. She was tall for a woman. He liked that. She'd fit perfectly against a man of his size, all their parts lining up just the way they should.

He pumped his hand up and down his shaft, feeling the tension building at the base. Closing his eyes, he concentrated on remembering every detail about her. Her waist-length, straight black hair would feel incredible sliding over his heated flesh. Her stormy blue eyes would take in every hard inch of him. He could imagine them widening before narrowing as she examined his body from head to toe.

Oh yeah. His cock jerked and fluid seeped from the tip. His fangs lengthened and his body threatened to change. Sweat beaded on his forehead as he fought the wolf for domination. The sac between his legs constricted and drew up closer to his body.

Then there was her delectable body. Meredith was slender but strong. Her hips were narrow, but her breasts were a handful. The creamy mounds tipped by a tender nipple of pale pink. He'd seen one, touched it, wrapped his tongue around it.

He increased the motions of his hand, squeezing and pumping faster. His chest was expanding and contracting quickly as he sucked in air. Thigh muscles tensed, his shoulders bunched.

Meredith. He whispered her name in his head, picturing her lovely lips parted in invitation. His back arched off the bed. His hand worked faster. Harder.

Her lips were soft and full and would be a thing of beauty wrapped around his cock. He groaned and bit back a howl as he came. His release spurted onto his stomach in a heady release. He kept pumping until there was nothing left. Releasing his shaft, he let his hand flop back on the bed.

His lungs were heaving as if he'd run for miles. Sweat coated his body. He needed a cold shower. He might have gained some physical satisfaction, but there was something missing.

Ignoring the growing emptiness inside him, he rolled off the bed and padded to the shower. He only hoped that took the edge off his hunger enough for him to sleep. He had a long day tomorrow.

Chapter Four

Isaiah sauntered into Riley's Garage at ten o'clock the next morning. It was a large brick building, kept in good repair, better than most on the street. Although it wasn't the only place that showed signs of being well-kept. There was nothing pretty about it, but it was solid. Much like the man who'd owned it for more than twenty years.

James LeVeau Riley had raised his daughter Alex here. Isaiah wondered how he'd managed to live in a city for that long and stay sane. But then again he'd had a powerful motivation—protecting his daughter. Isaiah had learned you could do anything you set your mind to if you had the right motivation.

He rolled his shoulders and emitted a soft sigh, suppressing a yawn that threatened. He'd passed a restless night and was more than a bit on edge. Even the large breakfast he'd eaten about an hour ago hadn't helped settle him. Of course, the two cups of coffee probably hadn't helped, but he needed the caffeine kick.

A man in his mid to late twenties looked up from the car he was working on and frowned. "Can I help you?" As he straightened, his fingers tightened around the wrench he was holding.

"Maybe." Isaiah kept his gaze on the man, but his peripheral vision on the wrench. He let his senses flare, but couldn't smell much beyond the oil and grease of the garage and the sweat and soap of the man. "I'm looking for Divine."

Suspicion grew in his eyes. "Divine hasn't come downstairs yet." He hesitated briefly before squaring his shoulders. He was a tall man, a little over six feet, but skinny. And certainly no match for Isaiah, even without his preternatural strength. "She doesn't do that anymore."

Confusion settled over him as he tried to follow the conversation. "Doesn't do what?"

The young man's cheeks flushed red and his lips firmed, but he didn't give ground.

"What Leon is trying so tactfully to say is that I'm no longer in the business of entertaining men for money, Mr...." She let the word dangle in the air.

He studied the woman who'd entered the garage from a door at the back. He knew who she was, but she wasn't quite what he'd expected. James had described her as a bleached blonde, a bit brash, but with a big heart. He'd had a picture of a woman with too much hard living showing on her face wearing revealing clothing and too much makeup.

This woman was a brunette and she was wearing jeans, sneakers and a blue sweater that hinted at attributes beneath. It was impossible to hide a bust that large, but she was obviously doing her best.

"Isaiah," he offered, holding out his hand.

She walked closer, her movements fluid, her hips swaying. Her eyes were cool and clinical as she studied him. There was the woman who'd spent years walking the streets, the woman who'd lost herself to drugs and alcohol before she found the inner strength to drag herself out. She took his hand and gave it a firm shake.

"Well, Isaiah, what can I do for you?"

"I need to talk to you." He glanced at Leon. "Alone."

Leon walked up to stand beside Divine. "I don't think that's such a good idea."

She patted his arm. "I'll be fine." She glanced at Isaiah. "I don't think he's looking to harm me. Are you?"

He shook his head, liking the feisty woman more and more with each passing minute. No wonder both Alex and James spoke fondly of her. "No, ma'am."

She laughed, a low, throaty laugh that hinted at many years of cigarettes and booze. "Come on up. I was just having a second cup of coffee."

Divine turned and headed toward the door at the back. He started to follow, but Leon stopped him with a hand on his arm. Isaiah glanced down at the hand and then at Leon. His cheeks were still red, but determination was etched on his face. "Don't do anything you'll regret." He removed his hand and slapped the wrench into his palm. The warning was obvious. Hurt Divine and he'd come after Isaiah with the wrench.

Damn, if he wasn't beginning to understand how James could stay here all those years. These people understood loyalty, like a pack.

"You coming?" Divine called.

He said nothing, but followed her up the stairs and into her apartment. He peered around with interest, curious to see where Alex had grown up. She talked about it often.

There wasn't anything out of the ordinary. A living room opened into a dining and kitchen area. He assumed the bedrooms and bath were down the short hallway. He could easily see James here. He was a man who didn't need much in the way of luxury.

On closer inspection, he could see a woman's touch in the

cushions on the sofa and a hot-pink throw tossed over a chair. A loud click yanked him from his musings and brought him back to the situation at hand.

"Who the hell are you really and what do you want?" Divine was standing behind the kitchen counter a 9mm held expertly in her hands.

Isaiah raised his hands in surrender and took a step closer. "I told you who I am." The bullets would hurt, but they wouldn't leave any lasting damage. He was a werewolf and would heal quickly.

She sent that thought out through the window with her next words. "I know you're one of *them*. You're not the first one to stop by to visit." She raised her hands slightly and aimed at his heart. "The bullets in this thing are coated in silver."

He froze, his respect for her growing in leaps and bounds. For a human female to challenge him in such a manner was astonishing. He could move quick enough to disarm her, but not without possibly taking a hit.

His acute hearing picked up a squeak on the stairs and he knew they were about to have company.

He lowered his right hand to his pocket.

"Leave 'em where I can see 'em," she ordered.

"Do what the lady said." Leon stepped into the room, rifle at the ready.

Isaiah shook his head. The situation would be funny if it weren't so ridiculous. "James Riley sent me. I figured I could call him and he could vouch for me."

Her eyes widened and her hand shook slightly before she steadied it. "How is Alex?"

He smiled. "Happily mated to my brother."

Divine frowned. "Phone her. I want to talk to Alex. But

make it slow."

Her eyes never wavered as he gingerly reached into his pocket with two fingers and drew out his phone. He dialed the number and held it to his ear, waiting impatiently for his brother to answer.

"Yeah."

"I need to speak with the little woman."

Joshua laughed. "Don't let her hear you call her that or you'll be in trouble. What do you need her for?"

Isaiah shifted slightly, keeping both Leon and Divine in sight. "Let's just say I'm having a little trouble with the locals. They seem to think I'm one of the bad guys."

His brother snorted. "They're smarter than I thought."

"Ha. Ha." For someone who hadn't shown much of a sense of humor his entire life, Joshua had certainly developed a warped one since he'd met Alex. "You're not the one with a rifle and a 9mm pointed at him. With silver bullets," he added.

Joshua gave a whoop of laughter and called for his wife. A few seconds later, Alex came on the line. "What's wrong? Joshua is grinning like a loon but won't tell me anything."

Isaiah silently thanked his brother for small miracles. "I'm going to put you on speaker. Hang on." He pressed a button and held up the phone. "You still there, Alex?"

Her voice came over the speaker load and clear. "I'm here. Now what's this all about?"

"Is that really you, Alex?" Divine's voice quavered and her eyes filled with tears. "I've been so worried about you and your dad."

"Divine?"

"Yeah." Divine swiped at her eyes with the back of her left hand, but kept the gun in her right. "Who is this guy?"

"He's my brother-in-law. He looks mean, but he's really a great guy."

Isaiah wondered if he shouldn't tuck his tail between his legs and just make a run for it. Between his brother and Alex his tough reputation was in tatters.

"Yeah? He does look mean. The way he moves reminded me of James. How is he?"

"Dad is good. He's enjoying being back home."

"So you're not coming back." Sadness tinged Divine's voice.

Alex's tone softened. "No, we're not coming back. I'll be back for a visit, but not until some of the heat dies down."

"Tell James that we had another one of those hunters down here, but Otto and his sons sent him packing." She paused and bit her bottom lip. "We also had one of them werewolves here. They were looking for you and wouldn't leave."

"What happened? You weren't hurt, were you, Divine?" Isaiah could hear Alex's concern in every word. He could also hear the love and respect that each woman had for the other.

"We took care of it." Her words were tough, but Divine paled slightly. It was then he knew she'd had a part in killing the wolf. She straightened her shoulders and continued. "Tell James the garage is still here if he wants it. I took his advice and Leon is working down there now. He doesn't have the same touch with cars that your father does, but he's good."

"The building is yours now, Divine." Alex brought the conversation around to his reason for being there. "Isaiah's there to pack up all our stuff and drive it back home." There was a pregnant pause. "I really can't tell you where, Divine. I'm sorry."

"Don't be." She laid the 9mm back into a kitchen drawer and shut it. Off to his left, Leon slowly lowered the rifle he was holding and disappeared out through the door. Isaiah heard his muffled footsteps on the stairs as he went back down to the garage. "It's probably better that way."

"I miss you."

Divine sniffed. "I miss you too, but don't you start bawling on me. I changed my hair color. You wouldn't recognize me now. I decided that brunettes have more fun than blondes."

Isaiah clicked the button to take Alex off speakerphone and held out the phone to Divine. "Here."

The older woman hurried over and took the phone before scurrying back to the kitchen to talk. Knowing they might be a while, he wandered over to one of the windows. He could see part of the city from here.

He wondered what Meredith was doing this morning. Had she slept as poorly as he had or had she forgotten him the moment he'd left? She was on the other side of the city, but she was probably up and about, doing whatever it was needed doing. He had no idea of the amount of work that went into running a club. There were probably an enormous number of things to take care of on a daily basis. Everything from cleaning to ordering supplies for the kitchen and booking acts. Not to mention the paperwork.

He closed his eyes and pictured her in his mind. What would she be wearing this morning? Not the skin-hugging, sparkling dress that fit her like a glove. Jeans maybe. Or perhaps black dress pants. Something classy, yet casual. That was more likely. His heart beat heavily, his jeans grew uncomfortably snug and his fangs tingled.

He rolled his shoulders, but there was no way to dispel the tension growing in him. He had to see her again. Tonight.

But for now he had work to do. His family came first. Always.

"Call me anytime. You take care of yourself, Alex."

He turned around as Divine was ending the call. She handed the phone back to him. He took it and tucked it back into his pocket.

Divine swiped at her eyes and quickly squared her shoulders. "I already packed up Alex's apartment and gave her notice to her landlord." Grabbing a set of keys, she headed to the door. He followed silently behind her. "All her stuff is in here."

She unlocked a rather large storage room at end of the hall. Furniture and boxes were piled almost to the ceiling. "Otto Bykowski, who runs the bakery up the road, and his sons, helped me." She nodded toward the downstairs. "Leon is one of his sons.

"I wasn't quite certain what to do with James's furniture, but I boxed up all his belongings and put them in here too."

"You can do whatever you wish with his furniture." James had told him to let Divine have whatever she wanted. Said she'd deserved it for all that she'd done. Isaiah had been skeptical at the time, but now he believed she more than deserved the furniture and the building. "Keep it or sell it. It's up to you."

Divine pointed to a gaudy purple chair in the corner. "I put that piece in here. James might not want it, but it was Alex's favorite."

"Thanks."

They left the room, Divine locking up behind them.

"I'm going to watch the garage for a few days before I bring in a truck."

Divine crossed her arms over her chest and looked thoughtful. "That's a good idea. Listen," she began. "If you want to be doubly safe, Otto can bring his bakery truck down some night and put it in the garage. No one would think anything of it. They'd just assume that Leon was fixing something for his dad. We could load up the truck and drive it to another location to make sure no one is watching. You could have a truck waiting and transfer their belongings to it." She tapped her bottom lip with her finger as if thinking the logistics through. "That would work."

Once again, Isaiah was impressed with Divine. "That's smart."

She gave him a wry smile. "I have my moments."

He grinned back. "I'm sure you do."

She gave a short laugh and winked at him. "That's what we'll do then." She walked past her apartment door and down the stairs to the garage. "You let me know when you're ready and I'll talk to Otto."

"You're sure he can be trusted?" Isaiah hated depending on anyone other than his brothers.

"I trust them more than I trust you." She turned to face him when they hit the bottom of the stairs. He glanced into the garage to make certain Leon was alone before he entered. Divine was all business now, all hint of laughter gone. "Ask James if you need reassurance."

"I will." He might respect Divine's strength, but he didn't *know* her. And the hunters could sometimes be persuasive—in a very violent way.

She shrugged. "Suit yourself. Just let me know when you're ready."

"I will." He started to leave, got halfway across the garage and swore under his breath. He spun around on one heel. "Thank you for being a friend to Alex and James."

She gave him a sad smile. "They've more than repaid it over

the years."

He gave her a curt nod and left. He moved quickly, wanting to be seen by as few people as possible. If any hunters or wolves were watching, they would see him and follow him. Which is exactly what he wanted. He was tense and could use a good fight to work off some of his aggression.

Prowling down the street, he slipped into a rundown apartment building and made his way to the roof. Settling in, he watched the day pass in the neighborhood.

On the other side of the street a man with a set of binoculars took note of the tall stranger. He yanked out his cell phone and hit a number on the speed dial.

It was answered on the first ring. "It's Warren, boss. That guy is back."

"Watch him," came the quick reply.

"Will do." Warren ended the call and settled in for the morning. Jones was relieving him at noon. Collins would take the night shift. Quinn wasn't on watch rotation yet because he was the new guy. Macmillan didn't care how well vouched-for the guy was. He didn't get left alone until they were one hundred percent certain of his loyalty.

The stranger at the garage moved with a fluid grace that was common in werewolves. Maybe he was just an uncommonly graceful human, but Warren didn't think so. There was a sense of barely controlled menace about the guy.

No, he was a werewolf and he was here for a reason. The mission was to find out what that was and who was involved. Raising his binoculars, he took another look at the doorway before lowering them. He could easily watch the entrance from here.

He wanted a smoke, but couldn't risk someone noticing the smell. Those werewolves were wily bastards with enhanced senses. He glanced at his watch and sighed. Noon wouldn't come fast enough.

Meredith checked her liquor order for the third time. Nothing was adding up today. She blamed that on her poor night's sleep. And that was Isaiah's fault.

Just the thought of his name sent a tingle down her spine and caused her sex to clench. She dropped her clipboard on the bar and tugged on her hair in frustration.

"You okay?"

She'd been so caught up in her thoughts she hadn't noticed Benjamin coming out from the kitchen. He was wearing faded jeans and a T-shirt that should have been consigned to the scrap bin months ago. They all dressed casually when the bar was closed. All except her. As she dealt with suppliers and such, she opted to wear a pair of black dress pants and a tailored white blouse. Classic and simple.

"I'm fine." She offered him a smile, but his blue eyes, so much like her own, still looked concerned. "I didn't sleep well last night," she offered, hoping he'd leave it at that.

"I'm not surprised." His gaze went to the front windows and he peered out at the busy street. "We're all a little tense and will be until we're sure this Striker guy is gone for good." He stopped behind her and put his hands on her shoulders, his fingers digging at the knot of muscles there.

She groaned as he worked on a particularly tense spot. "I don't think we've seen the last of him." That was what had kept her awake most of the night. She vacillated between never wanting to see him again and desperately wanting to see him. It was no wonder she couldn't sleep. Her thoughts had circled round and round until she'd wanted to scream in frustration.

Of course, the arousal heating her skin, making her body pulse and tingle, hadn't helped either. She stepped away from her son, not wanting him to become aware of the heat coursing through her body.

His gaze narrowed, but he thankfully said nothing.

"It was quiet last night." She picked up the clipboard and held it in front of her breasts. She should have worn a sweater instead of a blouse. Her nipples were plainly showing through her bra and the thin material.

"Yeah." Benjamin raked his fingers through his shoulder-length black hair.

He kept it tied back with a leather cord when he was working, but otherwise he let it flow free. It was straight like hers. Both her boys took after her more than their father. That had always been a sore spot for Maxwell.

"Listen, Mom," he began. He stopped and paused, glancing out the window again. "I know this time of year is hard for you."

Oh, God. The last thing she wanted to talk about with her son was the fact she was going into heat. But she'd always prided herself on being honest and straightforward with them. It was a biological fact of their species. And there were two women in this pack so they needed to be aware of it. But still.

Thankfully, Neema had Teague to help her get through it when it was her time. Heck, they enjoyed it. And why wouldn't they? They loved one another. She'd never had that. Never known what it was like to be with a male who loved her. Maxwell had wanted her. But he hadn't loved her. Nor had she loved him. That made all the difference.

Benjamin was waiting and looking more than a little disconcerted. She laughed to try to ease his tension. "That's an understatement," she answered wryly. As she hoped, he grinned and some of the discomfort left him.

"It's a fact of life and we've dealt with it before," she reminded him.

"Not with an eligible male wolf sniffing around."

Meredith tensed and glared at her son. "So that's what this is all about. You're afraid I'll let my hormones rule my judgment."

He shook his head. "No. Yes. No."

She straightened her shoulders and met her son's gaze head on. "Which is it?"

"I don't know," he blurted out. "I love you and I'm worried. You didn't see the way that guy was looking at you last night."

What was left unsaid was the way she'd looked right back at Isaiah. Her sons were very intelligent, astute men. And so were the rest of the pack. There could have been no mistaking the spike in her arousal around Isaiah.

"I'll handle it." She was alpha. It was her job to handle the tough situations. She'd been doing it for years.

Benjamin brushed a lock of hair over her shoulder and offered her a smile that didn't quite reach his eyes. "I hope so."

He plucked the clipboard from her hands. "Let me finish that. Why don't you go and take a nap. Otherwise you're going to be beat by the end of tonight."

Meredith didn't argue with him. She skirted past the tables with the chairs piled on top, ignored the clang of pots and pans coming from the kitchen, and hurried by the office where Kevin was hard at work.

Her apartment, which was usually her haven, seemed stifling today. She longed to shift, to run. But that was impossible, especially now with the pack on high-alert.

Still, she could shift. She hurried into her bedroom and

kicked off her shoes. Slipping out of her clothing, she tossed them onto the chair in the corner. She closed her eyes and embraced her female wolf.

Her skin rippled and tingled and she fell forward, her hands touching the floor. Bones cracked as her limbs reformed. Her jaw elongated as black hair grew from her skin, covering her body in a thick pelt.

Meredith glanced into her floor-length mirror, studying the large black wolf that stared back. She was still in there, but the wolf, with her instinct to run, was at the forefront. It took all her control to keep the wolf from racing to the front door and clawing at it until she was free.

The bed beckoned, but she couldn't bear the thought of lying there. Not where she'd spent the night thinking of *him*. Padding out to the kitchen, she lay in a beam of sunshine, soaking up the warmth. Exhaustion beat at her and she closed her eyes, curling her body until she was comfortable.

The wolf's thoughts pushed her own to the background, allowing her to focus solely on the physical. The wolf was physically aroused, felt the call, the lure of the male werewolf she'd met last night. But he wasn't here now. Eventually, she settled enough to drop into a light doze.

Her last thought before she gave into sleep was that she hadn't seen the last of Isaiah Striker.

Chapter Five

Isaiah walked into Haven at a little past eleven o'clock that night. He'd fought with himself for hours, forming one argument after another as to why he should stay away. None of them mattered. He needed to see Meredith.

And there she was. As though she sensed his presence, she turned her head away from the couple she was talking to and their eyes met. He'd thought that last night was an anomaly. That seeing her again wouldn't feel like taking a punch to the heart and a roundhouse kick to the gut. He was wrong.

If anything, the impact was even more striking, her appeal even more pronounced. Like last night, she was wearing a slinky, form-fitting dress. This one was silver and was slit all the way to the top of her thigh on the right side, allowing him a glimpse of her long, shapely leg as she sauntered across the room. Her movements were unhurried. Graceful.

Her hair was up in some kind of twist and anchored at the back of her head. Isaiah's fingers itched to tug away the clips holding it and watch her glorious locks cascade down around her.

Her eyes seemed darker and more mysterious. Probably a trick of the lighting, but effective nonetheless. Long, thick lashes framed them, brushing against her high cheekbones when she blinked. Her lips were stained a dark burgundy color that highlighted their sensual shape. But there was no welcoming smile to be found.

All the fatigue, all the aggravations of the day washed away as adrenaline coursed through his veins, pumping up his muscles and sending much needed energy racing through his body. He felt alive with anticipation.

Her gaze flicked over his shoulder and he knew he was about to get some unwanted company.

"You were told not to come back."

Isaiah turned and faced Hank. Waves of aggression rolled off him. The younger male had been away from his post when he'd arrived. It was wishful thinking to imagine he'd go unnoticed for long, not with them watching for him.

"I didn't listen." He started to give Hank his back, to let the other werewolf know he didn't view him as a threat. A low growl rose up from the younger man.

"Control yourself," Meredith hissed, placing her hand on Hank's arm. "The last thing we need is one of you out of control." She included him in her scowl, but Isaiah knew she wasn't worried about him losing it, but the younger male.

"And you," she whirled on him. "What are you doing here?"

He raised his hand and stroked two fingers down the soft curve of her cheek. "I came to see you. I told you I'd be back."

Waves of frustration, anger and, finally, acceptance rolled off her. "You've seen me. Now leave."

He shook his head. "I haven't eaten since this morning." He hadn't taken the time after he'd slipped away from his surveillance of Riley's Garage. He'd hit his motel room long enough to shower and change before catching a cab to the club. The fact that he hadn't walked, hadn't taken the time to stretch his legs was telling. He hadn't been able to get here fast enough to suit him.

He glanced around and saw a table for two over near the edge of the small dance floor and started toward it. Hank made to follow him, but Meredith stopped him. "You need to keep a watch on the door."

He frowned as he caught an underlying tone of fear from Meredith. What was she afraid of? He heard the swish of material and the click of her heels on the hardwood floor and knew she was right behind him. A whiff of her perfume assailed his nostrils and his dick immediately stood at attention. No doubt about it. There was some powerful chemistry between them.

He stood by one of the chairs, his hands on the back of it as he waited for Meredith to sit. She gave a frustrated huff and slid onto the seat. The last thing she wanted to do was bring more attention to them so he knew he'd win this small battle. Isaiah took the chair nearest the wall. The vantage point gave him a good view of the entire club.

"You can't stay," she began.

He leaned across the table and caught her chin between his thumb and forefinger. "What's wrong?" Her skin was so soft, so inviting. He wanted to kiss away the worry lines between her brows. He shook his head. This was so unlike him. He knew he should be concerned about what that meant, but he couldn't work up the energy to care.

"What's wrong?" she repeated, looking at him like he was out of his mind. "I'll tell you what's wrong. A male I don't know has come sniffing around and I don't know what his game is." She glanced around to make certain no one could hear them before she continued. "Why are you here?"

Isaiah sat back in his chair and studied her. He figured he had about two minutes before another male member of her small pack made his presence known. Her sons had already been alerted to his presence and were glaring at him from behind the bar. The other males he'd met last night were stationed on either side of the club, their eyes glued to him and Meredith. The young female werewolf was nowhere to be seen.

He shook his head and sighed, knowing she probably wouldn't believe him. "I came here on business for my pack and I happened in here by accident. I never came looking for you, Meredith. Nobody sent me. I'm no danger to you or yours.

"I had to see you again," he continued when she sat there watching him. "There's something between us." He raked his fingers through his hair in frustration. "Damned if I can explain it."

"I'm nearing heat," came her wry reply.

Isaiah chuckled. "Yeah, I caught that. But it's more than that. I was drawn in here by your voice, by you."

"You 'bout ready to leave?" The challenge came from off to the left as one of Meredith's sons stepped up beside her.

"Michael." Isaiah could hear the warning note in her voice.

The younger male shook his head, a muscle in his jaw rippling as he clenched his teeth. "He needs to go."

"All this focus on me is attracting attention," Isaiah pointed out. "That's exactly what you don't want."

"If you don't leave, I can give you some help," Michael threatened.

Isaiah bared his teeth. "You're welcome to try."

"Enough." The words were softly spoken, but they were solid steel. Meredith stood and pushed in her chair. "Get something to eat. Stay and enjoy the music. But we're done."

She turned her back on him and headed toward the bar. Michael shot Isaiah a triumphant look over his shoulder as he rested his palm on his mother's back to guide her.

Isaiah tensed. He knew Michael was her son, but he didn't like seeing any male touch her. Jealousy was a new emotion for him. He didn't like it. He didn't like anything that made him feel as though he was out of control.

He thought about leaving, about getting up and walking out of here, out of Meredith's life forever. Except he couldn't make himself do it. For the first time, he had an inkling of what Joshua felt for Alex.

Not that he planned to mate with Meredith, even if she'd have him, which he suspected she wouldn't. She was too used to running the show, to being alpha. He suspected there was a darn good reason why she, a beautiful werewolf in her prime, was running around without a male beside her.

All he wanted was one night in her bed. Maybe two. The sexual attraction sizzling between them was off the charts. She felt it as much as he did. The trick was to get her to acknowledge it.

The same waitress from last night hurried up to his table and placed a menu in front of him. "Meredith sent me to take your order."

A slow smile turned up the corners of his mouth. She must not want him to go if she was encouraging him to have a meal. Either that or she was trying to rush his meal so he'd leave.

Isaiah opened the menu and began to order. He was starving. "I'll start with a double burger with the works, fries and a basket of ribs and wings." He rattled off the rest of his order. Tammy's eyes grew wider the more he ordered. When he was done, she took the menu and headed toward the kitchen.

Two hours later, he was pleasantly full and enjoying the three-piece jazz combo as they wound down for the night. The food had been excellent and he'd had the added attraction of watching Meredith all evening.

Every muscle in his body was tense with arousal. He'd had an erection the entire time, a testament to the attraction he felt for her. It had been both arousing and torturous to watch Meredith laughing and chatting with patrons. She had an easy stride, more of a glide as she circled the room over and over again, checking on people. A word here, a pat on the shoulder there. Bringing a smile to everyone.

Everyone but him.

She'd made a point of avoiding him. He didn't know whether to laugh at her audacity or drag her over his knee and spank her for torturing him all night long.

At least the rest of the pack had settled down. Oh, they were still all watching him, but they weren't quite so obvious about it. Even the younger female werewolf returned to work, although she kept to the far side of the floor, serving customers well away from him.

The club was filled with people having a good time. Laughter and chatter surrounded him. The smell of perfume, sweat and arousal mixed with that of the liquor and uneaten food, creating a scent that was unique to such places.

He should have hated it. Shouldn't have been able to last a half hour, let alone several. To say he disliked being closed in and surrounded by humans was an understatement. Yet, he felt none of the clawing pressure to escape that he usually did. Both he and his wolf were content to watch Meredith. Her mere presence seemed to calm the agitation that constantly plagued him.

Either that or he was desperate to get laid.

He wanted to believe that. There was no future for him here. Meredith had an established life and seemed quite happy without a male butting his nose into her business. There was no way he could permanently settle in the city. Impossible.

But that didn't mean they couldn't enjoy one another's company, burn up the sheets and make some very pleasant memories. He pondered for a bit and wondered if he could convince her of that.

The band announced their last song of the night. He hated to see it end. Meredith chose that moment to walk across the dance floor. She was obviously heading for the stage, but he rose quickly and intercepted her. "Dance with me."

Heat rolled off his body in waves as desire punched him in the gut. She was getting closer to going into heat. She smelled ripe and desirable. He wanted to rip off her clothes right here, right now, and mount her until they both yelled in pleasure.

Sweat popped out on his temple as he slowly ran a finger over her bare shoulder, down her biceps and back up again.

"I shouldn't," she began, and he knew she was going to say no.

He forestalled that by putting one hand on the small of her back and urging her closer. She put a hand on his chest in protest, and he captured it and began to sway with her in his arms. "Just one dance," he murmured.

She bit her bottom lip. He could practically hear her mind working through the pros and cons of the situation. He held his breath and breathed a sigh of relief when she finally nodded.

She didn't look at him, but stared at his chest as if she found it totally fascinating. The tension gripping him eased slightly as they began to move, their bodies swaying easily as though they'd danced together a hundred times. There was none of the awkwardness usually associated with a first dance. The floor wasn't quite full, but there were other couples taking advantage of the final song. It was slow and mellow, with an undertone of sensuality that stoked the already burning embers between them.

He nuzzled her hair, loving the feel of the silky softness against his rough cheek, the fresh scent of her shampoo teasing his nose. It was something floral that made him think of a patch of wildflowers in a summer meadow. His palm made circles around the small of her back, urging her even closer.

There was no way she couldn't notice his rather large erection pressing against her belly. She swayed and her breasts rubbed against his chest. He caught his breath and gave a low growl.

Her head came up and her lips twitched. The little she-wolf was laughing at him. She knew very well how damn aroused he was. In retaliation, he released his grip on her hand and ran his fingers down the thin silver strap at her shoulder, following it down the slope of her breast and into the deep vee of her cleavage.

Her lips parted on a low moan and a surge of arousal hit him. He could smell the sweet cream dampening her panties and knew it was because of him.

Isaiah danced her to the edge of the floor and beyond, tucking them into a dark corner behind a post. She tensed, but she didn't protest. He leaned down and touched his lips to hers.

This was crazy. Meredith had no idea what madness had led her to agree to a dance with Isaiah. Not that she'd actually agreed. It was more that he'd pulled her into his arms and started moving. Not that she'd protested.

There was something about the tall, pushy male that drew her. She'd watched him sitting alone at his table, all the while doing her best not to let him or any of her pack know what she was doing. He, on the other hand, made no pretense that he was doing anything else but watching her.

For hours, she'd felt his eyes on her body as she moved through the club. It had been as potent as a physical caress.

Although she'd smiled and chatted with customers and friends, her breasts had swelled until her dress felt unbearably constricting and confining.

And her sex. Dear heaven, she ached so bad she wanted to scream. Her underwear was soaked and every step she took was torture as it rubbed the crotch of her panties against her swollen clit.

By the time Isaiah had put his hand on her, she'd been ready to jump him and climb on top of his rather impressive erection. It didn't matter how many times she told herself it was simple biology. She wanted him.

Dancing with him simply continued the foreplay they'd been indulging in all night long. Because that's what this was, and they were both mature enough to understand that.

She'd made sure he was able to watch her as she'd chatted and worked tonight. All but taunting him to come and get her. A male in less control of himself would have either left or made an overt play for her. He'd done neither. It was then she'd known she was dealing with a mature male, one who was a skilled tracker and hunter, able to wait patiently for his prey.

Knowing that, she'd have been much better off leaving the floor of battle and retiring to her room for the night. But she'd never been a coward, not since the day she'd taken her sons and run, and she had no intentions of starting now.

And, if she was being honest with herself, there was a part of her that enjoyed being chased by such a virile male. For the first time in her eighty-five years, she felt a longing for a particular male. It scared her even as it lured her.

By the time he drew her into the darkness, she'd expected him to ravage her. He'd surprised her yet again by barely touching his lips to hers. Bastard. He knew that would make her want even more.

Even knowing that it was a sensual trap set by a master, she went up on her toes and deepened the kiss. He made a low growl that went right to her core, making her inner muscles clench with need.

She touched her tongue to his and he slid his along hers and into her mouth. His large hand cupped the back of her head, tilting it slightly for a better fit. Oh, he tasted fine. Hot and masculine. Relentless.

She loved his eyes. They were the color of bittersweet dark chocolate—her favorite kind—and fringed with thick lashes that did nothing to detract from his masculinity.

His heart was pounding beneath the hand she had pressed against his chest. He was as aroused as she was. She could feel the heat coming off his big body, the tension in his thick muscles.

Raising her hands, she glided her palms over his heavy biceps and shoulders. His hair was down around his shoulders and she sifted her fingers through it.

He responded by yanking her lower body more firmly into the curve of his. Her mound rubbed enticingly against his erection. *Oh, that feels so good.* She hooked her right thigh over his hip, grateful for the slit in her dress that allowed the motion.

With his hand on her ass guiding her, she rubbed her mound over his hard shaft, imaging how good it would feel if they were both naked, her pussy gliding over his thick shaft.

She sucked in a breath and started to push away, knowing she had to stop this madness, but Isaiah worked his hips against hers. The movement sent his erection sliding over her sex in such a delicious way she gasped. She tilted her head back as she tried to get enough air into her lungs to keep from passing out.

It was too good. It wasn't nearly enough.

The band stopped abruptly and some of the houselights came on. Meredith gasped again, this time with dismay instead of arousal. She pushed on his chest. "We have to stop."

She pulled her leg down and her dress settled around her. Isaiah's grip tightened briefly and she held her breath. Would he release her or would he try to hold her? After what seemed like an eternity but was probably only a few seconds, he dropped his hand by his side. Immediately, she felt cold without his touch, even though it was what she'd wanted.

Flustered, she brushed a hand over her hair and straightened her dress straps. Anything but look at Isaiah. His hair was slightly rumpled where she'd run her fingers through it and his eyes were slumberous and inviting. There was no mistaking the hard-on pressing against the front of his jeans.

"You have to go." It seemed as though she was a broken record when it came to Isaiah. Not that he ever listened to her. But she had to get him out of here before she did something stupid like invite him up to her apartment. That would not go over well with the rest of the pack.

He frowned and raised his hand to touch her face. She took a step back.

"I was hoping we could continue this at your place." His voice was thick with arousal and steeped with sensual promise.

She pressed her thighs together to ease the ache that never seemed to leave her these days. Being around him seemed to heighten it. But that was no surprise. Mother Nature did her best to make certain the male and female of the species wanted to mate.

But she had to be smart. She had a pack, mostly filled with

half-breeds. Would he still want her if he knew? Worse, would he attack her and her children? She couldn't risk it.

Dragging her tattered composure around her, she faced him. "You had your dance. The club is now closed."

While she'd been standing there dealing with Isaiah and the aftermath of what had happened between them, her family had cleared out the last of the patrons and staff. She sensed concern emanating from all of them and knew Isaiah's continued presence here was undermining her authority with the pack.

"It's past time for you to go." She put on her haughtiest voice and manner as she waved toward the door.

Instead of getting angry, Isaiah gave her a look filled with understanding and a touch of pity. That fired her anger. "And don't come back. We're done."

He started past her, pausing long enough to whisper in her ear. Not that it mattered. With their preternatural hearing and the deathly quiet in the club, the others could hear him as easily as if they were standing next to them. "I've told you before. We're far from done."

She didn't turn to watch him leave, but she knew the minute the door closed behind him. The atmosphere was different. The room felt...empty.

Taking a deep breath, she turned to face her family. They were all watching her with varying degrees of concern. There was also a tinge of fear and anger.

She held up her hand. "I'm not talking about this tonight. We'll take watches again like last night. Michael, you're first. Work out a schedule amongst yourself and call me if you sense anything suspicious."

No one spoke as she strode past, but she could feel their gazes on her as she left the room. Isaiah had created this tension in her pack. No, that wasn't exactly true. She had. She'd allowed this male, this stranger, to disrupt their lives. And it had to stop.

Now if only she could make her body and her emotions listen.

She let herself into her apartment and shut the door firmly behind her.

Chapter Six

Meredith tilted back her head and enjoyed the autumn sunshine beaming down on her face as she meandered down the street. She'd needed to get away from the club, away from the constant tension that seemed to permeate the place these days.

True to his word, Isaiah had come back to the club last night and the night before that. And she had no doubt that he'd be there again tonight. It was enough to drive a woman stark raving mad. And considering how her hormones were jumping around these days, she didn't have far to go.

So she'd done what any sensible woman in her situation would do. She'd gone shopping. Other than sex, that was the one surefire way to work off some stress.

She'd hit her favorite vintage store and found a gorgeous black dress that shimmered with threads of silver. It was from the twenties and fit her like a dream. The boutique had also had a sexy pair of sling backs in silver. And what do you know? They'd been just her size. Surely a sign that she was meant to buy them.

The walk around her neighborhood relaxed her. It reminded her of why she'd bought property and settled here in the first place. It had been a rough area of the city back in the mid-eighties when she'd purchased the building. Many of the surrounding buildings had been derelict or close to it. But even then she'd seen the changes happening to the area. The artists had been moving in, bringing with them a creative, eclectic vibe that still existed today. She'd hated to leave and had missed the place all the years she'd been away. Coming back twelve years ago had been like coming home.

"Good morning, Miss Meredith." Ivan Prentski, who owned a local deli, greeted her as she passed. In spite of the fact he'd lived in America for forty years, he still had the accent from the land of his birth. She liked that. He was out sweeping in front of his shop, which he usually did several times a day. Meredith figured it was a way for him to get out of the shop and check what was going on around the neighborhood.

"It certainly is, Ivan."

He leaned on the handle of his broom. "We have fresh salami and pastrami, perfect for sandwiches." He paused for effect. "And Mama made fresh pastries."

Damn him, he knew her weakness. "You're an evil man," she groused. His mother might be nearly seventy, but she baked like a dream.

He threw back his head and gave a booming laugh as he held the door open for her. His sheer joy made her smile, pushing her worries aside. What the hell. She'd treat herself to a half-dozen pastries. Maybe even a dozen. Maybe she could eat away the sexual tension that was her constant companion.

Before she hit the counter, she'd been stopped by a local musician trying to book a gig. She'd said hello to a woman she knew and chatted with a local artist whose work she hung in the club. It was something she did with several artists. She liked to support local talent.

Meredith hurried the conversation, not committing to seeing the artist's new pieces. She knew her body and she was very close to having to shut herself in her room for a day or two. It was dangerous for her to be out on her own with her body emitting such powerful pheromones, but she hadn't been able to bear being inside. Not this morning.

Ivan stared at her from the other side of the counter, worry in his gaze. "You okay? You look a little flushed."

Heat rolled over her skin and sweat popped out on her brow. Damn she needed to get home. Now. "I'm fine. I've got to go."

"What about your pastries?" Ivan called as she turned to leave.

"Another time." She burst out of the store and hurried toward home, ignoring the calls of her name behind her.

Damn. What had possessed her to leave her apartment this morning?

She ignored the trembling in her limbs as her long legs closed the distance to her home. She knew darn well what had made her leave her apartment. *Isaiah*. Memories of his eyes watching her, his fingers caressing her. That's what. She'd known she was close, but she hadn't been able to bear being alone in her bedroom with her fantasies.

She heaved a sigh of relief as the club came into view. She was practically running now, chest heaving, muscles aching.

Hank was outside and saw her. He started toward her, but she waved him back. His eyes widened when she got within ten feet from him.

"Oh, shit." He might be her adopted son, but he was also a male and this was a difficult time for him as well, as it was for all her adopted sons. Only her biological sons were immune.

Meredith would have laughed at the look on his face, only it wasn't funny. Her clothing was torture against her skin. She wanted to claw it all off and run naked through the streets. Which would get her arrested and charged with public indecency. And wouldn't *that* be fun.

Instead, she raced past him, shoving her bags at him as she went by. She didn't pause as she hurried through the club and up the back stairs. Michael called out to her, but she ignored him.

She was panting hard and yanking at her shirt by the time she shoved open the door to her apartment. She slammed and locked the door behind her.

"Oh, God," she moaned as a wave of desire hit her like a bolt of lightning, knocking her to the floor.

Moaning, she waited for it to pass. She pressed her thighs together and wrapped her arms around her body. There was nothing she could do but ride out the ripples of pure, unadulterated lust. It was worse than it had been in years. Yet something else she could blame on Isaiah. Having him around, being attracted to him, made the situation much harder for her to bear.

When the episode finally eased, she dragged herself to her feet, almost clunking herself with her purse, which miraculously was still hooked over her shoulder. She staggered into her room, dumped her purse in the chair and kicked off her shoes.

She tore her shirt off, ignoring the ripping sound. Her bra came next. She heaved a sigh of relief as the cooler air hit her nipples. Jeans and panties quickly followed.

Naked, she climbed onto the bed and sank into the mattress. She wedged one pillow between her thighs and held the other in a death grip. When the next ripple of arousal shot through her, she buried her face in the pillow and moaned.

It was going to be a hell of a long day.

Isaiah strode into Haven. Once again, Hank had been on the door. The bouncer had growled, but allowed him to pass. The young male knew trying to stop him would only bring trouble and attention and that was exactly what they didn't want.

Tammy, the human waitress, waved at him as he settled at a table. This was the third night since his dance with Meredith. Heck, he was almost a regular at this point.

He glanced around but didn't see the object of his desire anywhere, but that wasn't unusual. She might be in the office or checking on something in the kitchen. He knew from his past visits that she wouldn't be away from the club floor for long.

His phone rang and he reached into his pocket, knowing who it was even before he answered. Only one person ever called him. "What?" The band chose that moment to begin playing a song, but thankfully it was an acoustic folk group tonight so he could hear his brother on the other end.

"Where the hell are you?"

"A club. I'm getting something to eat." He hadn't told his brother about Meredith. He hadn't told anyone.

"Should I be worried?" Joshua asked. "It's not like you to voluntarily go into a crowded bar. Takeout is more your speed. And why are you still in Chicago? I figured you'd have been home two days ago."

"I'm not ready to leave yet."

The silence on the other end was deafening. After a long minute, Joshua finally spoke. "Should I send someone else?"

Those few words sent him reeling, but Isaiah absorbed the blow. It was the first time in his life his brother had ever questioned his ability to carry out any task. And damn it, it hurt worse than he'd thought.

"I need a few more days. Is that too much to ask? Alex will get her stuff."

"Are you sure you don't need me to come to Chicago?"

Isaiah released a low growl of warning. "If you don't trust me to do the job, send whoever the hell you want." He almost ended the call. Almost. But habit and instinct were too entrenched to be denied, so he waited.

"I'm worried about you, not the damn job," Joshua snarled.

The anger flowed out of him as quickly as it had arisen. He'd been tense the past few days. Arousal was riding him hard.

He spent all his days watching for rogue werewolves and bounty hunters and his nights with a raging hard-on with no relief in sight. Meredith had been giving him the cold shoulder since the night of their dance. Still, he'd managed to steal several hot kisses. The woman wanted him no matter how she tried to ignore it.

"You still there?" his brother prompted.

"Yeah. I'm still here." He appreciated Joshua's concern, but the last thing he needed was his brother running around the city and maybe discovering Meredith and her pack. It was important to her to keep her small pack off the radar of the bigger ones. He respected that even if he wasn't quite sure why she did it. There was safety in numbers. "I'm just tense. I haven't seen anyone, but the back of my neck is tingling."

"Good enough," Joshua said. "Give it another day or two and, if you still feel that way, leave it and we'll try again in a month or so."

"Will do. Talk to you soon." Tammy set his beer on the table as he finished his call with his brother. He clicked off and tucked his phone away. "Thanks, Tammy. Where's Meredith?"

The blonde waitress was amused by his pursuit of Meredith and the way both her sons watched and glared at him all night long. It was nice to have someone on his side. Tammy chewed on her bottom lip. "Benjamin said she was sick. But I've worked here for almost a year and Meredith has never taken a sick day. She shows up every night, even if it's just for an hour or two."

Fear clenched his gut, but he let none of his concern show outwardly. "Thanks." He sat back, picked up his glass and sipped his beer. Over the rim, he studied the men working behind the bar. Competent was the word that came to mind. Tough was another.

What had led them here? It was a question he'd asked himself about a hundred times over the past few days. Sitting on the rooftop by Riley's Garage watching for bounty hunters and rogue werewolves gave him plenty of time to think. He was a man of action and all this downtime was starting to get on his nerves. He wanted an enemy he could face and fight.

Barring that, a bout of long, hot sex would do.

He shifted in his chair, doing his best to ignore the permanent bulge in the front of his jeans. He'd been forced to take himself in hand, so to speak, several times over the past couple of days. It eased the stress for a short while, but the moment he saw Meredith the sexual desire came storming back.

Where was she?

He didn't bother to order anything to eat. He'd grabbed a pizza on the way back to his motel room and devoured it before he'd showered and changed. The only thing that could quench his hunger was Meredith and, so far, she was proving to be elusive.

The lean redhead with the tats and piercings worked his

way around the room and headed toward his table. He hadn't had much contact with this member of the pack. There was a barely suppressed air of violence surrounding him, as though he was hanging on to his temper by a thread. Teague was his name. He'd learned all their names and a little bit about them. Tammy was a font of information.

He seemed unlikely to be mated with gentle Neema, but there was no doubting the devotion between the pair. There was also no doubting that Teague would kill anyone who threatened his mate. Isaiah could respect that.

"You need to go home." Teague wasted no time on pleasantries and got straight to the point.

He lifted his glass and took another sip of beer. "I'm just enjoying a drink."

Teague clenched his jaw and frustration crossed his face. "You need to leave Meredith alone."

Isaiah studied the younger man. They were all younger than Meredith. By how much, he couldn't be sure. But none of them seemed that old. He'd guess most of them to be in their thirties or early forties, barely adults in his world where childhood ended in the early twenties. Because they lived so long, they matured slower, not hitting their stride until they were in their fifties.

There was still no sign of Meredith. Whether she was sick or just avoiding him, he had to know. He also didn't want to stir up the pack. Anything could happen without her calming influence.

Draining his glass in one swallow, Isaiah pushed back from the table and stood. He was bigger and stronger than the younger man, but Teague didn't back down. A grin tugged at Isaiah's mouth. Teague reminded him of his younger brother, Simon, more guts than common sense.

"I'm going." He held up his hands and Teague slowly eased back from the table. Isaiah felt several pairs of eyes on him as he made his way to the entrance. He waved at Tammy as he left. The music faded as he stepped out onto the busy sidewalk. The night air was cool with just a hint of a bite to it. The perfect night for a run.

His skin rippled as his wolf clamored to be released. Years of practice allowed him to master the beast and assert control. Hank watched from the doorway of Haven as he prowled down the sidewalk. Isaiah kept going for several blocks to make sure Hank hadn't decided to tail him before ducking down an alleyway and doubling back.

No way was he leaving without checking on Meredith. The thought of her being ill was unacceptable. He wanted her to be healthy and happy all the time. An impossible feat, but he wanted it nonetheless.

Isaiah kept all his senses on high alert at he circled round the back of the building. The cool air did little to disguise the smell of garbage emanating from the dumpster, or the stench of fuel and exhaust fumes as vehicles of every description traveled up and down the road.

Then there was the noise. The constant hum from the electrical wires, cell phones ringing, music from the club, people talking and the rumble of traffic. There was never any peace to be found from the constant din.

He worked his way closer to the building, his sneakers making no sound on the dirt and gravel as he walked with care and purpose. A metal fire escape sat near the back on the right side of the building. It suited his purpose just fine. He bent his knees and then leapt. The muscles in his thighs and calves bunched and stretched as he jumped. He extended his long arms, hands ready. He hoped the bottom rung of the stairs was strong enough to hold his weight.

Metal bit into his palms as he made contact. Closing his fingers around the rung, he didn't wait until he was steady, but reached for the next one and pulled his body up. In seconds, he was on the first landing, crouched next to a window.

He paused and listened. The noise of the city continued on around him. There was no indication that anyone had seen or heard him. Still, he waited another ten minutes before he was finally satisfied he was alone.

Easing forward, he peered through the window. The room was dark, but that was no barrier for him. He could see as well in the dark as he could in a clearly lit room. It was obviously a living room. The sofa and chairs were a chocolate brown and grouped in a conversation area. A flat screen television perched on an entertainment center.

He shifted and looked further into the room and could see the kitchen. It was neat and tidy, but comfortable and homey. Much like Meredith.

His ears perked up as a low moan reached them through the glass. *Meredith.*

Placing his hands on the window, he applied a steady pressure until the lock gave with a pop. It would have been quicker to break the damn glass, but that might have brought someone running. It would also piss off Meredith if she had to replace her window. He'd fix the lock himself before he left.

Isaiah shoved the window up and threw one leg over the sill. He pulled his body inside and staggered, his back hitting the wall as a blast of erotic perfume assailed him.

Meredith was in full-blown heat.

As though dragged by an invisible rope, Isaiah headed toward the bedroom, his keen sense of smell leading the way. The door was closed, but he shoved it open. The panel hit the wall, bounced and started to close again, but he put out his hand to catch it before it hit him in the face.

The rest of the room faded around him as his gaze zeroed in on the woman writhing and moaning on the bed. The forest green comforters had been kicked to the floor and she was sprawled naked on her back, her hips undulating, her legs moving restlessly. Her fingers tugged on the sheets as her head rolled from side to side.

Her hair was a black curtain across the pale green sheets. Her skin was coated in a light sheen of sweat, making her skin glow in the light from the street lamp drifting in through the window. Her nipples were pebbled and her pussy glistened with cream.

Isaiah licked his lips in anticipation of tasting her. He'd never seen a more beautiful sight in his life.

Finally sensing his presence, she opened her eyes and stared at him. He didn't move. It had to be her choice. She had to invite him.

Even if it killed him.

His cock was jerking and throbbing, wanting out from his confining jeans. His lungs worked hard to suck in much needed air. His nostrils hummed with her unique scent. He couldn't tear his eyes away from her.

"Let me help you." He almost didn't recognize his own voice. It was guttural, almost animalistic.

"I won't let you claim me," she gasped, panting hard between each word.

He shook his head. "I wouldn't. Not like this." And he realized it was true. As much as he wanted her to belong to him, he wouldn't claim her when she was in heat, when biology was pushing them both toward it. He wanted it to be her choice.

He shook his head. What the hell was he thinking? He didn't want a mate. There was no place in his life for one. Let alone one who came with so many built-in responsibilities. He'd proven when he'd allowed his sister to be taken by bounty hunters that he wasn't fit to protect anyone. It was why he'd never taken the mantle of Striker with his pack. Why he'd devoted his entire life to protecting what family he had left, to the exclusion of all else.

Just the mere thought of tying himself down to a female, of staying in the city permanently, should have sent him running.

He took a step toward the bed.

She licked her lips, her hips arching. She moaned and Isaiah couldn't hold back a groan as he was bombarded with another wave of sexual desire. Her scent was so thick in the air he could almost taste her on his tongue.

"Meredith?" He couldn't wait any longer when she cried out. Pain tinged her cry of longing.

Isaiah yanked his shirt from the waistband of his jeans, dragged it over his head and tossed it aside. His lungs were working like a bellows now. In and out. In and out.

He kicked off his sneakers and tugged at the button of his jeans, but his hands paused on the zipper. Damn his misplaced sense of honor.

He strode to the side of the bed and reached down, cupping her face with his hand. "Look at me." She closed her eyes and shook her head. He gave her a small shake. "Look at me," he commanded.

She swallowed hard and opened her eyes. They were blue-gray pools of need. Like an ocean in the middle of a storm.

"Let me help you. I promise I won't try to claim you."

He could sense how torn she was. He slid his fingers down

her neck, tracing her delicate collarbone. His hands hovered over her breasts, her nipples straining toward his palms.

"I won't let you," she panted.

He withdrew his hand. Pain tore at his gut and his heart ached at her rejection. He tried to swallow the lump in his throat but it was too large. He took a step back even as every instinct screamed for him to stay. His wolf growled and pushed against his skin, struggling for release.

Isaiah gripped his hair with his hands and tugged. He had to get out of here before he did something he'd regret for the rest of his life.

"Won't let you," she said again. "Not claim me." She held out her hand to him. "Help me. Be with me."

Happiness surged through him. She wasn't rejecting him, just being permanently claimed and mated in the way of their kind. He could live with that. The happiness was followed by a bolt of lust so great it almost doubled him over.

He didn't need to be asked twice. He dragged down his zipper and stripped off his jeans and socks. Since he didn't wear underwear, he was now naked.

His cock rose up from the nest of curls at the base, strong and proud and more than ready to pleasure her. The thick veins pulsed and his shaft jerked as he crawled onto the bed. He kept going until he was straddling her on his hands and knees.

Reaching her hand up, she grabbed a hank of his hair and yanked him down to her. He gave a sharp laugh, her enthusiasm pleasing him no end. It quickly died when their lips met. Laughter faded, replaced by an overwhelming need that would only be assuaged when he had his cock buried in her hot sheath, fucking her until neither of them could stand it any longer.

Meredith didn't know where Isaiah had come from. Like someone in a dream, she'd been lost in a maze, her sexual desire swamping her. It was worse than it had been in years. Her body recognized there was an eligible male close by. One she wanted in spite of the fact he was mostly a stranger.

Thankfully, her family knew what was happening. Hank would have told them what kind of shape she'd been in earlier today. She was confident they'd handle the club for the next two days. It certainly wasn't the first time this had happened, even though it was one of the worst.

There was no way they'd tell Isaiah what was going on. They'd made no secret of the fact they wanted him gone for good. But somehow he'd come to her anyway.

He climbed atop her, holding his weight off her body, supporting himself on his knees and hands. God, she needed him. Needed his mouth on hers, his hands on her skin and his shaft buried deep in her tight, slick channel. Fisting her fingers in his hair, she yanked his mouth down to hers. She heard him laugh and then their lips met and nothing else mattered. He tasted musky and male and so inviting.

She tugged his head back and they stared at one another, both of them panting hard. Her body yearned to be covered by his. She sucked in a deep breath and took the plunge, knowing it would be too late to stop him once they started. She would have to trust him not to claim her.

"Help me."

Isaiah growled and swooped back down, his mouth taking hers in a brutal kiss.

Chapter Seven

Meredith thought she could handle sex with Isaiah and maintain a safe emotional distance, stay slightly detached. After all, it was just sex between two consenting adults.

But she was wrong. His lips ate at hers, his teeth tugged on her bottom lip, his tongue invaded her mouth until the only breath she had was his.

Her head swam. Her body craved more. Everything else ceased to exist. There was only Isaiah and the pleasure he was making her feel.

With a growl, he pulled away and stared down at her. They were both panting hard. "You are so beautiful." He lifted one of his hands and smoothed it over her hair. He peppered her forehead, cheeks, nose and chin with kisses. He nibbled at her jawline, working his way to her ear. His sharp teeth nipped at her lobe, tugging on the small gold hoop she wore there.

Her skin tingled where he touched her. The sensation worked its way down her torso and settled between her legs. She smoothed her hands over his chest, loving the play of the thick muscles beneath his skin. He was so strong, so hard. His shoulders bunched as he leaned closer and used his tongue to trace the whorls of her ear. She sucked in a breath, loving the sensual caress.

She arched up while using her grip on his shoulders to pull

him down. The firm plane of his chest brushed against her breasts. She sighed at the light caress. The tips of her nipples were red and her breasts ached.

"Touch me." She hooked her right leg around his thigh and tugged until his body was covering hers. The hair on his legs tickled the sensitive skin of her inner thighs. His heavy erection pressed against her sex, wringing a moan of pleasure from deep within her.

He was so large. So substantial. She felt feminine, almost delicate next to his bulk. An unusual sensation for her considering she was only an inch off six feet.

He arched his hips into her, working his erection against her slick folds. She spread her legs wider to accommodate him and earned his praise. "Yeah, that's it, baby. Let me in."

Isaiah slid a hand beneath her, cupping her butt and raising her into his thrusts. The smooth, firm weight of his shaft rubbed against her clit, setting off a series of fireworks inside her.

She began to pant like she'd been running for miles. Every inch of her body ached and she knew she was close to coming. She wanted to hold out, to make it last. But she'd been primed by days of his teasing kisses and the sheer magnetism of his presence. Combined with the thick mixture of hormones coursing through her and it all proved too much.

She cried out, her eyes closing and her head kicking back, as the first spasm hit. Clutching at his butt, she silently urged him not to stop. He kept working his cock against her clit, sliding through the swollen, damp folds until she was spent.

Damn, she'd orgasmed and he hadn't even been inside her yet. She opened her eyes to find him watching her, a tiny smile playing around the corners of his mouth.

"Now that the edge is off, I want to taste you." Putting

actions to his words, he dropped a quick, hard kiss on her lips and nuzzled his way down to her breasts.

Damn, she was hot. His head was still spinning from watching her orgasm. Hearing her soft whimpers of need followed by her cry of passion, seeing her lips parted, wet and enticing, smelling her lush perfume as she found release was a complete rush.

The head of his dick was wet, a reminder of how close to the edge he was. But he didn't want to enter her. Not yet. Not until he'd tasted her.

Her chest was still noticeably rising and falling, but her breathing was beginning to even back out. He lapped at the swell of her breast, tracing the edge of the mound with his tongue.

He shifted his weight so that his cock wasn't touching her. Too much of that and it would be all over for him. He turned his attention back to Meredith, ignoring the insistent need pounding at the base of his erection.

Her breasts were perfect. Plump mounds, tipped with pale pink nipples that were now puckered and red. Ripe. She reminded him of a raspberry bush. There were plenty of thorns, but the juicy red berries were well worth the effort it took to get them.

He touched the tip of his tongue to one ripe bud. She gasped and pulled at his hair, urging him closer. He took what she offered, opening his lips and drawing the nub into his mouth and sucking.

Her soft cry was music to his ears. He continued his sensual torture, flicking at the tip with his tongue before releasing it. She whimpered in protest and he blew on her damp flesh, pulling another cry from her.

"More," she commanded, tugging on his hair. He loved the way she wanted him and gave her what she needed. Working his way over to her other breast, he gave it the same attention.

She wasn't still for a moment. Her entire body moved under and around him. Her hands clutched at his hair and then his shoulders. Her nails lightly scored his skin in a way that made him want to throw back his head and howl his pleasure.

She ran her hands up and down the length of his spine, touching him wherever she could reach him. Her legs were restless and she wrapped her left one around him.

Isaiah couldn't remember a time in his life when he'd felt this alive. This damn good. And he savored every moment of it.

Giving her plump nipple one final kiss, he worked his way down her torso. His hands followed the slight curve of her hips as his lips licked and sucked over her stomach. He circled her belly button with his tongue, dipping in briefly before continuing his journey.

He situated himself between her spread thighs, widening her legs with his broad shoulders. This was what he'd been waiting for. Her pubic hair was damp. He buried his face against it and breathed in her scent.

His cock jerked so forcefully he was afraid he was going to spill himself then and there. He gritted his teeth and fought through the wave of lust that pounded in him like a runaway heartbeat.

Spreading her thighs as wide as they could go, he lapped up one side of her slick folds and down the other. Meredith moaned, arching her hips against his face.

Yeah, this was what he wanted. He sucked and tasted every inch of her pussy, reveling in every cry, every whimper of pleasure. Her fingers had a death grip on his hair, as though she was afraid he'd leave her.

No chance of that. Her cream was like nectar, an erotic cocktail that made him drunk with pleasure. She tasted sweet, like honey, but spicy too. A hint of cinnamon maybe. Mixed with a musky feminine scent of desire.

He slowly pushed one thick finger into her sheath. Her inner muscles fluttered around it, gripping it hard.

"*Yes*," she hissed.

He glanced up and marveled at the sensual picture she made. One arm was thrown over her head while the other held him to her. Her lips were parted on a low cry. The soft mounds of her breasts swayed with each breath she took, her nipples red and puckered. Her head was tilted back and her eyes were closed.

Growling low in his chest, he doubled his efforts. She had to come now. He couldn't wait any longer. His sense of urgency seemed to fire hers. She bucked her hips when he sucked her clit between his lips and flicked the hard nub of nerves with his tongue.

"So close," she moaned.

He pulled back and blew on her heated flesh. "Come for me, Meredith. Come now."

He pushed a second finger into her sheath, working both digits in and out of her hot core. The first ripples came a few seconds later and he felt the gush of her release coat his hand.

There was no time to wait. He had to be in her. Had to feel the slick walls of her channel tightening around his dick. Sitting back on his heels, he withdrew his fingers and brought them to his mouth.

She watched him, her blue eyes dark with passion, as he thrust them into his mouth and sucked, licking her cream from them, not wanting to waste a single drop.

"It's not enough," she panted, biting on her bottom lip. "I need you inside me."

Gripping her hips, he dragged her toward him, draping her thighs over his. Angling his body, he guided his cock to her opening and pushed.

Meredith was finding it hard to breathe. The heady scent of sex permeated the air, pushing her desire higher. She'd come twice already and he hadn't even been inside her yet. Never had she experienced anything like this.

She'd been married. She'd had lovers. But she'd never had a male make love to her as though her pleasure was all that mattered. It was erotic and enthralling. A woman could easily become addicted to it.

Maxwell had been all about his pleasure. If she'd found some, that was all well and good, but certainly not a prerequisite. Being in heat was the rare time she'd enjoyed sex with him. She'd found some pleasure with her human lovers. A sense of well-being and satisfaction. But this blew the doors off all her notions of what sex could and should be.

She knew she should be frightened out of her mind just thinking about the kind of power Isaiah could wield over her. But right now, she honestly didn't care.

She felt as though her body was experiencing what it was meant to for the first time in her life.

His hard thighs supported hers as he angled his thick shaft toward her channel. The broad head of his penis pushed past the constricted muscles banded around the opening. She gasped as the blunt tip of his cock forged into her.

He paused, his dark eyes watching her carefully. His powerful chest was heaving and she sensed his control was about to snap. And suddenly that's what she wanted. She wanted him out of control. As lost to the passion swirling between them as she was.

Meredith lifted her hips, driving him a bit deeper. His cock was broad and stretched her slick sheath. It had been quite a while for her, and she'd never had a lover as well endowed as Isaiah.

He emitted a feral growl, his lips drawing back and exposing his gleaming white teeth. The muscles in his neck corded and his strong hands gripped her hips.

She squeezed her inner muscles around him and his control snapped. He thrust his cock into her, not stopping until he was buried to the hilt.

Pleasure mixed with a twinge of pain as her body softened to accommodate his girth and length. Meredith panted hard, concentrating on trying to relax and accept him.

His head dropped down and he took several deep breaths before looking at her. "You okay?"

Now that the initial shock was over, her body was humming with pleasure. Her sheath was rhythmically squeezing and releasing his shaft, the slick, wet walls expanding and contracting. The initial pain vanished, quickly replaced by pleasure.

"I'm wonderful," she all but purred.

Isaiah kept his gaze on her as he pulled back until only the head of his cock was inside her. Then he plunged back in again.

Oh, yes. This was what she wanted. What she needed.

Hormones surged through her bloodstream. He continued to thrust, slow and deep. A fire flared between her thighs and only he could quench it. "Harder," she pleaded.

Isaiah banded an arm around her waist, his hips pumping faster. His cock powered into her, his thrusts growing shorter.

He seemed to go deeper as he angled her hips upward.

She cried out as the head of his cock dragged over a sensitive spot on the inside of her sheath. She dug her fingernails into his ass. "More."

He shifted suddenly, rolling with her.

Fear shafted through her. Was he going to try to get her on her stomach so he could claim her? She resisted, but stopped fighting him when he ended up on his back with her on top of him.

"Shhh," he ran his hands over her back and sides, calming her struggles. "Take what you need from me. Ride me."

She sat back and the motion drove him deeper inside her. They both groaned and then Isaiah gave a short laugh. "That is if you don't kill me first."

Meredith wasn't quite sure what to think of him. She'd never laughed with a man in bed before. Sex was serious business. It still was, but she hadn't realized it could be fun too.

Isaiah was opening up a whole new world for her. But it would be a short-lived one. He wouldn't be staying. That thought put a damper on her desire until he cupped her breasts and thumbed her puckered nipples. Then it came roaring back like a freight train running down a mountainside. There was no stopping it.

"Ride me," he urged her again.

She planted her hands on his chest and her hair flowed over her shoulders, pooling around him.

He groaned. "I love the feel of your hair on my skin. I want to feel it everywhere."

She had a flash of wrapping the long, black length around his cock as she sucked the tip. That surprised her. She'd given oral sex many times before to satisfy her partners, but she'd never gained much pleasure from the act. Somehow she knew it would be different with Isaiah. Just thinking about going down on him was pushing her buttons.

He gently tugged on her nipples and her entire body jerked. Pressure was building inside her that needed to be released. Her hormones were clamoring for him to come inside her. Only that would ease the ache that had been building inside her for days now.

Isaiah let one of his hands slide down her torso and delve between her thighs. He touched her clit and a shot of pure pleasure went through her.

Up and down, she raised and dropped her body over his. Her channel was slick and he slid easily in and out of her. She began to move faster, pushing down harder with each stroke.

She found a rhythm that worked for her and kept it up. Isaiah continued to fondle her breasts and touch his finger to her clit with each down stroke she made.

It was perfect. It was beautiful.

And it couldn't last.

Her entire body clenched. Paused. And then exploded. She spasmed around him. His cock swelled inside her. He grabbed her hips and arched his pelvis right off the bed, lifting her with it.

She cried out his name as another wave of pleasure raced through her. She felt the ripple surge up his shaft and then the hot spurt within her as he found his release.

He growled and rolled, taking her beneath him as he bucked his hips. Once. Twice. And one final time.

Another spasm rocketed through her and she orgasmed again. She clutched him to her, never wanting him to leave. He collapsed on top of her, burying his face in the curve of her neck.

She could barely breathe but didn't care. She was completely exhausted and totally replete. She curled her toes and toyed with a lock of his hair, smiling when she felt his lips brush her neck in a gentle kiss.

Isaiah was the first to move, shifting his torso off hers. Their bodies were so sweaty they stuck slightly. She couldn't help herself and she laughed. His hair was standing on end in one spot where she'd tugged on it. Both of them were sticky and smelled of sex. They were totally debauched.

Isaiah smiled and rubbed his nose against hers. "I take it that means you liked that?"

She kissed him because his lips were there and they were so very kissable. "I did."

"Good. That means you won't mind trying it again." He slowly disengaged his body from hers. He wasn't quite as hard anymore, but he was still semi-aroused. She gasped and then groaned when her body emitted a small sucking sound as if trying to keep him inside her.

He rolled onto his back and flung an arm over his head. Even at rest, his biceps were huge. She let her fingers walk over his chest and tangle in his chest hair. It was nice just to lie here together after such an explosive experience.

Isaiah covered her hand with his and flattened it against his body. "Too much more of that and you won't get a shower before I'm in you again."

She glanced down and, sure enough, instead of getting soft, he was getting hard again.

"Maybe we can have a shower while you're in me. Kill two birds with one stone, so to speak."

He grinned and it quickly became a full-fledged smile.

Meredith felt her mouth drop open. Isaiah had been compelling before, in a rugged way, but now he was drop-dead gorgeous. Her hormones were already rising to sing a song of thanks and encouraging her to get more of him before he was gone.

Reality descended with a heavy thud. He didn't live here. He had a pack of his own and was only here for business. Once that business was completed, he'd be going.

And she couldn't leave the city. Her pack and her life were here. She had to protect the secret of her pack at all costs.

They'd also had unprotected sex. Not that she had to worry about sexually transmitted diseases. Werewolves couldn't catch them. And the chances of her getting pregnant were slim to none. It was a miracle she'd carried both her sons to term when so many females around her had been losing their unborn children. Why that thought depressed her when it should have reassured her, she had no idea.

"Hey, you okay?" Isaiah rolled onto his side and propped himself up on one arm. She'd never met a man more in tune with her moods.

She pushed away all negative thoughts. It was too late to back out now. They'd already made love. He knew where she and her pack lived and worked. Deep down she trusted him to keep their existence a secret. She wouldn't have had sex with him otherwise.

Their affair was finite. That was a given. But that didn't mean she couldn't enjoy their time together. It was only one night. One night of pleasure. One she'd remember for the rest of her life.

"Meredith?"

She'd been silent for too long. She reached up and feathered her fingers through his hair. "I'm fine. How about that shower?"

He frowned, so she pulled him down for a kiss. It started out light and she felt him start to tug away. Fearing questions she didn't want to answer, she plunged her tongue into his mouth, putting everything into the kiss. All the years of loneliness, the need she felt for him.

By the time she pulled back they were both breathless and very aroused. Isaiah rolled out of the bed and lifted her into his arms as easily as if she weighed no more than a child. His sheer, virile strength made her hot. That was the primal wolf inside her, drawn to the strongest male, the one who could provide for her, protect her and give her children.

Well, she was a modern female and provided for herself, protected her pack and already had two children, which was more than most female werewolves ever had in their entire lifetime. She didn't need him at all.

But oh, how she wanted him.

"Which way?" he asked.

She rested her head on his brawny shoulder and pointed the way. Wistfully, she wondered what it would be like not to have to be the strong one all the time.

Then he angled his head down and kissed her as he carried her into the bathroom. She returned the caress, determined not to let such thoughts spoil their one and only night together.

Tomorrow was time enough for reality.

He released her legs and let her body flow over his until her feet touched the floor. He was hot and heavy and aroused. She turned on the taps and when the water was the right temperature, she stepped into the wide stall and held her hand out to him.

Chapter Eight

Isaiah woke, as he always did, completely alert and aware of his surroundings. Meredith was draped over his body, her limbs wrapped around him, her head nestled on his shoulder.

He rubbed his hand up and down her supple spine, loving the feel of her soft skin beneath his palm. Her long hair tangled in his fingers and he stopped, not wanting to tug on it and wake her. This moment was special. One he wanted to capture and remember.

Last night had been phenomenal. They'd made love in the shower before tumbling back to bed again for round three. Meredith was a generous lover, not holding back anything. He knew part of that enthusiasm was due to the fact she was in heat. She'd been insatiable and both of them were going to be a bit sore today.

Not that he minded. It was a reminder that he'd satisfied her, brought her through the peak of her needing time. Now that it had passed, he wanted to hold her in his arms and enjoy the quiet. He, who was usually the first one out of bed and gone from his previous lovers' homes, felt no inclination to leave.

He frowned, not wanting to delve too deeply into that. They were both adults. He genuinely liked Meredith. Admired the way she was fiercely protective over her small pack, the way she'd built a life for herself in the city. She was loyal, smart and strong. What wasn't to like?

She was also sexy as hell and twice as hot. There were several times last night he'd expected the sheets to start smoldering.

None of that meant they were making any kind of commitment to one another. They were simply enjoying their time together. Both of them knew it was limited. He would be leaving soon, his job here almost at an end. If he couldn't attempt to pick up Alexandra and her father's stuff soon he'd have to abandon the attempt for now and try again another time.

The thought of leaving Meredith made his guts twist into a knot. She was a beautiful woman and would eventually take another lover. A low growl rumbled deep in his throat and he tightened his grip on her. He didn't like the idea of another male, werewolf or human, waking up in bed next to her, being the recipient of her sensual generosity in bed, or out of it.

She lifted her head and stared at him, her blue eyes sleepy and sated. "Morning." She turned her head and yawned. He admired her profile, the tender slope of her jaw and her high cheekbones.

He rubbed his thumb across her bottom lip and she stilled, her breathing hitching for a brief moment before resuming slightly faster. Immediately, his dick responded, springing to attention. He'd always had an insatiable sexual side, seeking human lovers in nearby towns back in Wolf Creek to try to satisfy it, but this was different. Meredith brought out the primal aspect of his nature. The wolf.

He realized then that he wanted to claim her. That's why his body eagerly responded to her every move. He, who had no problem sleeping with women and leaving them, who had no place in his life for a mate, wanted Meredith. Permanently.

The concept stunned him. That's what all the possessiveness he was feeling was about. The way she was able to soothe him in the midst of a crowd of humans. How he wanted her above all other females and couldn't imagine ever wanting another. She was his mate.

"You're thinking awfully hard about something," she teased. "I can practically see the wheels in your head turning."

He patted her butt and curled his hand around one firm cheek while trying to order his chaotic thoughts. "I'm fine." And he was. She wasn't his mate. This was only about phenomenal sex. Nothing more. No wonder he usually left before morning. Staying just messed with his head.

"You're better than fine." Her voice was low and sultry, making his dick flex. She laughed. "I can see you're not the only one awake." Reaching down, she stroked her hand over his erection. His hips rose to meet her and all thoughts and worries disappeared.

Not to be outdone, he dipped his fingers between the crease of her butt and found her sex. The tender folds were slick and damp. The gentle catch of her breath was followed by a breathy moan.

"Again?" She gasped as he slipped one finger in and out of her channel.

"If you're not too sore." As much as he wanted her, he didn't want to push it if she was tender. Last night had been a vigorous workout for both of them.

"I'm not *too* sore." She slid her hand from the base to the tip of his shaft and back down again.

He noticed she didn't say she wasn't sore and hesitated, removing his hand. He cupped her face in his hands. "Are you sure? We can wait."

Her gaze softened and her lips parted. "I'm sure."

She leaned down to kiss him, their lips almost touching.

A loud banging on her front door made her jerk so hard her forehead clunked his. She scrambled back and stared at the bedroom door, a look of horror on her face at the sound of the front door to her apartment being unlocked and opened. Heavy footsteps walked through the outer room, heading for the bedroom.

Isaiah heaved a sigh. There went his chance at sleepy morning sex and sure as hell ruined any chance he had of having breakfast with her.

Meredith scrambled for the sheets, tugging them to her chin. Isaiah leaned back against the headboard and waited. His preternatural sense of smell picked its way through the overwhelming perfume of sex that permeated the room and he scented the intruder. Not that he needed any special powers to know that it was one of her sons. Whether it was the more levelheaded Benjamin or the more aggressive Michael remained to be seen.

There was a short knock on the door. "Mom." He knocked again. "Mom, you okay?"

Michael. Isaiah sighed, knowing this wasn't going to be simple.

"I'll be out in a minute, Michael." She shot him a worried glance, but didn't speak. Isaiah could have told her it was pointless to try and hide from her son. Michael's sense of smell would kick in at any moment.

As if on cue, the door flew open and a furious Michael filled the doorway, his fists clenched at his sides and his wolf rippling under his skin. "What the fuck are you doing here?" he demanded, glaring at Isaiah.

"I think that would be obvious." Isaiah had no idea why he was baiting the younger man, feeding the flames of his temper instead of trying to extinguish the fire.

Maybe it was the way Meredith stayed silent beside him. Was she ashamed of what had happened between them? His ego and his pride took a hit and he shoved back the sheet and rolled out of bed, doing nothing to hide his aroused state.

"Michael, you need to go downstairs." She shooed him with one hand while keeping the other clenched around the sheet.

Isaiah could have told her it was useless. The sheet might cover most of her body, but there was no disguising the red marks on her neck from where the stubble on his jaw had abraded the tender flesh. Nor was there any way to hide the state of the bed and the smell of sex in the air.

Her son ignored her. "You sonofabitch," he roared and attacked. Isaiah was ready for it, knew it was unavoidable. He was handicapped because he didn't want to hurt Michael. That would just piss off Meredith and ensure he'd never get back in her bed.

Michael, on the other hand, felt no such restrictions. He pulled no punches as he swung at Isaiah. The wolf inside Isaiah went on alert, every sense acute, every instinct screaming at him to protect his woman. He ducked the punch and moved swiftly, coming up behind the younger man. Slipping his arms beneath Michael's, he yanked up and clasped his hands behind his opponent's neck, locking him into an unbreakable hold.

"Don't hurt him," Meredith cried as she all but leapt out of bed. Isaiah had no idea which one of them she was talking to, but she suspected it was him.

Michael must have thought the same thing because he growled and threw himself back, slamming Isaiah back against the wall. The entire room shook and a picture crashed to the floor, but Isaiah hung on. He had to get the younger man to calm down before he released him. He didn't want to have to hurt him, but he would if he didn't soon stop.

Her son was a strong man, big too. But he was no match for Isaiah who was several inches taller and a hell of a lot meaner. He'd been hunting bounty hunters and rogue wolves when he wasn't much older than Michael.

"Isaiah!" Meredith's frantic cry broke through the haze of his memories and he realized that Michael had stopped struggling. In fact, he was damn close to breaking the boy's arms.

He took a deep breath and released him. To give him credit, the younger man moved slowly and the only sign he gave to the pain he must be in was a measured roll of his shoulders. Michael was tough, he'd give him that.

"I think you should leave." The material wrapped around Meredith rustled as she walked toward them, her eyes pinned on him. "And you—" she turned on her son, "—we'll talk about this as soon as I'm dressed."

"You slept with him," he spat.

She calmly nodded. "Yes, I did. And I don't need your permission to do so. I'm still alpha of this pack."

"Maybe not for long," he challenged.

Isaiah bristled at the implied threat to Meredith and growled. She slapped her palm on the center of his chest, not taking her eyes off her son. He caught a glimpse of pain in her gaze before it disappeared behind a wall of calm.

"That may be, but for now I'm alpha. Go downstairs and wait. I won't tell you again."

"Mom," he began, but broke off and shot an angry look at Isaiah.

She shook her head and nodded toward the door. Michael whirled around and stomped out of the room and down the hall.

She winced when the front door slammed behind him.

"Well, that went well." She secured the sheet around her, walked to her dresser and tugged open a drawer.

"Meredith," he said her name, not quite certain what he was going to say. There was no way he was going to apologize for fighting with her son. Not that it was really a fight. Hardly even qualified as a scuffle. More posturing than anything. He was damned if he was going to let the young pup attack him and not defend himself.

She shut the drawer and turned, panties and a bra clutched in her hands. "I don't want to talk about this. Not now." She glanced toward the open bedroom door. "I have to talk with my sons and the rest of them."

"What about us?" He was a fool for asking, but couldn't seem to stop himself.

She laughed, but it wasn't a happy sound. "There is no *us*. You're passing through town." She waved a hand toward the bed. "This was an affair. One I'd hoped to keep quiet."

It stung. Even though he'd expected it, it still hurt. His chest ached so badly that he almost glanced down to make sure he hadn't sustained an injury in the altercation with Michael, even though he knew he hadn't. He resisted the urge to rub the area over his heart.

She continued, seemingly oblivious to the pain she was causing him, each word hammering at his body and soul, injuring him worse than any hunter or rogue ever had.

"This shouldn't have happened. We both know it." She raked her fingers through her long, tangled hair. "You're a stranger passing through town and I..." She took a moment to find the word she wanted. "I was vulnerable."

"Are you saying I took advantage of you?" She might as well stab him through the heart with a silver-bladed dagger. He was

Isaiah's Haven

many things—a cold-blooded killer among them—but never in his life had he done anything that could be construed as harming a woman. That went against every code of honor he lived by. He protected. It was who he was.

"No! No," she repeated more softly. The fact that she seemed as horrified as he did by the thought appeased him somewhat.

"I'm saying I let my hormones rule my good sense. I invited you into my bed last night. You gave me a choice. Now I have to live with the consequences."

"It's not all bad—"

"Not for you. You're leaving Chicago and going back to wherever it is you come from."

"North Carolina," he interjected. He wanted her to know more about him even as the security-minded part of his brain argued against it. The less she knew, the safer she was.

"Wherever. My point is that this is my home. This is my pack and I've put them all in danger by bringing a stranger into our home. Into my bed."

Isaiah frowned. He understood caution. That was only smart, and Meredith was a very intelligent woman. But he'd been hanging around for days now. She'd trusted him enough to sleep with him. Surely she knew he wouldn't betray them to bounty hunters. What was she hiding?

"I need to get a shower and you need to leave." She sidled past him on her way to the bathroom. She was so close he could feel the heat from her body. He could also smell himself on her and it made him hard.

He ignored his erection as he tracked her path to the bathroom.

"This can't happen again." She shut the door quietly and he

117

heard the snick of the lock. They both knew he could easily break down the door. The lock was more symbolic than a physical barrier.

"The hell this is over," he muttered as he snagged his jeans from the floor and tugged them on. He winced as he tucked his dick to one side and carefully pulled up the zipper. Swearing, he sat down on the edge of the bed, ignoring the inviting pillows and the cozy comforter that was half on and half off the mattress. He pulled his socks and sneakers over and put them on, his mind working as he tied the laces.

He picked up his shirt and pulled it over his head, not bothering to tuck it in. As he stood, his gaze went to the bathroom. The shower came on and he closed his eyes. His entire body tightened as the memory of a naked, wet Meredith filled his mind. Her pale skin glistening, her dark hair slicked over her back like a sleek pelt. He wanted to see her in her wolf form. Felt cheated that he hadn't. She'd be lean and her fur would be the color of her hair. He just knew it.

His feet moved of their own volition, leading him to the bathroom door. He placed his fingers against the wood, wanting more than anything to be in there with her.

Swearing, he whirled away and stalked from the room. This wasn't his problem. He'd had a great night of sex. Why couldn't he leave it at that? Why was he worried about what was going to happen with Meredith and her family? And what secret was she hiding from him about her pack?

He paused in the living room and stared at the window latch. There was no way he could leave here with it still broken. Muttering to himself, he went into her kitchen area and tugged open all the drawers until he found a screwdriver. It wasn't much of a fix, but he reattached the latch from where he'd popped it off the night before.

When he was done, he dropped the screwdriver onto the counter next to a notepad that was sitting by her phone. He grabbed a pen and wrote a quick to-the-point note that told her to get better locks for her windows.

He stalked back to the window and went out the way he'd come in only hours before. Such a short time, but he felt as though the experience had changed him in ways he couldn't even comprehend.

"Whatever," he grumbled as he pulled it partially shut behind him. He didn't close it all the way because he wanted her to notice it and lock it behind him.

He went down the fire escape, landing lightly on his feet as he hit the ground. He should go. He had work to do. It was already past the time where he should be watching Riley's Garage. He was neglecting his responsibilities to his own pack. And that just wasn't like him. His brothers were his family. Nothing came before them and he was here to help his brother and sister-in-law, not to have hot sex with some sexy she-wolf.

Still, he eased back into the shadows on the far side of the neighboring building. He couldn't leave, not until he knew her apartment was secure.

His patience was rewarded some fifteen minutes later when Meredith appeared in the window. She closed and latched the window. Pausing, she stared out the glass right at the area where he was standing. He couldn't be sure if she saw him. Not that it mattered. A second later she turned and left.

Isaiah shoved away from the brick wall and headed down the alleyway to the sidewalk. He wondered what was going to happen between her and her pack.

"None of your business," he told himself. Problem was it very much felt like his business.

What he needed was a shower and a hot breakfast. He was

already running behind so he flagged down a passing cab and climbed in. Giving directions to his motel, he leaned back against the seat and closed his eyes.

"You okay, buddy?" the cabby asked.

"No, but I will be," he responded. He had to be. He was here to do a job and leave. Nothing more. Nothing less.

But he suspected it was way too late for that now. It had been too late from the moment he'd first heard Meredith's voice.

Chapter Nine

Meredith's hands shook as she closed the living room window and latched it. So that was how Isaiah had gotten in. She'd been so caught in the web of her sexual needs last night she hadn't thought to question how he'd gotten into her apartment.

He had to be angry with her after the way she'd dismissed him and put her family ahead of him. Not that she could do anything else, she told herself. Yet he'd fixed her window latch before leaving, taking the time to ensure her safety.

He was like no male she'd ever met before. The calm, matter-of-fact way he'd handled her son, controlling him without hurting more than his pride was an indication of just how powerful and dangerous he was. The way he fixed her window before leaving told her he had a deep sense of responsibility.

She sensed him standing in the shadows. Watching. Making certain she closed and locked the window before she left her apartment, as per his instructions. It was both infuriating and seductive. She'd never known a male, other than her sons, to make her feel protected and special. And this was totally different. Lying in his arms this morning, she'd felt safe, wanted to burrow closer instead of running away. A first for her.

Turning from the window, she strode across the room.

There was no space in her life for a male, especially not one who had a life elsewhere. It was one night and one night only. She'd known that going in. And if her heart ached and her wolf howled in protest, she'd ignore both.

Right now she had bigger worries, and they were waiting downstairs. Not one to put off the hard tasks any longer than necessary, she let herself out of her apartment and went down the stairs and into the club. As she'd thought, all of them were waiting for her.

Michael was pacing back and forth, his lips compressed into a thin line. Benjamin was leaning against the bar with his arms crossed over his chest. He appeared more thoughtful than angry, but with her youngest son it was sometimes hard to tell what he was really thinking.

Hank was sitting on a barstool, using a whetstone on his hunting knife. Great, that was all she needed. Hank was a good fighter, especially due to his time in the military, but she had no doubt that he was nowhere near a match for Isaiah.

Kevin, the calmest male of the bunch, busied himself behind the bar putting on a pot of coffee. She gave a mental prayer of thanks. She was going to need more than one cup to get through this confrontation.

Teague sat next to Neema at a table, his knee moving up and down with nervous energy. His childhood of growing up in the back alleys of the Bronx had given him serious street-fighting skills. Neema appeared to be more concerned than angry and it was she who caught sight of Meredith standing in the doorway.

Everyone else sensed the change in the room and turned toward her. Meredith felt pinned by six sets of eyes that varied from deep concern to outright hostility. Oh yeah, this was going to be fun.

Michael shot toward her, but Benjamin caught his brother's arm, holding him back. "Listen to what she has to say first," he cautioned.

Meredith cocked one brow and went on the offensive. "What should I say? I'm a healthy female who took a male to her bed for the night. You can't tell me you haven't had your share of women."

"That's different," Michael retorted.

"And why is that?" She strolled forward and stopped at the edge of the group.

"Because," Michael sputtered. "You're my mother."

"I've had lovers before."

"But you've never had them here." He dragged his hand through his hair, making the short black strands stand on end.

"You've never taken a lover as dangerous as this male. You've stuck to humans, never one of our kind." Benjamin, in his usual thoughtful way, went to the heart of the matter. "This could come back to bite us all."

Guilt assailed her. This had been her concern with Isaiah, yet she'd disregarded it for a night of pleasure. "I'm aware of that. But I don't think it will. Isaiah is no threat to us."

"Not now," Teague countered. "But what if he finds out what some of us are?" The word half-breed was left unsaid as he drew his mate into his arms, cradling her against his chest.

Meredith knew that Neema was Teague's anchor in this world, the only thing keeping him from turning into a rabid wolf. He'd been close to wild when he'd found Neema and she'd changed his life. But it was still touch and go on some days, especially when he felt Neema might be threatened.

"I trust Meredith," Neema said. "After all, none of us would have a permanent home or would have been safe all these years without her. And even before that, when we were still moving around, she kept us all safe, taught us how to control our wolves and keep the hunters and rogues at bay."

"Thank you, Neema." She could barely speak past the lump in her throat. The years had been hard since she'd taken her sons and run from her pack. Adding half-breed children into the mix as she'd discovered them along the way had only made the job more difficult. But there was no way in hell she could have left any of them behind. They were hers. Just as her sons were.

"Mom." Michael stood before her, tall and proud and strong, a male of worth. Someday he would make a female a wonderful mate. If he could find one, that is. There were fewer females than males and their numbers were dwindling with each passing decade.

She'd lose him then, most likely. He'd probably join his mate's pack. She tried not to think too hard about that day. She wanted both her sons happy, but she prayed they'd both want to stay with their small pack.

The others wouldn't leave. There was little acceptance for half-breeds in most werewolf packs. It was rare and there was no way to find out how a pack felt without putting yourself in danger. That was why they kept to themselves and maintained a low profile. Something she'd put in jeopardy.

"Damn it," Michael swore. "The pack has to come first. Isn't that what you've always taught us?"

"Yes, it is." That was the first rule they'd all learned. And it was the most important. Their safety hinged on everyone obeying it.

"Yet you chose to ignore it," her son challenged.

"Michael," Benjamin cautioned, pushing away from the bar, his body tense.

Hank stilled his movements and sheathed his knife, his muscles coiling for action.

"No." Michael brushed off the hand Benjamin laid on his arm and faced her. "I'm not sure you're fit to lead this pack any longer. Not if all it takes is for some wolf to tumble you into bed to make you forget the rest of us."

Pain lanced through her, but she gave no outward sign that his words hurt her. She heard Neema gasp and several of the others emitted low growls of challenge.

Straightening to her full height, she faced her eldest son. She'd known this would happen eventually. If not over this, then over something else.

He was at the age where his hormones were charged, pushing him to exert his independence, his dominance. It was only natural for a male werewolf. She'd been expecting it for the last five years, but was still shocked by how devastated she felt. This was her son. She'd carried him in her body, had raised him single-handedly after escaping from her pack.

It was Hank who stepped forward, placing himself between Michael and her. "I think you need to take a step back and cool off," he cautioned.

"What are you going to do if I don't?" he sneered.

"Enough." Her voice cracked like a whip in the room. She stepped around Hank and faced Michael. "It is your right to challenge. We'll go to the park tonight after the bar is closed." There were quite a few large parks in the heart of the city, and they sometimes shifted and ran through them, one or two at a time while the others kept a watch.

Michael's eyes widened as recognition hit. "I'm not going to fight you." He sounded horrified by the very thought.

"Yes, you are." She turned in a slow circle, addressing them all. "Michael has challenged my leadership of the pack and the challenge will be met."

"This is crazy." Benjamin came forward, holding out both his hands in supplication.

She shook her head, knowing she couldn't give in. There was too much at stake. Deep down at their core, their wolf nature demanded that the strongest, the fittest lead. The rest wouldn't follow a weak leader. Either she'd win or her son would defeat her. No matter the outcome, the leadership of the pack would be secure. That was all that mattered.

If she didn't accept the challenge, there would be unrest in the pack and more challenges to come. This way, there would be stability, at least for another year or so.

She feared this was only the beginning. Michael was too much of an alpha, too much like his father, and her for that matter, not to want to lead the pack. She'd known it was inevitable. She'd only hoped for a few more years to give him time to mature into the man she knew he could be. Right now he tended to be a bit hotheaded and impulsive. And that was a dangerous combination.

"Tonight," she repeated. She walked behind the bar and helped herself to a cup of coffee from the freshly brewed pot. Behind her, all of them lingered, still in shock over what had just happened.

This was the first internal threat to their pack they'd ever dealt with. Up until now, they'd all been focused on a common enemy and that alone had kept them unified. But things had changed. Isaiah had done that.

No, that wasn't fair. She'd done it by allowing him into her life and her bed.

She'd been unable to resist his rough charm, the way he'd made her feel. For the first time in years, she'd felt like a female instead of simply the alpha.

She brought the cup to her lips and sipped. Kevin hovered near her and she sensed his anxiety. He was such a sensitive soul. She offered him a smile. "Everything will be all right, Kevin. You won't lose your home. The pack will survive this."

"I don't like it," he muttered, shooting Michael a glare.

She lightly touched his arm. "No, don't blame him. It's his right to question my decisions, my leadership ability. It's the way of things among our kind. Only the strongest can lead."

"I think you're doing just fine."

She smiled and leaned up to kiss his cheek. "Thank you." She turned back to the rest of her family. "Now, if this drama is done for now, we have work to do." She glanced at her watch, shocked to find the morning almost gone. "We open in an hour. I'll be in the office if anyone needs me."

Benjamin made his way to her side. "Mom, you can't be serious about this."

"A challenge is deadly serious. And it has to be treated as such." Because he was her son and she loved him, she tried to reassure him. "We probably won't kill each other tonight."

"If that's meant to calm my fears, it's not helping," came his wry reply.

"Go to work, Benjamin. Michael and I have to work this out between us."

As she left the room, she heard their voices raised in discussion. She shut it all out. They had to learn that there were repercussions to all actions, just as she had. She'd known there was a good chance her family would find out about Isaiah, but she'd taken him to her bed anyway. Now she had to face that.

Michael had challenged her authority in front of the rest of the pack. She couldn't let that stand without answering it or her leadership was worthless. They would all start to doubt and question her loyalty, her ability to protect them and hold their pack together.

No, as much as the thought of fighting her son made her sick to her stomach, she had no choice. One way or another, the pack would survive with a strong leader at the helm. Whether it was her or her son remained to be seen.

Meredith turned on her computer and sipped her coffee as it fired up. She was eerily calm for someone with so much upheaval in her life. A week ago her life had been predictable and safe. Now it was out of control.

A part of her regretted being with Isaiah, allowing his presence to cause such a rift in her family. A bigger part of her was anything but sorry. She felt more alive than she had in years. It was as though he'd awakened a part of her that had been dormant for far too many years. The friction between her and Michael had been growing. Just little things here and there, but enough for her to know this was coming.

Meredith set her mug down on the corner of her desk. Like her life, the desk was tidy. Organized. No matter what happened, she'd set a good foundation for her pack. One that would continue whether she led them or not.

That made her feel better about the situation. But not much. She still had to face her son on the field of challenge.

"Damn." She rubbed her hands over her face, suddenly wanting to do nothing more than go back to bed and pull the covers over her head. But there was no do-over and the facts were what they were.

Heaving a sigh, she called up her accounting program and went to work. It was going to be a long day.

Isaiah sat with his back against a crumbling brick wall, the cool of the stone seeping through his shirt and into his skin. He ignored the discomfort and watched the garage and the street beyond. People came and went with regularity. He'd been watching for days now and was starting to get a feel for the place. It had a predictable rhythm.

Otto Bykowski was the first to open shop every morning. The yeasty, sweet smells from his bakery wafted out through the vents in his building, competing with the odors of gasoline and garbage. Gradually, others would wake and find their way out into the world. Leon would show up at the garage around eight o'clock. The barbershop opened at nine. Divine would usually head down to the bakery somewhere between ten and eleven. The bar stayed closed until two in the afternoon.

He'd made his decision in between showering at his motel and arriving here this morning. It was time to pack up the truck and head out of Chicago. The attraction he had to Meredith couldn't go anywhere.

It was one night of hot sex between willing adults. Nothing wrong with that.

He absently rubbed his chest. "Everything wrong with that," he whispered. Meredith was so much more than just a quick roll in the sheets. Just the thought of leaving her was making him crazy. He worried about her and her small pack. Would they be okay? What would happen if hunters found them? Did they have some kind of escape plan in place?

So many questions with no answers. They hadn't talked about such things because he wasn't a part of her pack. He was just some wolf she'd taken to bed to help ease her when she was in heat.

He didn't believe that either.

He'd caught a glimpse of the pain in her eyes this morning. Seen the yearning as well. She felt as troubled by what was happening between them as he was.

A car pulled up outside the garage and a tall, lanky man with cropped blond hair stepped out. Isaiah shoved aside his personal problems and catalogued the stranger. The man glanced around, his eyes skimming over the rooftop Isaiah was situated on, but not stopping. He sauntered into the garage and a few minutes later, Leon strode out with him and popped the hood of the engine.

Must be a legitimate customer. Still, Isaiah watched for anything suspicious or out of the ordinary. An hour later, money exchanged hands and the man was on his way again.

The day progressed slowly. The sun rose to its peak and began its slow descent. By the time it finally sank, Isaiah was more than ready to move. His skin itched with the need to shift.

He dug out his cell phone and dialed. A woman answered. "Hey, Divine. I'm going to bring a truck in about an hour and load James's and Alexandra's stuff."

"You sure it's safe?" Her voice was raspy and filled with concern.

"You see anything to make you think it wasn't?" Because of the life she'd lived before inheriting James's building, he knew Divine had good instincts.

"Nothing I can put my finger on."

"I think we're clear."

"Why don't we do what we talked about earlier? I'll go downstairs and ask Leon to get his father's truck. We can load everything and then he or his father can drive it to another location where you can transfer the load to your truck. Better safe than sorry."

Isaiah once again marveled at how these humans were willing to put themselves in harm's way to help a bunch of werewolves. "Sounds good to me."

"Okay, I'll go down and talk to Leon. Watch for the truck. I assume you're close by."

"You assume right. See you in a bit." He ended the call and then placed another one. It was picked up on the second ring.

"Striker."

"I'm loading the truck tonight." He saw no reason for preliminaries or pleasantries. He wasn't feeling real sociable right about now. He hadn't left the city yet, and already he missed Meredith. The thought of never seeing her face, touching her soft skin, kissing her lush lips or losing himself in her body was untenable.

"No sign of trouble?" Joshua was always concerned about security.

"None I can see." Which left what he couldn't see. He couldn't quite shake the feeling that someone was out there. Watching. Waiting.

He explained to Joshua what the plan was. "I'll leave the loaded truck for a day or so to make certain no one is watching. If I see anything suspicious on my tail when I leave, I'll dump the truck somewhere along the way and we can pick it up later."

"Do you need any help?"

His fingers gripped the phone so hard his knuckles began to turn white and he forced himself to relax his hold. Part of him wished his brother was here beside him and that they were close enough for him to talk to. But he'd been reserved for years, keeping to himself, and they didn't have that kind of relationship. Suddenly he wished it were different. He wanted to ask his brother about his mate, how he'd felt when he first met Alexandra.

"No, I'm fine."

"Okay, see you soon." Joshua disconnected and Isaiah was left listening to a dial tone. He pressed the off button and tucked the phone back in his pocket just as the Bykowski Bakery truck pulled up in front of the garage.

Isaiah hurried across the roof, down the interior stairs of the building and out the back door. He paused, listening for anything that seemed out of place. When he was sure he was alone, he worked his way over to the garage and slipped in through the smaller door. The truck was already inside, the large garage doors closed.

Divine was there along with Leon and his father, Otto.

"Let's get started," he growled. Quicker they were done, the quicker he could go see Meredith. There was no way he would be able to leave the city without going to see her first.

"Everything is upstairs." Divine led the way up the back staircase. They all followed behind her, Isaiah bringing up the rear.

Maybe he'd be able to see her again when he came to Chicago. It wasn't so far away that he couldn't come up at least once a month. Yeah, like a classy lady like Meredith would settle for something like that. Not a chance.

"You okay?" Divine had stopped to wait for him, her expression concerned.

"Yeah." She really was a great lady, for a human, and he told her so. She laughed, her blue eyes twinkling, and the moment passed.

The mound of boxes and furniture was substantial so he grabbed one and started back down the stairs. He heard the men chatting with Divine as they all fell to work loading the truck.

Isaiah's Haven

From his vantage point down the road, Collins noted the truck driving into the garage. He also noted the way that Leon looked up and down the road before shutting the door.

It had been genius of him to loosen a few wires under the hood earlier this morning and drive to the garage to get the problem looked at. It had allowed him to introduce himself to the man working there. Leon Bykowski was quiet, but competent. But most importantly, he was human. There was none of the fluid grace when he moved and his senses were no more than normal. He'd lightly blown on a dog whistle when Leon's back had been turned just to be certain. Not loud enough for anyone outside the garage to hear, but loud enough to get a reaction if Bykowski had been a werewolf. The man hadn't jerked or shown any reaction at all.

When Collins had asked about the former owner, James Riley, Leon had shrugged and said he didn't know much about him. He'd simply rented the garage from the new owner of the building.

Still, he hadn't been able to shake the sense that the man was holding something back. Quinn had taken the afternoon shift but seen nothing. Collins had switched cars and driven back to take up his watch for the evening. From the looks of things, their luck was about to change. He shifted his lanky body and yanked his cell phone out of his back pocket.

He thumbed a button and waited while it rang. It was picked up on the third ring. "Yeah?"

He was glad he answered to Jones instead of Macmillan. That bastard creeped him out. "There's a lot of activity at the garage tonight."

"Okay. Keep a watch. I'll bring the boss up to speed, then I'll round up Warren and Quinn and we'll stay ready if you need us."

"Sounds good." He wouldn't mind getting a little action. It had been a while since he'd bagged a werewolf and his trigger finger was getting itchy.

"If you see that tall bastard, don't lose him."

Collins winced. Warren had seen him but lost him last night. Macmillan hadn't been happy.

He rubbed his hand over the stock of his rifle that lay on the seat beside him. "Don't worry. I won't."

Chapter Ten

It was late by the time Isaiah reached Haven. Too late. The club was already closed. Isaiah swore under his breath. Taking care of business had taken much longer than he'd anticipated. The bakery truck had gotten a flat on route to the parking lot where he'd stashed his truck. By the time they'd fixed that, driven to the lot, shifted everything from one truck to the other and moved his truck to a parking garage, Leon and his father were ready for a meal and a drink. And they'd wanted to talk with Isaiah.

He'd been unable to refuse them.

They'd done so much for James and the pack they deserved his respect. They were also genuinely nice men. They'd put themselves in harm's way just to help a friend.

Otto had driven them to a pizza place where they'd devoured two large pizzas. Well, Otto and his son had shared one. He'd managed one on his own. He hadn't realized how hungry he was until he'd started eating.

Two hours later, Isaiah had managed to extricate himself and say his final goodbyes to the two men. Divine had been waiting for him downstairs at the garage with a letter for Alex, which was currently stuffed in his back pocket. He'd said goodbye to her as well, not flinching when she'd reached out and hugged him.

He liked these people, but he didn't plan on coming back anytime soon. At least not to the garage. Meredith's club was another matter altogether.

Right now, the building was locked up and the security lights were on. Damn, he'd rushed as fast as he could, even opting to take a cab to the edge of Meredith's neighborhood before hot-footing it the rest of the way. The back of his neck was tingling and his shoulders were tense. Something was very wrong.

Isaiah heard a sound and ducked back into the shadows. Hank's voice drifted over the night air, followed by a low mumble. Possibly Teague, but he couldn't be certain. He didn't make his presence known, uncertain of his welcome after this morning's incident.

Then he heard a sound that went straight to his groin. Meredith. Her low, sultry voice washed over him. He closed his eyes and was savoring the sound when it occurred to him they were getting distant. They were leaving the building. He wasn't just hearing them through an open window. Their voices were moving away from him.

Where were they going this time of night?

Keeping his back flat against the wall, he took a quick look around the corner. Sure enough, the entire family was walking down the road. Thankfully, he was downwind. That and the usual stench of the city should block his scent from detection.

Did this have anything to do with the secret Meredith was keeping from him?

He had no idea. All he knew was he had to follow them. If nothing else, he needed to talk to Meredith before he left the city in the morning. He'd told his brother he'd probably wait a day or two, but if everything stayed the same there was no reason for him to remain any longer.

Meredith had made it clear this morning that last night wouldn't happen again. His muscles bunched and rippled in his shoulders and his fists clenched at his sides. He wanted the opportunity to change her mind.

He shoved that distraction aside and concentrated on where they were going. He noted that Meredith's sons seemed to be talking intently as they brought up the rear. Meredith led the way with Hank keeping pace beside her. The other three strode in the middle of the pack. He sensed the tension in the air and quickened his pace.

They eventually reached Wicker Park. The green space was the namesake of the neighborhood. It was a nice little bit of nature in the heart of the city, even though it was cultivated and not wild as he preferred.

Keeping them in his sight while maintaining enough of a distance so they wouldn't detect him wasn't easy, but he managed. For one thing, they weren't vigilant enough. Isaiah wanted to kick Michael and his brother for not keeping better watch on the back trail.

What if he was a hunter?

Meredith should be more cautious. Sure, they were werewolves and therefore stronger than humans, but those hunters were wily bastards. He'd seen them kill strong werewolves before. And most of her pack was young. Not a single seasoned fighter among them.

They walked past the iron fence and into the park, skirting alongside the fountain and moving deeper. He followed, staying hidden in the shadows.

Isaiah breathed a sigh of relief when they stopped among a stand of trees. Meredith disappeared behind one of them and Isaiah sprinted forward, his sneakers making no sound on the grass. What the hell was she doing leaving the safety of the pack?

Suddenly he knew. Relief blasted through him as she came into view. He gave thanks for his preternatural vision as she kicked off her shoes and shimmied out of her jeans, revealing her firm, slender thighs. She folded the pants neatly and set them aside.

Her sweater came next and then the shirt she wore beneath it. More of her pale skin was revealed with each layer she stripped off. She was wearing only her underwear now, a pair of pale green panties and a matching bra that cupped the mounds of her breasts. He could almost see the goose bumps on her skin brought on by exposure to the sudden chill.

He wanted to warm her skin against his.

She didn't linger, but efficiently removed her bra and panties, dropping them atop of the mound of clothing. Her breasts swayed as she took a deep breath. Then the change began.

Bones cracked and shifted, some lengthening while others shortened. Her jawbone reformed, becoming long and straight. Fur sprouted from beneath her skin, covering her entire body. She fell onto her hands as they changed.

He'd seen female werewolves change before but none had ever affected him like this. It wasn't an erotic act, so much as a functional one. But his dick obviously didn't know that. It was as hard as a rock.

Meredith was a gorgeous woman and she was just as beautiful in her wolf form. She was strong and sleek, muscles rippling beneath her skin as she prowled back out to the small clearing. Her fur was as black and glossy as her hair. She carried herself like a queen, her eyes watchful, her gaze filled with innate intelligence.

He tracked her movements, prowling closer. His fingers dug

into the trunk of a tree, almost shifting into claws as his wolf clamored to get out. Sweat broke out on his brow. He wanted to run. With Meredith.

The others were waiting. Only one of them had shifted. Michael. He looked a lot like her, but bigger. The rest ranged around on the grass. He sensed their nervousness, tinged with anger. Isaiah could understand their nervousness, but why were they angry?

Teague kept looking over his shoulder, the trio of earrings in his left ear glinting in the artificial lighting that managed to find its way into the clearing, while Kevin kept his eyes moving over the park beyond. It was dangerous to shift here. This wasn't exactly a huge park. A human could come by at any time. He couldn't sense one at the moment, but that could easily change.

Isaiah's skin itched but he resisted the urge to scratch. His wolf wanted out, especially since it sensed others of its kind. Who was he kidding? He wanted to shift because he wanted Meredith to see his wolf. Wanted to run with her. Protect her.

He was debating what he should do when Michael and Meredith faced each other and the rest formed a loose circle around them.

Hank stepped between the two wolves. "Challenge has been issued and, although I'd like to personally beat Michael to a pulp, it must be met."

Meredith shot Hank a glare and gave a low growl.

"Sorry." He raked his hand through his short, blond hair. "Michael has questioned Meredith's right as alpha of the pack."

"Shit," Isaiah swore under his breath even as he was kicking off his sneakers. This was about him. He'd known Michael was upset with his mother, but enough to challenge her? Actually fight her?

No fucking way.

He tore his shirt over his head and practically yanked his jeans from his body, throwing himself into the change just as Hank finished speaking.

"Let the challenge begin."

Isaiah felt his bones shifting and reforming, felt the cool grass on the pads of his feet. Muscles coiled and his ears shot up as he strained to hear any signs of fighting.

He loped forward, catching sight of the group. Michael and Meredith were circling one another. She growled, baring her fangs at her son. He growled back, but made no move to attack.

Meredith struck first, nipping at Michael's flank. He responded instinctually, striking back. She barely moved out of the way in time to keep from getting struck by his lethal front claws.

Isaiah didn't slow, didn't hesitate. He jumped, flying from between the trees, a silent, deadly shadow, and went on the attack. Teeth barred, he spun to face Michael. The younger wolf backed up a step in surprise, but quickly recovered and launched himself at Isaiah. Savage pleasure filled Isaiah as he met his opponent, more than ready for a fight.

Collins was all but quivering with excitement as he pulled his truck into an empty space by the park. He grabbed his phone. "We got 'em," he said as soon as it was answered. "Wicker Park. He followed another group in there. Could be more than one wolf."

"We're right behind you. Two minutes."

Collins closed his cell phone, grabbed his rifle and slid out of his car. The others could have the rest of them. He wanted that big bastard for himself. He tucked the rifle beneath his long trench coat and headed into the park.

Meredith didn't know what was happening at first. One moment she'd been squared off against her son, the leadership of their small pack hanging on the outcome of this night. The next, another wolf had come from out of nowhere, attacking her son.

Isaiah.

There was no doubt as to the identity of the huge male wolf. He was enormous. Larger than her son. Fur, mostly brown with patches of black, covered a massive, muscular body. Menace poured off him in waves as he growled at her son and attacked.

Michael hesitated and then jumped into the fight. A yelp filled the air and she knew it was from her son and not Isaiah. He fought with a savagery that could only come from years of practice. None of the males in her pack were any match for him.

Benjamin stripped of his clothes, shifted and jumped into the fray. Isaiah twisted his body at the last second, getting out of the way of Benjamin's powerful jaw. Saliva dripped from his teeth as he whirled around to face his two attackers.

She had to stop this before anyone was hurt. She charged between the males and emitted a low growl. He sons ignored her, inching forward, their muscles coiled for attack.

Meredith faced Isaiah and one look in his eyes told her there was no appealing to him to back down. He was not the sort of man, or wolf, to back away from any fight.

She did the only thing she could think of that might stop them. She shifted. The fur on her body receded. Her bones snapped and reformed. Muscles lengthened and hands reformed. She pushed herself to her feet, her long hair fluttering around her, the cool air caressing her skin.

Standing between three ferocious wolves, she put out her hands. "Stop. Please stop." She made sure she included the rest of her pack in that order. Hank and Teague were already inching forward, ready to shift and wade into the fight. Kevin stood beside Neema, his arm around her slender shoulders.

Michael lunged forward, huge jaw snapping. Isaiah used his massive body to knock her down, standing in front of her, protecting her from her own sons.

She reached up and grabbed him around his thick shoulders. "Please don't hurt them," she begged. She had no doubt that he was capable of killing both of them without hesitation. There was a wildness in Isaiah, a darkness. It drew her to him even as it sometimes frightened her. She hadn't been around a male werewolf this aggressive since she'd fled her pack years ago. She'd forgotten just how dangerous they could be.

God, how had this happened? Her pack was in turmoil. She dug her fingers into Isaiah's fur and dragged herself up beside him. "Please."

Her son shot her a glare. She could see and sense the wounded male pride. She wanted to smack him. She'd had enough male posturing to last her a lifetime, and she still had about four hundred years left to live, give or take a few decades.

"Stop it," she told both her sons. "You're no match for him. Not yet. Maybe in a few years."

Isaiah snorted, and she dug her fingers into his fur in warning and was surprised when he subsided. His teeth were still bared, but at least he was no longer straining against her hold.

"Everyone back off and get dressed so we can sort this out." This was such a mess. She glanced around when she sensed them all hesitating. "It's too dangerous to be exposed for this long," she reminded them.

That did the trick. Both her sons whirled around and disappeared. She sighed with relief, slowly releasing the chokehold she had on Isaiah. She didn't know whether to laugh or cry. Her life had turned upside down.

Isaiah took her hand in his mouth and tugged.

"No way am I going with you. I have to get dressed." She shivered. It was cold this late in October.

She yanked her hand from his mouth and stalked off. His feet padded silently behind her, but she knew he was there. He didn't stop, but disappeared into the bushes beyond where she'd left her clothing.

She dressed quickly, knowing she wouldn't have much time. The rest of her family was waiting in the clearing when she arrived. Michael was angry. He was pacing, the muscles in his jaw working furiously. And Benjamin, her calm son, didn't look much better.

Teague was on full alert with Neema tucked beneath his arm. Kevin was quiet. Watchful. Hank came immediately to her side. "Are you okay?"

She was anything but okay, but she nodded. "Thanks."

Michael stopped pacing and everyone froze as Isaiah strode into the clearing, taking up a stand beside her. It irritated her even as it warmed her that he'd stand beside her during a challenge. Still, he shouldn't have interfered and she told him so.

"This isn't your business," she began.

"He attacked you. That made it my business." That calm, skewed male logic made her want to scream.

She ground her back teeth together to keep from doing just that. When she'd regained some semblance of calm, she went on the offensive. "You're not a part of this pack. Just because we had sex, it doesn't give you any right to interfere in my life. Challenge was issued and was being met when you jumped in."

A blast of cold hit her and it wasn't from the cool autumn air. Isaiah's dark brown eyes went almost black and his glare was icy. There was no sign of the playful lover from last night. This was a very dangerous wolf who was used to taking orders from no one. She wondered how he fit into his own pack, as it was obvious he was not a follower.

She wanted to back away from his frigid glare, but stood her ground. His gaze swept over her small, ragtag pack. Most of them were barely adults in their culture. The oldest was forty, which was around late-twenties in humans. She had no idea how old Isaiah was, but she sensed he'd never been young. Whatever had shaped his life had turned him into a fighter, hardening him against the world at a young age.

She hated hurting him, but it couldn't be helped. He was going back to his pack and she was staying here with hers. Or what was left of it. After tonight, she had no idea what would happen.

"Forgive me for overstepping my boundaries." His formal tones dripped with disdain. "I should have realized I was nothing but a quick fuck. Glad I could be of service."

His brutal words sliced her to the bone. But that's what she'd done to him. She'd taken something beautiful between them and reduced it to a few hours of meaningless sex.

She reached her hand out to him, blinking back tears that threatened. He stepped out of reach as if he didn't want her to touch him, as though it was somehow distasteful.

She bit her bottom lip and watched as he turned and walked away. No fanfare. No anger. That was worse than if he'd stomped off. It was as though he'd dismissed her, indeed all of them, from his thoughts and his life.

He looked so alone as the night swallowed him up. She wanted to cry for him, for her and for what they might have had together.

The pain almost brought her to her knees. His name was on her lips but she fought to keep it inside her. Even if she wanted to be with him, she couldn't risk the lives of her four half-breed, adopted children. Isaiah was so powerful, so deadly, that if he objected to half-breed werewolves, as most did, he could easily kill them.

Her body began to shake. The trembling began in her knees and worked its way up her body until her teeth were chattering. She was so cold.

"Mom." It was Michael. His arm went around her and she glanced up at him. He sucked in a breath, making her wonder just how devastated she looked.

"Come on. Let's go home." All his anger seemed to be gone.

Suddenly, she was tired. No, she was beyond tired. Bone-deep weariness dragged at her. For decades, she'd kept her small pack safe from hunters and those werewolves who would want some of her children dead. The only moments of true peace she'd experienced in all that time was in Isaiah's arms and she'd just sent him away.

"Mom?" Michael sounded concerned now. All of them were. She could see it in their faces as they looked to her for direction. For the first time ever, she couldn't care enough to reassure them.

Benjamin took over. "Come on. Let's get moving." His eyes tracked around the woods. "I'm feeling exposed all of a sudden."

The tinge of fear in his voice snapped her out of her depression enough for her to notice how quiet it suddenly was. Too quiet. She caught a scent on the air and it made her blood run cold.

"Run," she yelled, just as a shot cracked the air. Benjamin gave a cry, clutched his shoulder and fell to the ground. Hank ran to his side.

Meredith saw red, tearing at her clothing and shifting on the fly, she headed for the direction of the shot, ignoring the frantic cries of her sons behind her.

Chapter Eleven

Ice encased Isaiah as he walked away from Meredith. Obviously he'd been wrong about what had happened between them. Or maybe it was all one-sided. Maybe he was the only one who'd experienced the soul-deep connection.

With each step he took away from her, he felt as though his guts had been torn out and were dragging on the ground beside him. His chest ached and his brain wanted to explode.

Not his business. Not his business.

Her words echoed in his head, beating at him like a sledgehammer. He wanted it to be his business.

She was surrounded by males who didn't know the first thing about fighting, about protecting her. Who would have taught them? Meredith was an alpha female without a male. They would have been all children beneath her rule. There was little wonder she'd been able to hold them together all these years. Where had the rest of them come from? Werewolves were fiercely possessive when it came to their children. It was obvious that only Benjamin and Michael were blood relations to her.

Not his business.

He wanted to physically remove those three words from his head and crush them beneath his heel.

He strode out of the park and down the cracked sidewalk,

ignoring the light traffic and the few people who were still out and about at almost three in the morning.

The challenge had been over him. Her son had questioned her leadership because she'd slept with him. Still, he'd wanted Meredith to choose his side over that of her sons in their fight. Wanted her to stand beside him with pride.

And how fucking stupid was that? He was just passing through Chicago, he wasn't moving to the city. Wasn't mated with her.

"Damn it." He stopped and stood with his head down, hands on his hips. The farther away he got from Meredith the more tense he became. "She doesn't want you," he reminded himself.

That sure as hell wasn't true. She'd definitely wanted him last night when she'd arched against him and screamed his name.

He was panting hard now, as though he'd been running full out for miles. He could still feel her body wrapped around his, her slick, tight channel squeezing his cock.

"Fuck," he swore again. He wouldn't go back. If nothing else, he had to retain some sense of pride. The woman had sent him packing. She couldn't get any plainer than that.

It was then he got a tickle on the back of his neck that went down his spine. "Shit," he muttered as he dove to one side and rolled, ending up at the mouth of an alleyway. Maybe he was overreacting. Maybe it was just one of Meredith's pack following him to make sure he left the area. Whatever it was, his instincts were screaming at him to take cover.

And they'd kept him alive too many times for him to ignore them now.

Concrete shattered near his head, several shards hitting his face just as a muffled sound reached his ears. Someone was shooting at him. Definitely not Meredith's pack. Not unless they'd had some concealed weapons he hadn't seen.

There was another distinct sound of a gun being fired, this one in the distance. Meredith and her pack were under attack.

His breathing slowed, his senses becoming even more acute. He listened even as he began to move, keeping low to the ground. He didn't shift. Not yet. He didn't know who he was dealing with—humans, hunters or werewolves. He was exposed out here on the streets and couldn't risk changing, not unless he absolutely had to.

Either way they were dead. No one shot at his woman and lived.

Isaiah loped forward, sniffing the wind. He could scent gunpowder and sweat and veered off to the right. This shooter was closer and had to be the one who took the potshot at him.

"Come out, wolf. I know you're in there."

Isaiah raised his brow at the man's stupidity. A hunter, but not an experienced one otherwise he'd never have given away his location. Either that or he was smart and had a partner ready to take a shot when Isaiah exposed himself.

Both hunters and wolves knew they didn't have much time until the cops showed up, and none of them wanted to deal with the authorities. The hunters had no respect for government or its employees, but neither faction wanted to kill a cop. That would bring too much unwanted attention to both groups.

He skirted down the alley toward the hunter, using a dumpster for cover. Scenting the air, he listened for any telltale sound. His nostrils filled with the stench of trash. But just beneath it he could smell anticipation, sweat and gunpowder.

Isaiah didn't hesitate. He jumped, propelling himself up onto the lid of the dumpster and launching himself at his attacker. The hunter had been expecting such a move and was waiting, rifle raised and ready. Isaiah twisted his body, praying he'd reach the hunter before he could get off a good shot.

Time froze. The hunter seemed to move in slow motion, the barrel of his rifle tracking Isaiah's movements. A shot rang out. He waited for the pain to kick in. Sure as hell, the hunter had silver bullets—bullets that would kill him instantly if they hit his heart or slowly poison him if they hit him elsewhere.

He felt nothing but the collision of his larger body with the hunter. Isaiah didn't hesitate. He gripped the man's neck and twisted. The crack was unnaturally loud, echoing in Isaiah's ears.

He dropped the hunter's body to the ground, panting heavily. It was then he saw the blood staining the front of the hunter's chest. Someone had shot him.

Isaiah slammed his back against the wall as his eyes tracked the rooftops around him. He caught a glimpse of a shadow above him and then nothing. Who the hell had shot the hunter?

That was a riddle to puzzle over later. Someone was shooting at Meredith and the others. Leaving the hunter lying in the dirt and filth of the alley without a backward glance, he sprinted toward the park.

His heart pounded frantically. He was afraid. Not for himself, but for Meredith and her small pack. He heard grunts and groans as he raced past the iron fence and fountain and deeper into the park. His preternatural senses helped him catalogue the situation immediately.

Benjamin was down. Hank was beside him, his shirt off, desperately trying to stop the bleeding. Neema was beside him, doing what she could. Teague and Kevin had shifted and were guarding the small group. Meredith and Michael were missing.

"That way," Hank pointed when he saw Isaiah.

His legs were pumping, but not going fast enough. Was he going to be too late once again to save someone he loved? Despair threatened, but he shoved it back. Meredith wasn't a child like as his sister had been. She was a mature woman. She'd held her pack together alone for years. She was a fighter. And he was no longer a young wolf. He was a male in his prime. He would protect what was his.

And whether she ever admitted it or not, Meredith was his. Isaiah was past fighting his instincts.

Sweat rolled down his temple. His shirt clung to his torso as he sped toward Meredith. A man was down on the ground, his neck ripped open. Meredith stood over him, blood dripping from her fangs. Michael was nowhere to be seen.

Isaiah skidded to a stop and stared at her. Pure despair filled her gaze as she looked back at him. He knew that she'd hated taking this hunter's life, even though she'd had no choice. Unlike him, she'd suffer for this night's work. The way he figured it, they'd come hunting. They deserved what they got.

Meredith was softer. Kinder. Not that she wouldn't do what needed to be done. The evidence of that truth was lying on the ground in front of him. But it hurt her to do it.

"It's okay." He eased forward, hands out in front of him. "He's gone. I got another one in an alley just outside the park."

He heard a sound and spun around, catching the scent of another wolf. Michael loped up to his mother and shifted back into human form. "I got one just beyond the basketball court." Hurrying to the base of a nearby bush, he grabbed his clothes and began yanking them on as fast as he could.

Sirens sounded in the distance. They had to get out of here. This place was going to be crawling with cops within minutes.

"We've got to go." He wanted to pick Meredith up into his

arms and carry her away from all this death. But he couldn't. He wasn't her mate.

She lowered her head and raced off. He quickly followed with Michael on his heels. Only Kevin was waiting when they reached the original clearing. "The others took Benjamin home. He's still bleeding."

Meredith stepped out from behind a tree fully dressed but disheveled. "We've got to hurry." Isaiah fell into step beside her. She shot him a glare. "What are you still doing here?"

He ignored the pang in his heart and kept his features level. "You ever remove a silver bullet before?"

She bit her bottom lip as they swung out of the park and shot across a street and down an alley just as the first cop car pulled up outside the park. "No."

"I have."

Nothing more was said as they took a circuitous route back to the club, ducking in through the kitchen door in the back. Isaiah kept an eye on their back trail just in case, but sensed no one following them.

Meredith hurried up the stairs and burst through the door on the left side of the hallway. "Benjamin!" She called her son's name as she ran.

"In here, Mom." His voice was weak, but the fact that he was able to talk was a relief. She stumbled and Isaiah reached out a hand to catch her, but she shook him off.

Blood stained the bedclothes even though Teague was keeping pressure on the wound. Isaiah took charge. "Do you have any medical supplies?" Most packs kept some basic stuff on hand for situations like this.

Hank came in behind them, a large plastic tub cradled in his arms. "This is everything."

Isaiah flipped open the lid and began sorting through packages and boxes. He pulled out a disposable scalpel, some forceps, bandages and some sutures. "I need to wash up."

Meredith pointed toward a door off the bedroom. "In there."

Meredith wanted to curl up in a corner and cry. She'd killed a man tonight. It hadn't been the first life she'd had to take, but that didn't mean it got any easier. Michael had also killed a man.

She sought out her eldest son and found him standing silently in a corner watching his brother. Benjamin was injured. In all the years they'd been running, none of them had been seriously hurt before. They always ran rather than stand and fight. This time there'd been no choice. It was fight or die.

Water ran in the background, a stark reminder of what was about to happen. Isaiah was about to operate on her son. Meredith moved to the side of the bed and sat. Benjamin turned to her, his face pale and wan.

"It hurts more than I thought it would."

Her heart squeezed. He sounded like a small boy looking for reassurance from his mother. "Everything is going to be okay," she promised. At least she hoped it would. She brushed a lock of his thick dark hair away from his face.

Benjamin nodded and closed his eyes.

Isaiah came back into the room, a rolled-up towel in his hands. "Teague, hold his shoulders." He glanced at Hank. "You hold his legs."

"What about me?" She couldn't find it in her to object to his heavy-handedness. Not when she was expecting him to save her son's life.

"Hold his hand, but be ready if I need anything."

She nodded and gripped Benjamin's hand in hers.

"This is going to hurt like hell." Isaiah's movements were sure and brisk as he eased aside the bandage and studied the wound. "Are you ready?"

Benjamin nodded and Teague and Hank both gave the go-ahead. Isaiah brought the rolled-up towel to her son's lips. "Bite on this."

When the towel was clenched firmly in Benjamin's teeth, Isaiah took the scalpel in his hand and made a cut. Blood seeped from the wound, making her stomach lurch and her head spin. She wasn't usually squeamish, but this was her son's blood.

"It's a shoulder wound, so it's not too bad." Isaiah talked as he worked. She focused less on his words than on his tone. He didn't seem overly disturbed and that calmed her somewhat.

She trusted him. Deep down on a cellular level, she trusted him with her son's life.

He took the forceps in his hands and dug into the area he'd opened up. Benjamin's entire body jerked, a muted cry coming from between his clenched lips. His limbs started to shorten and coarse hair appeared on his arms.

"Benjamin." She took her son's face between her hands and stared into familiar blue eyes, so like hers and filled with so much pain. "Fight it. You can't change. Not now."

He nodded and closed his eyes once again. He took a deep breath and his limbs returned to normal.

"Got it." Isaiah dumped the slug on the bed and went back to the wound, picking out pieces of cloth and bone fragments. Meredith thought he'd never finish, but finally, he picked up the sutures and set several stitches. "The bullet didn't go through. It did cause some slight damage to the bone when it hit. Whoever got him wasn't using a rifle, but a smaller caliber weapon."

All the better for the silver bullet to stay in and poison him. Still, it could have been worse. If Benjamin had been hit in a vital spot or if Isaiah hadn't been here and able to operate so quickly—she broke off from those thoughts. Benjamin was going to be fine.

Isaiah's hands were steady and competent as he stitched her son back together. "He should shift as soon as I'm done if he has the energy. It will help the chipped bone repair itself."

He stepped back and dumped the needle onto the bedside table, his hands covered in blood. "His werewolf genetics will heal the bone, but it will take a bit longer than normal because of the silver coating the bullet. Make him rest a few days at least. A week would be best."

"I will," she promised. She removed the towel from between her son's lips. "Can you shift now?"

Benjamin struggled to answer. "Think so."

"If you can't, don't push it." Isaiah rested his hand on Benjamin's forehead, his concern obvious. "You can rest and try again later."

Benjamin shut his eyes. His face contorted with pain. Beads of sweat popped out on his forehead. She was just about to call a halt when his body began to shift.

He cried out in agony, but didn't stop. By the time he'd finished shifting, Meredith was soaked to the skin in sweat. She'd felt every inch of the change her son had experienced.

The black wolf on the bed shut his eyes, his chest moving up and down in an even rhythm. Isaiah studied the wound to make sure it hadn't broken open during the change. "We should move him and change the sheets so he'll be more comfortable."

"We'll take care of that." Meredith ran her hand up and

down her son's side before placing her hand over his heart to feel the steady beat.

"How did the hunters find us?" Michael stepped away from the corner where he'd been standing silent and watchful during the entire operation.

Everyone in the room stilled. Tension rose as Michael confronted Isaiah. "We've lived here for more than a decade and we've been fine. You're here for a few days and we have hunters after us. Do they know where we live?"

Meredith gasped as the implication of tonight's attack hit her. She'd been so worried about getting her pack away before the cops arrived and frantic about Benjamin's injury, she hadn't thought beyond.

"Oh, God!" Neema cried. "What if they come for us? What if they told other werewolves?"

"Neema." Teague's voice was sharp, something it rarely was with his mate.

She bit her bottom lip and burst into tears, covering her face with her hands. "I'm sorry." She glanced at Meredith, remorse in her eyes.

Meredith hoped Isaiah hadn't picked up on Neema's slip of the tongue.

"They attacked at the park, not here at the club. You have to assume it was pure bad luck they found you tonight. Maybe they patrol the parks regularly." Isaiah figured if there were hunters in the city, they probably did check out the green spaces on a regular basis.

"Maybe they followed you?" Michael stepped forward, fists curled, shoulders thrust forward, more than ready for a fight. "Or maybe you sent them?"

Isaiah's lips thinned and Meredith could see he was

grasping for patience. "Why would I do that? I was shot at tonight too."

"So you say," Michael sneered. "We only have your word on that. And as to why..." He pointed to the bed. "Maybe so you could come to the rescue and play hero. But we don't need you. We took care of the hunters who attacked us on our own."

"Michael," she began, even as her mind started picking through the facts.

"You can't dismiss this as coincidence," her son insisted.

All eyes were on her now. She had a decision to make that was too important to all of them for her to make a mistake. "No, I can't dismiss it."

Michael inclined his head and she could see the look of triumph in his eyes. Isaiah just stared at her, his eyes blank.

"Do you truly believe I'd knowingly bring the hunters to your doorstep?" Isaiah asked. He grabbed the towel that Benjamin had held clenched between his teeth and used it to wipe his hands. Hands that were coated with her son's blood. He'd saved Benjamin's life. None of them could have removed that bullet, not without possibly causing even more injury. They just weren't skilled enough.

She owed him respect and honesty, if nothing else. "No. I don't believe you'd knowingly bring bounty hunters down on us." He sighed and his head dropped down, his chin almost to his chest. She hated the blow she was going to have to deal him, but she had no choice.

"But what about unknowingly? You said you're in the city on business, but you never said what kind. Could the hunters have been following you and stumbled on us?"

He raised his head and she read the indecision in his eyes. He wasn't certain. Oh, God. This had happened because of him.

Everything came tumbling down on her at once. One son was injured, the other one had been forced to kill to protect them. If the hunters knew where they were all their lives were in danger. Their livelihood was threatened. Their home. Where would they go if they had to leave Chicago? It was home.

Fury blasted out of her and she spoke before she could think. "This is all your fault. I wish you'd never stepped foot inside Haven. I wish I'd never laid eyes on you."

Even as her heart was screaming for her to stop, the bile spewed from her mouth in an unending torrent. She needed someone to blame. Even though she knew it wasn't intentional. Even though she knew she was to blame for not protecting her pack better.

What had she been thinking to go to a park so close to home, a small park at that, to settle the challenge between her and Michael? It could have waited.

She'd always known it was inevitable for either hunters or other werewolves to find them eventually if they stayed in one spot for any length of time. Still, she couldn't stop the anger that was boiling over inside her.

She'd fought her entire existence for the peaceful life she'd created here with her family. And now it was gone. Forever.

"Go." She pointed to the door.

Without a word, Isaiah marched to the door, shoulders stiff, head held high. He didn't look at her as he walked away. This was an eerie replay of their last parting. Except this time she knew it was for good. He wouldn't be back. Not this time.

Pain crushed her and she fell to her knees. Michael put his hand on her shoulder, but she jerked away from him. She couldn't bear for anyone to touch her.

Her skin hurt, her entire body ached. Inside, her wolf howled in pain. She'd just sent away the man she loved to protect her pack. She'd struck out at him instead of getting on her knees and thanking him for saving her son's life. The responsibility of protecting her six children was crushing her. But she was strong and they were her life.

They needed to see her be a true leader, in command of the situation. Able to put the good of the pack first and make the hard choices that needed to be made.

She pushed herself to her feet, waiting until she was certain her legs would hold her before she spoke. "Let me know if there's any change in Benjamin." Her voice sounded as dead as she felt as she trudged out of the room. Hank started to speak, but she held up her hand. "Not now. Not..."

Meredith didn't remember how she made it across the hall to her apartment, but suddenly she was in her bedroom. The rumpled bedclothes from the night before were still there.

Isaiah's essence permeated the room. She doubted she'd ever be able to sleep in this room again without remembering the hours she'd spent in his arms. Tumbling down onto the bed, she closed her eyes.

The tears started as a trickle and soon became a torrent. She cried for her sons' loss of innocence. Until tonight their world had always been secure. Yes, the threat had been there, but it had never hit quite this close to home before.

She cried for her adopted children and the home they might all have to abandon.

But mostly she cried for herself. She'd lost something precious and irreplaceable tonight. Something special and fine. And the worst part of it was she'd do the same thing again. She couldn't put anything above the safety of her children.

What if she trusted him with their secret? a voice in the back of her mind asked.

It was too late for that. Even if she thought she could trust

Isaiah with such a huge thing, the time for that had come and gone.

Isaiah was out of her life for good. As quickly as he'd come, he'd disappeared. She didn't even know where to find him if she wanted to. North Carolina, he'd said. But that was a large state. Chicago was still their home, until they decided differently.

She'd only known him for a short number of days, but it didn't matter. In her heart she knew he'd lay his life on the line for her and for all her children. But realization had come too late, smothered by anger and fear.

Meredith had sent him away and he wouldn't be back.

She cried until she had no more tears left. Her eyes were puffy and swollen when she pushed herself off the covers without having slept a wink. The sun was rising and there was work to be done.

She stripped off her clothing and headed toward the bathroom. A shower and a cup of coffee would help, but she didn't think she'd ever feel fine again. How could she? She was a woman without a heart. She'd sent hers away with the man she'd publicly scorned.

Chapter Twelve

"What the fuck happened?"

Quinn held the phone away from his ear as Steve Macmillan continued to rant. When he finally ran out of steam, Quinn spoke. "We stumbled across a group of werewolves. Must have been a meeting of some sort. On neutral ground."

They'd been following one possible werewolf. They hadn't expected to find more. He glanced down at the rifle lying on the front seat of his truck. He'd started down this road. There was no going back now.

"Jones texted that there were two females in the group."

Quinn's gut clenched. "Yeah."

"Shit." They all knew that Macmillan was searching for one particular female. Quinn didn't quite know the details, but he knew it had something to do with the death of the man's father.

"Jones and Warren took the ones in the park, while Collins followed the big guy. I was on the rooftop, as ordered." Quinn threw that last bit in. He hadn't wanted to play sniper, but he was the new guy in this group and did what he was told. He hoped like hell he'd made the right decision by shooting one of the hunters instead of the damn werewolf. His life was getting more complicated by the second.

"Why didn't you get the sonofabitch?"

That was the question, wasn't it? And he needed a good answer. "He moved too damn fast. Then he took off for the park again. I didn't have a good angle and the cops were moving in."

All true.

A sigh came over the other end and Quinn could picture Macmillan rubbing his hand over his face and smoothing down his goatee. "Here's what you're gonna do. Keep an eye on the park and see if you catch a glimpse of any of them. I'm going to watch Riley's Garage myself."

"Sure thing, boss."

"And, Quinn."

"Yeah?"

"Don't fuck this up."

The rest of the statement went unsaid as Macmillan hung up. If he messed up again, he was dead. Quinn rubbed his hand across his eyes and pondered his options. From his vantage point last night, he'd watched the wolves run from the park. He'd seen them enter a building not far from where he was now.

He also knew the identity of the man that Jones, Warren and Collins had been watching for days. He'd seen him once before. That was twenty years ago, but he wasn't a werewolf you forgot. The only question now was what he was going to do about it.

He clutched his phone in his hand and made his decision. Macmillan might have his own agenda, but so did Quinn. Quickly, he dialed a number. He didn't wait for a greeting when the phone was answered on the other end. "I've got a problem. Isaiah Striker is in Chicago."

The voice on the other end swore. "Trouble?"

"Yeah. You know what to do." Quinn rattled off the address

of the club called Haven and prayed he was doing the right thing.

Steve Macmillan ended the call and then punched in another number. He didn't quite trust the new guy. He didn't know Quinn. He preferred to work with men he'd known for years.

"Yeah?"

"Mitch, you hear what happened last night?"

"Fuckin' wolves got Jones and Warren."

"Collins too." Macmillan added.

"What do you need?" That's what he loved about working with men he trusted, men who had the same agenda as he did.

"I got the new guy watching the park. I want you to send a couple of your men down to watch a club called Haven. Jones sent me a message before he died and said he thought he recognized one of the women from that particular club." Jones had been a fan of blues music and had gone to the club once or twice. "See what you can find out."

"I'm on it." The call ended as abruptly as it had begun.

Macmillan tucked his phone away. If the club had been established for years, then the female he was searching for wasn't there. That didn't mean if there was an infestation of werewolves it didn't need to be dealt with. He'd get the facts first and then plan his strategy.

Isaiah walked the streets for hours. He put one foot in front of the other, not caring where he was going. It was all the same to him. Each step was taking him farther from where he wanted to be.

With Meredith.

The sun rose and still he walked, his long legs eating up the concrete sidewalks. He wondered what she was doing. Was she hurting as much as he was or had she put him from her mind completely? The last thought almost paralyzed him. He'd never be able to forget her. Ever.

His phone rang. He reached into his pocket and hit the answer button without really thinking about what he was doing. It was automatic. Much like breathing. "Yeah?"

"You okay?"

He closed his eyes. Joshua. He didn't want to talk to anyone, but especially not his happily mated brother. For a moment, he almost hated him. But the feeling passed. His current situation wasn't Joshua's fault. He'd fucked up his and Meredith's relationship, such as it was.

"No," he answered honestly. He didn't have it in him to lie or pretend. He was still too raw. Maybe in an hour or two, but not now.

"What happened?"

Isaiah started to laugh, but it was bitter on his tongue. "Nothing for you to worry about. I'll watch the truck today and leave tomorrow." No way was he risking leading hunters back to his pack.

Bad enough he'd led them straight to the woman he loved and her kids.

This is all your fault.

Meredith's words beat at him like a hammer. But he deserved it. He'd been in such a hurry to get back to her, to see her, he'd ignored the niggling feelings he'd been having for days. He hadn't been as cautious as he normally was.

As usual, when he fucked up someone else paid the price. It had been his sister years ago. This time it was Meredith and her family.

Once again, he'd failed to protect someone he'd loved. And he did love Meredith. There was no denying it any longer. She was the one for him. He'd spend the rest of his life missing her, longing for her.

"Isaiah?"

He'd forgotten his brother was on the phone. He stared at it and simply ended the call. He didn't want to talk to anyone. He waited for it to start ringing again but thankfully, it remained blessedly silent.

His stomach growled, but he ignored it. He didn't care about eating. He didn't care much about anything. Not even his family.

That shook him, but didn't quite pull him out of the numbness that surrounded him.

The woman he loved had sent him away. The sheer terror he'd felt when he'd known she was in danger was unlike anything he'd ever known. Primal instincts—protect or die—had enveloped him until he'd been more beast than man.

Even her pack had found a home in his heart. He'd wanted to kill those hunters all over again for injuring Benjamin, and not just because it upset Meredith. He honestly liked her boys and the rest of them. They were young, but they understood loyalty. You could see the love and respect they had for one another. It reminded Isaiah of how life had been for him and his brothers before Rachel had gone missing.

Like his life, theirs was now changed forever. They'd been safe until he'd stumbled upon them. They'd lived here for years without any hint of trouble. Now they would always be worried, looking over their shoulders. They'd have to consider moving, leaving everything they'd built behind.

What if they told other werewolves? Neema's words kept

rolling around in his brain. Why would it matter? Were they running from a pack? Possibly. But only Meredith and her sons were family. From what little he'd been able to glean, none of them had been with her the same length of time.

Isaiah stumbled to a halt as the possibility struck him. Almost all of them had been kids when Meredith had taken them in. No way would werewolf children be running around on their own. Even if their parents were gone, the pack would raise them. It was too dangerous for a young werewolf to be out in the world alone.

There was only one reason why it would happen.

They were half-breeds. They'd been on their own and running because they hadn't known who or what they really were until Meredith had found them.

No wonder they'd been afraid of him. Some werewolf packs were just as bad as the bounty hunters, wanting to kill any half-breeds to protect the purity of the bloodlines. And how stupid was that considering they were a dying breed. But beyond that, children were to be protected. No matter what.

"Shit," he muttered under his breath and got a strange look from a passerby. It was only then Isaiah noticed that the streets were starting to get busy. The world was waking up to start their day and he was walking around in bloodstained clothing.

He glanced up and looked at his surroundings, catching sight of a street sign. He might not have paid any attention to where he was going, but his feet had. His motel was only a few blocks away.

Picking up his pace, he made quick time to his room, doing his best to avoid people. The last thing he wanted was someone to remember seeing a man with blood on his shirt. Not that there was much to be seen. Thankfully, he was wearing a black T-shirt. Still, he didn't want to take any chances.

When he reached his room, he heaved a sigh as he stripped out of his clothing. He padded to the bathroom and started the shower. When it was warm enough, he stood beneath the spray, letting it cascade over him. Isaiah grabbed the soap, worked it over his body from head to toe and rinsed. He did it twice more before he felt clean.

He didn't linger. He had things to do.

It didn't matter that Meredith didn't want him. She was his. His to love and protect. There was no way he was leaving the city until he knew he hadn't brought more hunters down upon them. If he'd found them, it was possible other werewolves would too. What if one of those two groups discovered their secret?

He yanked a clean pair of jeans out of his duffle bag, pulled them on and sank down on the side of the bed without bothering to zip them. His life as he knew it was over.

There was no way he could go back to North Carolina. No way he could leave Meredith and the kids vulnerable. Most folks would laugh to hear him call grown men kids. But that's what they were. In werewolf age, they were adults, but not by much. Furthermore, Meredith had kept them sheltered. They all needed training in self-defense.

Not that they'd accept it from him.

He leaned over and grabbed a clean shirt and pulled it on. This was his destiny. His resolve hardened as he took out his phone to make the call that would change everything.

Funny, but he wasn't the least bit upset about it. A sense of rightness coalesced inside him. This was what he was meant to do. The small pack living in the heart of the city was his to protect. It was where he belonged.

If he spent the next four hundred years of his life watching over them, then he'd done what he was supposed to be doing with his life. Didn't matter if they never knew he was there. He'd know.

What if Meredith eventually found and took a mate?

That thought stopped him cold. He couldn't even think such a thing. His fangs lengthened and his fingers turned to claws. He dropped the phone on the mattress before he accidentally crushed it.

Grabbing the ends of his hair, he bent down, putting his head between his knees. He sucked in air as he willed his wolf back into submission.

If such a thing happened, he'd have to learn to accept it. If Meredith ever took a mate, he'd leave and return to North Carolina. But until such a day came to pass, she and her children were his responsibility.

He raised his head and picked up the phone. His thumb pressed the necessary buttons and then it was ringing.

"Isaiah." The concern in Joshua's voice soothed him. His brother was Striker of the Wolf Creek Pack. They would be fine without him. And he would see them on occasion. Still, his heart ached. He loved his brothers fiercely, but he loved Meredith too. And she was as necessary to him as air was. More. Without her, he had no life.

"Yeah." He took a deep breath. "You need to send someone else to Chicago to pick up the truck." He rattled off the address where he'd left it. "Have them watch it for a day or so before they move it. I won't be able to monitor it today."

"What the hell is going on? And don't say nothing."

He had to tell Joshua something or his brother would be on his tail in a heartbeat. As it was, it sounded like his brother was in a moving vehicle. "Where are you?"

"Don't worry about me. Talk."

"I met a woman." He didn't know what else to say. He couldn't talk to Joshua about Meredith and what she meant to him. He was too raw. Too vulnerable and he hated feeling this way.

He'd blocked off his emotions for so many years it was as though they'd finally overflowed the dam and it was ready to burst.

"Yeah. Anyway, I won't be coming home."

"But you hate the city." He could hear the disbelief in Joshua's voice and it brought a slight smile to his lips.

"Life's a bitch, ain't it?" He had to end this and get back to Haven. He was also going to have to find a room to rent close to Meredith's place. "I know you'll take care of the pack and the boys."

His eyes stung and he rubbed them with his thumb. "I gotta go. I'll call you as soon as I'm settled. And don't worry. I'll contact James in a day or so to let him know I'm leaving the pack. I won't leave that for you to handle."

"Isaiah," his brother shouted. But he was done and ended the call. He turned off his phone and stuffed it into his back pocket.

He sat and stared at his empty hands. It felt strange not to have to answer to anyone but himself. He was truly a loner. He shook his head and pushed to his feet. Lone wolf. That was him.

Except it wasn't funny. A wolf without a pack was vulnerable. He rubbed his chest, trying to ease the ache there as he thought about Meredith alone for years with children to protect. She was one hell of a female. She was worth giving up everything for.

Grabbing his duffle, he headed out of the room. He hadn't unpacked, so he knew he was leaving nothing behind. Check out was fast and easy as he'd paid cash in advance. In a dive like this they didn't care how you paid as long as you did.

Isaiah stood on the sidewalk and squinted up at the morning sunshine. He needed food and a place to stay. He turned and made his way toward Wicker Park, his gait sure and steady.

His first plan of action was to get some food and a paper, preferably in a location where he could keep an eye on Meredith's building. He'd check the rooms for rent in the classifieds and find somewhere to dump his stuff after he fueled up.

The hunters would need time to regroup and wouldn't strike in broad daylight. He had time to take care of business and catch a few hours sleep before he had to stand watch.

Thankfully, money wasn't an issue. Living for ninety years had some benefits, one being that he had investments in many major companies, primarily oil, gas, pharmaceuticals and technologies. He'd never spent a quarter of what he'd made over the years and had banked it all. He could easily spend the rest of his life watching over Meredith. His needs were simple—a place to sleep, food and keeping Meredith safe. Everything else was extra.

By the time he hit Meredith's familiar neighborhood, his stomach was very vocal in its complaints. He'd been here mostly at night and the area had a much different vibe in the day. It was alive with sights and sounds and smells. Instead of making him feel claustrophobic, as they usually would, they made him feel closer to Meredith. This is where she worked and lived. These were her people.

A local café caught his eye—Bean There. Obviously, they specialized in coffee. But their outside menu board also boasted a soup and sandwich lunch special. The location was perfect, so he went in.

It was a pleasant place, painted in vibrant shades of yellow, cinnamon and green. It wasn't quite lunchtime so only three of the tables were occupied.

A young woman wearing a tie-dyed skirt with a bulky knit sweater smiled as he went to the counter. "Hi. What can I get you?"

"I'll take two soup and sandwich specials and a coffee." He studied the desserts in the glass case.

"You expecting company?"

Isaiah shook his head. "Just hungry." She laughed as he pointed to the case. "I'll have a blueberry turnover and one of those brownies as well."

"If I ate like that, I'd be as big as a house," the dark-haired woman groused. "You must have great genes."

"Something like that." He paid when she rang up his total.

"You can have a seat and I'll bring your food down to you."

"Thanks. By the way, do you sell the local paper?"

She shook her head and pointed to a small stand. "We don't sell them, but we have several copies. You're free to read, we just ask that you don't take it with you when you go."

"Fair enough." He grabbed one and headed to a table near the window, dumping his duffle bag on the floor. Usually, he'd sit in a corner with his back against the wall. But then he wouldn't be able to see Haven. He did manage to get a small table that allowed him a good view of the club.

He opened the paper and went straight to the rental listings. He was perusing likely places when the waitress brought down his meal. She smiled at him as she set two bowls of soup and a small mound of sandwiches in front of him. Coffee and the sweet treats followed. "If you need anything else, just ask."

On impulse, he showed her the paper. "Know anywhere I can rent a room around here cheap?"

She chewed on her bottom lip and studied him. "I saw a sign in the window of one of the boutiques just down the road. I can't remember which one, but I think they were renting out an apartment or room above them."

"Thanks. I'll check it out after lunch."

"No problem." The girl stuck out her hand. "I'm Amy."

He shook it briefly. "Isaiah."

"So, you're planning to stay around here."

"That's the plan."

She smiled at him. "Welcome to the neighborhood."

Chapter Thirteen

Meredith bent over Benjamin, checking him for about the hundredth time this morning. She stroked his fur gently, careful not to wake him. Sleep was the best thing for him right now.

"He hasn't stirred in hours." Neema sat in the corner, an open magazine on her lap. "Not since I took over from Michael."

It was just past lunch and Meredith was exhausted. She hadn't slept at all. Instead, she'd sent the rest of them to bed and gone downstairs to get everything ready for the club to open.

Michael had turned in when Neema had relieved him. The rest of them had gotten a few hours sleep and were now downstairs taking care of business.

"You should take a nap. You don't look so hot."

Meredith shook her head. She didn't want to sleep. Every time she closed her eyes, images of Benjamin being shot, of Isaiah walking away beat at her. She couldn't take it.

"She's right, Mom."

Meredith turned to see Michael walking across the room toward her. He put his arm around her and hugged her. She felt the weight of his arm, but no warmth. She was so cold. So numb.

"I'm fine."

Her son stared down at her, his eyes older and wiser than they'd been a day ago. She wanted to howl and cry at the knowledge that now lingered in them. But what was done was done. And it had truly only been a matter of time. Their lives were precarious at best. It was a miracle they'd gone as long as they had without detection.

"No, you're not." Michael caught her chin in his hand and lifted her face. Sadness filled his gaze as he stared at her. She didn't know what he was searching for, but he didn't seem to find it.

"Come on. I'm taking you to your apartment. If you can't sleep, you can at least rest." He turned to Neema. "Call me if there's any change."

"Will do."

Meredith allowed Michael to lead her from the room, mostly because she was too damn tired to care. They walked across the hall in silence. He shoved open the door to her apartment and waited for her to enter.

Her gaze went straight to her window. She hadn't changed the locks yet. She had Isaiah's note tucked away in a drawer. She hadn't been able to bring herself to toss it in the garbage.

Where was he now? What was he doing? Had he already left Chicago?

"Mom?" Michael stood next to her. Waiting.

"What?" She didn't know what he wanted and was too tired to figure it out.

"I'm sorry."

She frowned and studied her son. There were dark shadows under his eyes, but there was resolve in them. "For what?"

He gave a short bark of laughter. "For what? For questioning your leadership. For getting us into that mess last night. It was my fault. We wouldn't have been at the park if it weren't for me and my stupid resentment."

"Resentment?" Meredith was lost. Reaching out, she touched Michael's arm. "What did you resent?"

He shook his head and heaved out a sigh. "Not what. Who."

She frowned. "I don't understand."

"Isaiah." He shifted his weight from one leg to the other. "Anyone could see the way he looked at you." He paused. "And the way you watched him. The way he was working his way in to our lives."

"But you're my son." She was bewildered. "Nothing can change how I feel about you. Or Benjamin or any of you."

"I know that." He raked his free hand through his short hair, making the ends stand up straight. "It's just that you've never looked at a male like that before. He wasn't just some guy. He was a powerful male werewolf. An alpha. I struck out in anger, challenging you. Thinking I could do a better job at running the pack."

"You were afraid he'd take your place in the pack?" While she was alpha, Michael had always acted as her beta, her right hand, her second in command.

"Stupid, huh? And look where it got us. Benjamin is shot and everyone else is scared."

Meredith grabbed his shoulders and shook him. He was larger than her, but she was still his mother. "It wasn't your fault. You're at the age where you want to assert yourself. That's natural. No," she stopped him before he could speak. "I'm not done yet."

He subsided and she continued.

"You haven't lived around adult males before, so you don't know. That's on me too." She'd deprived her sons of so much by taking them and running from her pack.

"No." Michael shook his head adamantly. "I haven't missed anything. I don't want to be a part of a pack that would force you to mate whether you wanted to or not."

Meredith closed her eyes and gave thanks that she had such wonderful, understanding sons. She'd told them what had happened when they'd come of age and made their first change. She'd given them the option of returning to the pack, knowing their grandfather would welcome them with open arms, even as he sent assassins to kill her. Not that she'd told her sons that little detail.

But they'd both refused. Even more so when she'd told them about her former pack's stand on half-breeds, which was that the only good half-breed was a dead one. No way were they putting their brothers and sister in danger.

"You're a good son, Michael. A good man." She pulled him into her arms, hugging him. His arms banded around her. "This wasn't your fault. If it hadn't happened this time, it would have been some other time. Bounty hunters are everywhere. We risk detection every time we go to a park and change."

He buried his face in her neck, holding her close. "I'm sorry I was jealous of Isaiah. Sorry you felt you had to send him away."

She pulled back. "That was my decision. Right or wrong, I made it."

"Can you call him?"

"Why? What's changed since last night?"

Michael rubbed his hand over his stubbled jaw. "I had a lot of time to think while I watched over Benjamin. He was willing to protect you from me. He came back to the park last night and he didn't have to. He removed the bullet from Benjamin. But beyond that, he looked at you the same way Teague watches Neema."

Meredith's breath caught in her chest. She couldn't think about that. Couldn't think about what she'd destroyed in a moment's anger and pain. She swayed and the edges of the room began to close around her.

"Mom?" Michael caught her in his arms and picked her up, carrying her into her room. His gaze flicked over the tangled sheets, but said nothing. He could easily smell Isaiah's scent on them and knew she hadn't changed them.

He laid her on the mattress, tugged off her shoes and pulled the comforter over her. "Rest. I'll send someone up with something to eat in a few hours."

She closed her eyes and turned her head into the pillow, breathing in Isaiah's scent. She didn't acknowledge when Michael left. Meredith lay there, not sleeping, but remembering the hours she and Isaiah had spent in this room. Knowing it would never happen again.

She clung to the pillow and pulled her legs toward her chest, curling up as tight as she could. But nothing could dispel the pain or fill the empty, aching hole in her heart.

Michael was worried. Not only for his brother but for his mother. She'd always seemed so strong, so confident. She was the rock on which they all leaned. Now that foundation had been shaken.

He realized just how much he depended on her. How much all of them did. It was habit, he supposed. Left over from childhood. But that didn't make it right. It was time for him, for the other males, to step up and take more on their shoulders.

Hank had been trying to do it since he arrived. Maybe it

was because he'd been older when he'd found them. An adult male who'd spent time in the human military. Only Hank had pushed to make Meredith let him take on some of her duties. And she'd let him.

That should have been a sign. But Michael, like the rest of them, had ignored it. Each comfortable in their roles. Well, no more.

He found the rest of the guys sitting at one end of the bar. They had to open on time even though none of them wanted to. Their mother was adamant about that. They could do nothing to draw suspicion to them. Not until the commotion over the killings in the park blew over.

There were two dead men, three if you counted the one in the alleyway not far from the park. Isaiah hadn't been lying when he'd said he'd been attacked too. Hank had gone out early to get a paper and he'd also checked out the news on the local television station.

Hank's eyes practically bored a hole in him as he sauntered over and took a seat. "How is she?"

Michael thought about how much to tell them and decided to go with total honestly. They'd never kept secrets from one another in this pack and this was no time to start. "I don't know."

"Fuck." Teague tapped his fingertips on top of the bar, his entire body practically vibrating.

"That says it all." Kevin raised his coffee mug and saluted all of them.

"We made a mistake last night." Hank's pale blue eyes glittered like diamonds, hard and sharp. Deadly. "We were so caught up in the challenge we forgot to be cautious. Those hunters were on us before we knew it."

"That's on me." Michael sat on one of the tall stools and

rested his elbows on the edge of the bar. Kevin placed a mug of coffee in front of him and absently wiped a stain off the counter with the edge of his hand.

"Shit, man, there's enough blame to go around." Teague swung around on his stool. "None of us were paying attention last night. Too worried about the challenge and Isaiah."

"Yeah." Michael dug the heels of his hands against his eyes and sighed. That was another mess he'd helped create.

"Does Meredith know where to find Isaiah?" Kevin leaned back against the counter and crossed his arms over his chest. "'Cause I really think we need to talk to him."

Michael picked up his mug and sipped his coffee. It was hot and strong, exactly what he needed. "Nope."

"Shit." Teague echoed his earlier sentiment.

"That about sums it up," Hank added. "Everything is a mess." He faced Michael. "So what are we going to do about it?"

They all looked to him. Michael straightened on the stool and shoved his coffee mug aside. He wouldn't let his mother down. Not this time. "We watch and we wait. We don't do anything to bring attention our way."

"What about Isaiah?" Kevin asked.

Michael shrugged. Wasn't much any of them could do. They'd been so busy trying to get rid of him they'd never taken the time to learn much of anything about him. "Don't know. Maybe he'll come back. Maybe he won't. Either way, it's not our call."

Hank frowned, not looking pleased, but he nodded his agreement.

Teague nodded and slid off his stool. "I'm gonna go up and sit with Neema for a bit, help her watch Benjamin."

They all watched him leave, not blaming him for not

wanting his mate out of his sight.

Kevin picked up his half-full mug and headed toward the office. "I have some suppliers I need to deal with. You guys can open the club. I already called in the rest of the staff to cover the kitchen and waitressing duties for the day shift. It will be just family for the evening shift. Everyone should catch an extra few hours of sleep this afternoon." He didn't wait for a reply, but hurried off to take care of business.

Michael and Hank shared a look when they were alone in the bar. They would protect the rest of the family from whatever threat came their way.

A knock came on the front door. Hank stood and managed a friendly gesture as Tammy waved enthusiastically at him through the glass. "I'll get the staff started and take the first watch. I'll send someone up to wake you in a few hours. Get some rest."

Michael nodded and Hank went to unlock the door. It was time to start their day.

Macmillan was watching Riley's Garage when his phone rang. He welcomed the distraction. This was one hell of a boring job. After the depletion of his men last night, there was no one else to put on the job until reinforcements arrived. Mitch and his guys were working on a more important job for him.

"You're not going to believe this," Mitch began.

"Tell me something to make me happy." Macmillan shifted in the front seat of his truck, ignoring the cramp in his leg.

"Bob got up on the roof of the building next door and managed to get a look in one of the windows. He saw an injured wolf lying on a bed. There was a female sitting next to him, keeping watch. And that's not all."

"Go on," Macmillan prompted.

"He saw another guy carrying trash out to the dumpster behind the building. Said he was a redhead with tats and piercings. Moved real smooth. Like a werewolf."

"I've never heard of a redheaded werewolf."

"Could be a half-breed," Mitch speculated. "Bob's convinced he could be one of them. Said he prowled around the alley and sniffed the air before going back inside."

"Damn." This was gold. He hated the half-breeds even more then the pure werewolves. After all, some human man or woman had mated with one of those mutants. The products of such unnatural unions needed to be killed on principle alone. Macmillan thought for a moment and then smiled. He couldn't afford to waste any more men. Maybe there was a way to get rid of the werewolves who'd taken out his men and a few more besides.

"You gotta pen?" he asked Mitch.

There was the sound of rustling and then Mitch was back. "Go."

"Here's what I want you to do." After he finished his instructions, he disconnected and placed another call.

"Quinn."

"It's me. I've got a job for you."

Isaiah dumped his duffle bag on the bare mattress. The room was sparse, but clean. It wasn't really an apartment. More like a living space.

A small kitchen area was comprised of a sink, hot plate and miniscule refrigerator. The pitted blue countertop was about three feet long and there were two upper and lower cabinets.

A battered sofa, a desk and a tiny table with two chairs

that had seen better days furnished the place.

A closet and a basic bathroom with toilet, sink and shower completed the space. The walls and the cabinets were painted dull beige and the floors were scuffed planks.

The best thing about the efficiency apartment was the window that gave him a view of the street, of Haven.

It was everything he needed.

He went to the window and stared at the building across the way. His hand flattened against the glass. Meredith was only yards away, but she might as well be a million miles.

Sighing, he turned and surveyed his new home. His landlady had taken cash for the first and last months' rent and assured him he could pay her in cash every month if he chose. It was perfect for him.

As much as he wanted to crash for a few hours, he needed supplies. Food and some basic bedding at the very least. He glanced out the window again, seeing movement at Haven.

Tammy was banging on the front door. Moments later, Hank let her in, his gaze wandering up and down the street before he shut the door. Good, they were on alert at least.

He tore his gaze away from the window once again and strode to the bed. He unzipped his duffle bag and drew out a long, thin case from the bottom. He set it on the mattress and opened the latch. A rifle sat waiting for him. He had enough ammunition for now. What he shot at, he hit. It wasn't his preferred way to fight, but he'd do whatever he had to do to protect Meredith. Closing and latching the case, he took it to the closet and stored it on the top shelf.

He paused, closed his eyes and let his head fall back on his neck. He was so damn tired. Exhaustion tugged at him, urging him to curl up on the mattress for a few hours. "Soon," he promised himself.

Working his eyes open, he went into the bathroom and turned on the cold tap, flicking water on his face to try to wake himself up. He grabbed the tail of his T-shirt and rubbed it over his face. He peered at himself in the mirror. His eyes were bloodshot. His face was grim.

There was little he could do about how he looked. "Get on with it," he growled at his reflection. He turned off the tap and headed for the door. He'd get enough supplies to get him through a couple of days. Then he'd come back and catch a few hours sleep.

Bending down, he checked the knife in his boot. The deadly blade was coated in silver, so it worked well on werewolves and hunters alike. He wasn't taking any chances. Not with Meredith's safety.

Grabbing a flannel shirt from his duffle, he slipped it on and left his new home, locking up behind him. His first stop would be a hardware store to pick up a new lock. He wasn't taking a chance that anyone else had a key.

His sneakers made little sound on the treads of the narrow staircase. The entrance to the upper floors was around the back of the building, which suited him just fine. There was also access with another staircase at the front of the building, but the back worked better for him. Less chance of Meredith or any of her pack catching sight of him.

Not that he expected that to last. After all, he was living here now. They were bound to run into one another eventually. His gut clenched and a muscle beneath his left eye began to pulse. He'd deal with that when he had to.

For now, he had things to do and places to go. The quicker he got the necessary chores out of the way, the faster he'd be back to start his surveillance of the club for the evening.

He pushed open the back door and listened. He inhaled,

ignoring the stench from a nearby dumpster and the mixture of gas and pollution in the air. He heard nothing out of the ordinary, nor could he smell anyone. He stepped out and glanced around, scanning high and low.

Satisfied he wasn't being watched, he headed toward the street. He turned left and started walking, making a mental list of everything he needed.

His thoughts drifted to Meredith and he swore under his breath. A sense of urgency tugged at him. He didn't want to leave her, even for a few hours.

She was safe. For now. He had to believe that. She was surrounded by her pack and they were all on high alert. The bounty hunters would need time to regroup. She was in no danger, not until nightfall.

Still, that niggling sense that something was wrong wouldn't leave him. "There is no other danger," he assured himself. He dragged his hand through his hair and took a deep breath when he noticed several people looking oddly at him.

Talking to himself in public was not the way to stay unnoticed.

He noticed a thrift store on a side street. They would have blankets and sheets and maybe some basic kitchen stuff. He'd get whatever he could there. He could dump it back at his place and then go searching for a grocery store. There had to be something close by. Even a convenience store would do. He wasn't picky.

But there was no way he could leave the neighborhood. His instincts were screaming at him to stay close. So close he would stay.

There was always takeout and restaurants for food, and if the thrift shop didn't have what he needed, he'd sleep on the bare mattress.

Hell, he'd slept on the ground before. No big deal. He could always shift and curl up if had to. His wolf certainly wouldn't care.

Decision made, Isaiah relaxed slightly, but still stayed on alert as he pulled open the door of the thrift shop and stepped inside.

Meredith cried out. The sound woke her and she wrapped her arms around herself as she tried to shake off the remnants of her dream. It vibrated through her like a never-ending ache. Loneliness filled her, reminding her of all she'd lost.

She rolled over and glanced at the clock on her bedside table, surprised to see that five hours had passed. In spite of all the thoughts she had running through her brain, she'd eventually drifted off to sleep.

But Isaiah had followed her there, finding his way into her dreams.

It had started out so good. She'd been lying in bed trying to sleep, and he'd come to her. It had never occurred to her to question why he was here or why he was naked. She'd reveled in the sight of his wide shoulders, massive biceps, ripped abs and muscular thighs. He'd been aroused. His penis stood tall and proud, the tip red and wet as he moved toward her.

He belonged with her. She'd pushed back the covers to reveal her nude body, inviting him into her bed. He'd smiled at her then, a roguish smile filled with sensual promise. She knew he could smell her essence. She was wet between her thighs, ready to take him. There was no disguising her puckered nipples or the way her breasts swayed with each deep breath she took.

She shivered at the memory.

He'd devoured her with his eyes before kneeling on the bed

and starting with his hands and mouth. He'd touched and licked and tasted every inch of her skin from the sensitive curve of her neck to the tips of her toes.

The look in his eyes had aroused and frightened her at the same time. This was a male who wouldn't be denied.

And she didn't want to.

She wanted to give him everything. Share every aspect of herself.

"Roll over." His deep voice had washed over her. His command demanding her compliance.

She'd rolled over on her hands and knees. She known what was coming, had wanted him to claim her, to mate with her.

Meredith had waited, breath held, needing to feel his large body covering hers.

Nothing but cool air had hit her skin.

She peered over her shoulder only to see him fading into the shadows.

"You sent me away. You sent me away." His voice had become little more than a whisper until it disappeared totally.

She'd cried out and the sound had pulled her out of sleep.

She lay on the bed shivering, not with cold, but with barely suppressed desire. She didn't want to move. Her breasts ached and her sex throbbed, empty and aching.

She could easily have stayed in bed forever. Being surrounded by Isaiah's scent was almost as good as being held in his arms. But he wasn't here, his smell would eventually fade from the sheets and she had a family to protect.

Sighing, she shoved the comforter down and sat up. She felt groggy and it was difficult to string a coherent thought together. Her mouth was dry and she felt sticky and uncomfortable.

She'd slept in her clothes. How grungy was that?

Sliding her legs over the side of the mattress, she paused and took a moment to collect herself. No one had come looking for her. That was a good sign. Benjamin must be resting and there had been no further threats to the security of the pack, at least for the moment. Still, she had to know.

It took more effort than she'd thought to stand, but once she was on her feet she went straight to the kitchen and grabbed the phone. She had no idea where her cell phone was and didn't want to take the time to search for it. The phone rang twice before it was answered.

"Haven." Michael's voice came clearly over the line.

She tried to swallow and realized too late that she should have had a glass of water first. "Hey, honey." She cleared her throat and kept going. "How is Benjamin?"

"He's still sleeping. Everything is fine. Give me a sec." She heard him call out to Kevin and then the sounds of the club receded. The sound of footsteps echoed through the receiver. She turned toward her front door just as it opened and Michael walked in.

Meredith clicked her phone off and put it back in the stand. Michael tucked his phone into his back pocket and kept coming until she was enfolded in his arms.

"Did you sleep at all?" His voice was gruff with concern.

She pulled back so she could see him clearly. "I didn't expect to, but I did. Thank you."

He shook his head, a pained look in his eyes. "Don't thank me. It's no more than I should have done." He stuck his hands in his pockets and continued. "We called in the human staff to work the day shift. Hank and I took turns keeping an eye on things while everyone else rested. We figured it was better if only family worked tonight. Just in case."

He didn't need to finish that statement. They were all expecting trouble of some kind, sooner rather than later.

Meredith stifled a yawn. She really needed a cool shower to throw off the remnants of her nap, and her erotic dream. "Good thinking."

Michael smiled at her, reached out and brushed a lock of her hair away from her face. "Why don't you shower and come downstairs. Teague has a pot of chicken soup on the stove waiting for you."

In spite of his rough appearance, Teague was a wizard in the kitchen. And his chicken soup was her favorite. "I think I'd like that."

Her son leaned down and kissed her forehead. "Good."

"I'll check on Benjamin first."

"I wouldn't expect anything else." Michael kissed her again. "We've got it covered downstairs until you get there."

He left her standing in her kitchen, slightly bemused. There was a change in her son, a new maturity that hadn't been there before. Maybe something good had come out of this mess.

And maybe it was her fault he hadn't matured as quickly as he possibly should have. She'd been guilty of overprotecting all of them.

"What's done is done." She headed toward the shower, tugging off clothing as she went.

Chapter Fourteen

Isaiah had decided to have a quick bite to eat at a restaurant just down the road before going back to settle in to his watch for the night. He was enjoying a quick dinner of lasagna and garlic bread when the hairs on the back of his neck stirred.

He lowered his fork slowly, not daring to move, barely daring to breathe. Something was wrong.

His free hand slid down to the sheath strapped to his ankle, his fingers closing around the hilt of his knife. *Danger.* His instincts were screaming at him.

His first thought was bounty hunters. He scanned the room but didn't recognize anyone. Not that he expected to. They'd killed the hunters who had attacked last night. All except for the unknown sniper on the rooftop who'd gotten away.

A group of men followed a waitress to a table on the far side of the room. He studied the way they moved, the way their gazes scanned the room. Isaiah glanced down at his plate just in time to avoid being caught looking at them.

Werewolves.

There was no disguising the way they moved or their hyperawareness of their surroundings. It took one to know one. What were three werewolves doing here?

This neighborhood was getting very crowded with

paranormal creatures and hunters.

Coincidence? He didn't think so.

The smells of the humans and the spices of the food helped mask their scent. Which was a good thing. If he couldn't smell them, they couldn't know about him. He'd be fine as long as he didn't draw their attention.

He picked up his fork and forced himself to start eating. Using his preternatural sense of hearing, he tried to eavesdrop on them. It wasn't easy. He had to tune out all the other noise around him.

The men ordered dinner and said little until the waitress returned with their meals. A waitress came up to take Isaiah's empty dinner plate and he ordered coffee and a dessert he didn't want. But there was no way he could leave before these men. They'd spot him in a heartbeat. And while they were no danger to him, he didn't want them asking any questions about what he was doing here.

He would do nothing that might jeopardize Meredith and her pack.

After what felt like an eternity, but was probably no more than twenty minutes, one of the men shot a glance around the room and leaned in closer. Isaiah pretended to be absorbed with his dessert, but listened intently.

"...email...park..."

Isaiah swore under his breath. He needed to hear more. Had someone contacted them about what had happened in the park last night? Were they possibly here to search for more bounty hunters? That made sense. Werewolves hated the hunters with a passion.

"...wolves...female..."

A low growl threatened to escape him and Isaiah barely

managed to swallow it back. The muscles in his arms and shoulders rippled and bunched. He forced himself to breathe deep and slow. The last thing he needed to do was change and let his wolf rip out their throats. That would surely attract unwanted attention.

The metal fork in his hand bent and he carefully set it on the table by his plate. The men shoved away from the table and headed toward the front door. He studied them surreptitiously as they paid for their meal.

When the front door closed behind them, Isaiah was on his feet and across the room. He tossed his waitress the money for his meal and a substantial tip and exited the restaurant.

As the warm air and spicy smells receded, he peered up and down the street, catching a glimpse of the men as they turned a corner. Isaiah loped down the sidewalk. He had to know what they were doing. If they were friend or foe.

Opening all his senses, Isaiah took a quick glance around the corner before following the three men into a dark alley.

The smells that masked his presence also made it more difficult to follow the wolves. Thankfully, they weren't exactly sneaking around or he'd have had a much harder time.

Isaiah slipped through the darkness, keeping to the shadows. He ducked into a doorway just as one of the men turned suddenly. Shit, he was too close.

"This is the spot," said a large male with long brown hair, an experienced werewolf from the way he carried himself.

The other two looked around the ground. "The guy who contacted us said there were two females and several males in the park last night."

"Why would he email us?" the guy who'd almost caught Isaiah asked. That was the same question Isaiah wanted answered. He stood in the shadows, not moving a muscle.

"There's really only one reason why he would." He didn't elaborate, but kept on searching the ground. "I want to know what we're supposed to be looking for," the large man complained. "Why couldn't he have just given us the details in the damn email? This cloak and dagger shit is for amateurs."

"That's what you get when you're dealing with humans." The wolf who'd done the talking back at the restaurant ignored the other two while he scanned the ground. He suddenly pointed at a bottle. "I think there's a note in there."

The male who was closest stalked across the alley, grabbed the bottle and opened it. "Hmmm, looks like our friend has had several men watching the street all day and found what he was looking for." The male smiled and it wasn't a pleasant sight. Isaiah peered between a crack in the brickwork and waited with bated breath. Had they found Meredith and her pack?

"Show me." The largest male, and obviously the leader of the three, held out his hand. He took the note his friend offered and scanned it. "Seems as though our mysterious contact did more than find them. He had a guy watching and he saw something he thought would interest us."

"What?" the younger man asked. "Women?"

"Yup. And possibly a half-breed male. Maybe more." The leader of the three crumpled the paper in his hand and stuffed it into his pocket. "Gotta love online social networking. We're going to pay a little visit later tonight when the club closes down. I'm just glad we were close enough to Chicago to get here tonight."

"That's why they contacted us." The man who'd done the talking at the restaurant smiled.

"Why don't we just go and get them?" the younger male asked.

Isaiah's entire body tensed, ready to fight. No one was

touching Meredith or her family. Over his dead body. Or rather, over their dead bodies.

His fingernails elongated and his fangs lengthened. The wolf was close to taking hold. Protecting his mate superseded all else.

The big man smacked the younger one in the back of the head. "Because you never take the word of a human, one who is most likely a hunter. We don't want to destroy one of our own. Besides, it could be a trap for us. We'll watch until the club closes, then we'll pay our visit."

The three men continued down the alley and disappeared.

Isaiah released a breath he hadn't realized he'd been holding. Meredith was safe. For now. It had to have been the sniper on the rooftop who'd contacted these wolves. Either that or someone he was working with. Meredith's cover was truly blown.

Shit. He swore as he leaned against the wall of the building and hit the back of his head against the brickwork. This meant that both the hunters and a group of purist werewolves knew about Meredith and her family. This was turning into a clusterfuck of epic proportions. And it was all his fault.

There was nothing to be done about it. Their secret was out. The only thing he could do now was protect them. They'd have to be ready to move, and fast.

His heart hammered and blood surged through his veins. He longed for a fight. He needed an outlet for his anger and these males were it. He'd send Meredith and the rest of the pack to safety. Then he'd give these wolves a little something they hadn't been expecting.

Pushing away from the wall, he listened. He was alone. Still, he was cautious as he loped down the alley and back onto the sidewalk. He could see the lights of Haven down the street.

His heart ached at the thought of what he was about to do.

Meredith had sent him away after what happened. He'd be lucky if she didn't try to kill him, given the bomb he was about to drop on her.

Straightening his shoulders, he strode down the sidewalk. He glanced at his watch. It was still early. But he couldn't afford to wait.

Hank was leaning against the doorframe chatting with two women when he spotted Isaiah. He straightened and said something to the women that had them laughing and walking into the club.

Music, laughter and happy voices drifted out from the open door. Isaiah hated that he was the one who was going to put an end to it. For all time.

"I didn't expect to see you again." Hank spread his legs and rested on the balls of his feet, ready to fight.

"This isn't about Meredith and me. This is about the safety of all of you." He stopped two feet from Hank, hands at his sides. He wouldn't attack, but he would defend himself.

"You can tell me and I can pass your message on to her."

Isaiah shook his head. "We can do this the easy way or the hard way, but I'm going to see Meredith."

"What's going on?" Michael stepped out, eyeing Isaiah cautiously.

"He wants to talk to Meredith."

Isaiah studied Michael. He looked older, harder than he had twenty-four hours ago. He was sorry for that. He was sorry for all of it.

He couldn't change the past. All he could do now was try to minimize the damage from the fallout.

Meredith's son studied him. Isaiah didn't shift position,

didn't fidget under Michael's scrutiny.

"I thought you'd be long gone by now."

"You thought wrong."

Isaiah sensed no antagonism, no anger from Michael. The younger male actually smiled. That worried Isaiah. What the heck was going on?

"She's in her office. You know the way." Michael stepped back and motioned Isaiah inward.

Not hesitating, Isaiah walked into the club. The familiar sounds and smells surrounded him. It felt like home. He hated like hell that Meredith was going to have to leave it to protect her family.

Tammy waved at him as he passed by. Teague glared at him from his post just outside the kitchen door. Kevin was behind the bar, filling drink orders. He nodded, his gaze solemn, and went back to work.

Isaiah cut through the crowd like a shark through a pool of minnows. Everyone moved out of his way without his having to ask. He was throwing off don't-fuck-with-me vibes even an idiot could sense.

The narrow hallway closed around him and then he was in front of her office door. He didn't knock, didn't want to give her the opportunity to send him away without allowing him to see her first.

He gripped the handle, turned it and shoved the door open.

She looked tired. That was his first thought. Meredith was sitting at her desk working on her computer. She wasn't wearing her usual flashy, sexy dress, but a pair of jeans and a turtleneck sweater. The sweater was soft and clung to her breasts like a lover's caress.

She glanced up, her eyes widening as she jumped to her

feet. Her gaze went behind him and narrowed. "Did you hurt any of them?"

He took the punch to his heart without flinching. "I wouldn't hurt any of your children." And they all belonged to her, heart and soul.

She nodded and glanced down at her computer screen, downsizing whatever she'd been working on. Her hair was pulled back in a braid rather than flowing down her back. He wanted to release it, to set it and her free.

"We need to talk." He shut the door and the room suddenly felt smaller. The noise from the club muted and he could hear every breath Meredith took.

He could smell her too. Her soap and the essence that was pure female, pure Meredith.

His cock jerked to attention. Isaiah longed to go to her and drag her into his arms. He wanted to feel her feminine curves against the hard planes of his body, softening and accommodating his much larger frame. He wanted to inhale her scent into his lungs until it drove out every other smell.

Her lips parted and her tongue flicked out to touch the bottom one. He swallowed a groan as his balls drew up close to his body. Meredith had lips that were made for kissing, full and soft and sweet.

He clenched the muscles in his thighs to keep from walking across the room and sweeping her into his arms. The urge to take her, to make her his once again was overwhelming.

The only other urge that could take precedence, that could control the primal instincts beating at him, was the urge to keep her safe. Nothing was more important than that.

"I thought you'd gone." The words "for good" went unsaid. Tension crept over him, hardening every muscle in his body.

"No." He wouldn't tell her he'd rented a place and was watching her club for any sight of her.

"Oh." She fiddled with her pen, then tossed it onto the battered desk and squared her shoulders. "Why are you here?"

Meredith could barely breathe. She was finding it extremely difficult to slap together a string of coherent words. Isaiah was here.

He filled the room with his larger-than-life presence. The jeans he wore clung to his thighs. They were well worn and had been washed so often they were soft and supple, molding to the thick muscles. They also did nothing to hide the rather large bulge pressing against the zipper.

Her sex spasmed and cream dampened her panties. She resisted the urge to cross her arms over her chest to disguise her puckered nipples. Thankfully, the sweater she was wearing was thick enough to hide her arousal. Not that it mattered. If he got close enough, he'd smell it.

He was wearing a T-shirt with a flannel shirt over it. The inner shirt stretched taut across his abs, outlining his hard chest. Her fingers itched to touch him.

She wanted to run her hands through his shaggy hair and touch her lips to his. He looked tired. The lines radiating from the corners of his eyes were deeper than they'd been. His chocolate brown eyes ate her up as they stood watching one another.

She realized his gaze was on her lips and they parted of their own accord.

Isaiah sucked in a breath and took a step toward her before coming up short. He raked his fingers through his hair. "We need to talk."

"Okay." She managed to nod. Neither of them moved. She didn't know how she felt about him being here. She was elated and frightened at the same time.

She'd sent him away. A man as proud as Isaiah wouldn't come crawling back. That meant something had sent him here and whatever it was, it couldn't be good. Only his innate sense of responsibility would have brought him back to her.

"What is it?" She had to know. Her stomach was jittery and her palms were sweating. "Is it about what happened in the park?" She felt slightly ill. Had someone seen them last night?

"I overheard a conversation in a restaurant," he began. She nodded encouragingly and he continued. "There were three of them. Werewolves."

"Oh, God." She swayed, catching herself on the back of her chair. "What did you hear?"

"With the noise of the crowd, I could only catch a word or two so I followed them when they left."

Meredith swallowed hard. Maybe it was nothing. Maybe it was—

She stopped trying to kid herself. If it weren't deadly serious, Isaiah wouldn't be here.

"They stopped in an alley and found a note they'd been told to expect. Seems that the bounty hunters saw where you came from last night and set someone to watch your place today. They had a man on a nearby roof and saw Benjamin and Neema. They also saw Teague." He hesitated for a second and then continued. "They suspect he might be a half-breed."

This couldn't be happening. This was her biggest nightmare unfolding. "Oh, God," she whispered.

Isaiah's grim expression didn't give away any of his thoughts or feelings on the matter. "They also know there might be two werewolf females here."

Meredith flew around the desk, making for the door. Her kids. She had to protect her children.

Isaiah's muscled forearm shot around her waist, stopping her. She turned on him and struck out. He captured her arms easily, pinning them behind her. She brought her knee upward in a lightning-fast move, but he countered it. Shoving her against the wall, he leaned against her, holding her prisoner with his weight.

She glared at him, trying to ignore the feel of his body against hers. His thighs were on the outside of hers, squeezing them. That put his erection right at the juncture of her legs. His cock was hard and hot against her mound. His broad chest covered hers, making her nipples ache.

"The others are safe. For the moment," he added. He leaned down, touching his forehead to hers. "The wolves are planning to wait until closing to check out the situation. They want to make certain of their information before they attack. After all, the intel came from hunters."

That made sense. She took a deep breath, but relaxation was beyond her. "I don't understand. Why would hunters contact werewolves and why would the wolves have anything to do with the hunters?" That didn't make any sense. All wolves hated bounty hunters. It was bred into them from the day they were born. They were natural enemies.

"I've come across this before. The bounty hunters use the wolves to do their dirty work for them. They let us kill one another without putting any of their men in danger. And the purist werewolves don't care. All they care about is keeping the species line strong and untainted."

"That's crazy."

"Yeah, it is." Isaiah raised his head. "Considering how our

species is clinging to survival, every member needs to be protected."

Something deep inside her broke open and a warm, healing balm enveloped her. "Then you don't agree with them?"

A low growl came from deep inside Isaiah. "Hell, no. What kind of male do you think I am?"

Pain flashed in his eyes and then it was gone. He stepped away and she felt the loss of his warmth.

"That's why you didn't tell me." He glared at her and she felt the full weight of his displeasure.

Emotions pummeled her. Fear warred with desire, making her lightheaded. It took her a moment to make sense of his words. "You knew?"

"I suspected as much. It wasn't hard. You're a female alone with two pups. The rest of them would have been children or barely adults when they came to be with you. There's only one reason all of them wouldn't have been within the protection of a pack."

"I think I need to sit down." Her head was spinning. She lurched for the desk and sat down on the corner. Isaiah's hand shot out to steady her while she tried to absorb everything he'd told her.

The sensual tension between them sizzled, but she shoved it aside. Bounty hunters knew about them. Werewolves knew about the half-breed members of her pack.

It hit her with the force of a sledgehammer. Their home had been compromised. Chicago was no longer safe. Haven was lost to them forever.

Tears threatened, but she blinked them back. She'd done harder things than this before. She would survive. Her pack would survive.

But there was something she could do.

Isaiah wasn't a part of this. Nothing he'd said indicated they knew anything about him or his involvement with her pack. It might kill her, but she had to do this. She had to send him away again. And this time it had to be for good.

He was a pure werewolf with a pack of his own. He didn't need to be a part of this mess. She and her small pack would spend the next five or ten years running and hiding until it was safe to set up a home base again. She couldn't ask that of him.

Taking a deep breath, Meredith faced the male she loved. "Thank you for telling me this. We'll take care of it."

His expression went blank. "That's it?"

She forced herself to shrug nonchalantly though her heart was breaking. Her wolf was howling in pain at the thought of never seeing her mate again. Because that's what he was. And she would protect his life at all costs. "What else did you expect?"

"What else indeed?" he muttered.

He turned to leave and her hand automatically reached for him. He opened the door and she closed her eyes, not able to watch him leave again. This was the third time she'd sent him away. Maybe it was karma for what she'd done, for leaving her pack and taking her children with her. Being forced to do this to him was killing her even though she knew it was the right thing, the only thing to do.

The door closed softly and she let out a soft moan of pain. Wrapping her arms around herself, she hunched over as pain radiated from her heart to every part of her body and soul. Tears seeped from the corners of her eyes.

He was truly gone.

Warm arms surrounded her, pulling her gently against a

strong chest. Her head shot up and her eyes widened as Isaiah stared back at her. His expression was no longer blank. Fire burned from his eyes and determination filled his face.

"You cheated," she accused. "You didn't really leave." She couldn't believe he was here.

"So sue me," he growled. He swooped down, captured her lips with his and thrust his tongue into her mouth, devouring her whole.

Chapter Fifteen

Isaiah didn't know whether to shake Meredith or kiss her. The maddening female was going to send him away again. Or she was going to try to.

He wasn't going anywhere. Not this time.

He'd gotten as far as the door, when it had hit him what she was trying to do. Her eyes had been closed, so he'd shut the door softly and waited. The cry that came from her almost broke his heart. It echoed the loss, the pain that he'd felt when he'd walked away from her the last time.

No more.

They belonged together. She was his woman. His mate. He'd do whatever it took to make her see that.

He knew he'd rather cut off his right arm than hurt her. Taking her in his arms and kissing her senseless seemed like the only reasonable thing to do. So he did.

Her lips were soft, yielding to his. Her tongue tangled with his, stroking, touching. Their breath mingled, combined, until they were one.

Isaiah cupped her jaw, stroking her cheek with his thumb. Her skin was like the finest silk. She made a small sound in the back of her throat. Her hands touched his chest, branding him with her fiery touch. Her fingers slid over his shoulders, clinging to him through the thick fabric of his shirt.

His cock was throbbing, aching to be buried in her hot sheath. He had to have her. Now.

He tore his mouth from hers and grabbed the hem of her sweater. "I've got to see you." Sweat beaded on his forehead as desperation seized him.

"Yes." She raised her arms, allowing him to remove the garment. Before he'd tossed it aside she was dragging his flannel shirt down his arms. Their limbs tangled with the fabric and he fought to get the shirt off.

Meredith didn't wait for the shirt to hit the floor before her hands were buried beneath his T-shirt. He groaned as her hot hands stroked over his abs and up to his pecs.

"I love the way you feel. So hard. So strong," she murmured.

Desperate, he yanked the T-shirt off. She gave a low hum of contentment and leaned forward, licking one of his flat nipples.

Isaiah thought the top might blow off his head. He caught her long braid in his hand, winding it around his palm. Using his grip, he tipped her head back and kissed her. He could kiss her for the next four hundred years and never tire of her taste, of the way her mouth felt under his.

He released his hold on her hair and stroked his hands over her shoulders. Her skin was like cream and he wanted to lap her up. He hooked his fingers in the thin straps of her bra and slowly lowered them over her arms. The cups flowed downward, revealing her bountiful breasts.

Lowering his head, he kissed the swell of the lush mounds before drifting lower. Her nipples were already taut with desire. He teased one tip with his tongue. Meredith arched her back, offering her breasts to him.

Satisfaction flowed through him. She wanted him. And he wanted her. Nothing short of an all-out attack would stop him from having her.

He pulled back and surveyed his work. Her nipple was red and wet, like some luscious berry. He blew softly on it, wringing a moan from between her sweet lips. It was music to his ears and a balm to his ragged soul.

Too impatient for him to wait any longer, Meredith attacked the button of his jeans. Now it was his turn to moan. The zipper came down and her hand closed around his hard, hot flesh. She gripped the base and stroked her hand all the way up to the flared head.

A pearly bead of liquid seeped from the slit and she used her thumb to spread it over the tip. This was going to be over before he got inside her if he didn't stop her. He was too close, too needy. And he desperately wanted to be inside her when he came.

"I want to taste you." Her words went through him like a wildfire burning out of control.

He wanted that too. But not now. "Later," he ground out as he gripped her wrist and slowly removed her hand.

"Now," she countered, curling her lip into a seductive pout.

The woman was lethal. He moved, banging into a chair. He shoved it out of his way as he backed her against the nearest wall. "Later," he repeated. He went down on one knee before her and worked the fastenings of her jeans. Sliding his hands inside the opening, he savored the feel of her silky panties against his hands. He'd love to feel them rubbing against his cock, but he'd come for sure if he did.

Swearing, he thrust his hands beneath the waistband, trying not to notice how hot and supple her ass was as he pushed both panties and jeans down over her thighs.

The material bunched around her ankles and he swore again. His cock was bobbing in front of him, a stark reminder of how damn bad he needed to get inside her.

A soft laugh stopped him. He looked up and his heart turned over. Meredith was smiling at him, her blue eyes glowing with desire and something more. Something he couldn't quite put his finger on. All he knew was he'd never seen a more beautiful sight in his life. Her lips were red and moist and inviting. Her bra was shoved beneath her breasts, showcasing them to perfection.

He took a deep breath, struggling for control. He was tearing her clothing from her like some animal. And that's what he was. A werewolf desperate for his mate. He might be partially human, but the wolf half of him wouldn't be denied.

Her scent hit him like a sledgehammer. Sweet and musky and inviting. There was no doubt she wanted him. Her pubic hair was damp and her soft folds were slick with cream.

Isaiah dived between her thighs, lapping at her core. Meredith groaned, grabbing his shoulders for support. Her nails scored his flesh. He loved the bite of pain as he ate her pussy.

She struggled to move. At first he thought she was trying to get away from him. He couldn't allow that to happen. He gripped her hips, his hands holding her still so he could continue to pleasure her.

"Shoes," she gasped. "Get my shoes off so I can get naked."

His head jerked back. Good plan. Spectacular plan. She didn't want to get away from him. She wanted to be free from the tangle of clothing holding her ankles prisoner.

He pulled off one shoe, then the other, and tossed them over his shoulder. Her jeans and panties were next. The second she was free she lifted one leg over his shoulder, opening herself wide to him.

Oh, yeah. He was in heaven. Parting the slick folds with his thumbs, he sucked and licked and nipped at her sensitive flesh.

She writhed in his arms, her breath coming faster and faster. He felt drunk on her taste, her smell, the soft sounds breaking from her throat, the feel of her hands on his head, neck and shoulders.

"Isaiah." His name was a plea, a curse. He growled and sucked her clit into his mouth, teasing the hard bud with his tongue and teeth. She bucked against him and he lifted her other leg over his shoulder, using his strength and the wall to hold her there.

She tugged at his hair as he teased the opening of her slit with his tongue before plunging inside. She tilted her head back, exposing her long, slender throat.

His cock was leaking steadily now. His balls were tight and his shaft rippled. He was going to come any second.

But not before Meredith came.

He slid two fingers deep into her core. Her inner muscles rippled around them, squeezing, clutching. He flicked his tongue over her clit as he pulled his fingers almost all the way out and thrust them back.

She cried out, every muscle of her body clenching. Then hot cream coated his fingers, filling his mouth as she came. He licked and sucked and stroked, wanting to extend her pleasure.

Pressure built low in the base of his cock and he knew time had run out. He quickly lowered her to the floor and surged to his feet. Meredith started to slump. He lifted her, cupping her hips in his hands. He ground his hips against her mound, searching for her opening with the head of his cock.

He found it and squeezed inside. The constricted inner muscles around the entrance threatened to keep him out. He didn't hurry, but kept up a steady pressure. Her sheath finally relaxed and he pushed his cock head inward. She was so wet he slid balls deep, burying himself in her damp heat.

"Isaiah." His name was little more than a strangled whisper.

He gritted his teeth, unable to look at her. It was taking every ounce of control he possessed not to come. A light sheen of sweat coated his torso. His breath was coming hard and fast. His jeans were around his hips, the fabric rubbing against her soft thighs.

"I can't wait," he ground out.

Meredith's world was one of desire. Of lust. Of relentless need. Isaiah played her body like it was an instrument and he a master musician. His every touch was designed to ignite another burst of longing within her, to push her over the edge.

Her body was still shivering from her orgasm, but he wasn't giving her time to rest, time to come down from that high. Instead, he forged his way inside her until his cock was stretching her sheath, filling her completely.

The smell of sex, of musk and hot male mingled with the softer scent of her lotion and soap. The wall was hard and cool against her back, while he was hard and hot against her front. She leaned into him, licking his neck and breathing him in.

His cock jerked inside her. She raised her head. His eyes were dark with need. Brown fathomless pools of lust.

His gaze never left hers as he pulled back until only the thick head of his erection was inside her. She tightened her thighs around his flanks and squeezed her inner muscles hard.

Isaiah groaned and slammed back into her. They both groaned. She clutched his hair. "Harder."

He started moving his hips faster until he was hammering her against the wall. The sound of their wet flesh slapping together mingled with their heavy breathing and the grunts and groans of pleasure.

His hips pistoning, Isaiah took her hard, as she asked, and fast, as she needed. She clung to him, tangling her fingers in his thick, silky hair.

He moved in closer, his strokes getting shorter and faster. The tips of her breasts rubbed against his chest, abraded by the mat of thick, dark hair that ran from between his nipples before angling down in a thin line to his groin. His groin brushed against her clit with each stroke. She angled her hips to get more of his touch.

She was so close.

Gasping, she clung to him. Burying her face in the curve of his neck, she nipped at his skin, tasting the salty tang. She'd gone from thinking he was lost to her forever to being in his arms. This was where she longed to be.

Isaiah swore and she felt his shaft ripple, the hot surge of liquid filling her as he came. She whimpered and he thrust once more. Touching her clit just right.

Meredith cried out, her channel convulsing around his cock. He swore again and she felt his shaft pulse again. Her body tensed and released, shaking uncontrollably as she came.

She wrapped her arms around his neck, trusting him to keep them upright. He leaned his body against hers for leverage. His heavy breathing moved the tendrils of her hair from her neck and caressed her face.

She wanted to stay like this forever. Safe and warm and sated in Isaiah's arms.

He shifted position slightly and she gasped. She was tender and still a bit aroused. The man made her crazy. Turned her into a sex fiend. And she couldn't blame the fact that she was in heat this time. That biologically needy time was over, but she still wanted him like she'd never wanted another man.

His lips nuzzled her jaw and his hands smoothed over her sides. "Are you okay?"

His deep voice set off tiny spasms deep in her core. "I think so. You?"

"Never better." He put one hand on the wall for support and used his other to hold her butt as he straightened. His cock was still almost fully erect inside her and the motion drove him deep.

Meredith sucked in a breath and let her legs slide down his until her feet were flat on the floor.

"I'm going to try to move now," he warned her.

"Okay," she managed to say before he bent his knees and withdrew his semi-erection. She hissed as her inner muscles clutched at his shaft, trying to keep it inside her. Their bodies made a loud, sucking noise as they disengaged.

Isaiah rested his forehead against hers and heaved a sigh. "I hadn't exactly planned to toss you against a wall and rut like a stallion in heat," he muttered.

Meredith giggled. She couldn't help herself. It surprised her as much as it seemed to surprise him. She was a serious, mature woman. Only girls giggled.

It didn't seem to matter. She looked at him, at the incredulous expression on his face and lost it. "Worked for me," she said as she gasped for breath.

A slow smile curved his lips and his eyes twinkled. Nothing could soften his hard features, but he appeared relaxed and happy. She'd done that for him.

"I'm glad." He glanced down at their damp, mostly naked bodies and then toward the door. "We should probably get dressed."

She sobered immediately. For a brief few seconds, she'd

forgotten that her family was just beyond that door, not to mention a club full of patrons. Then there was the problem of the bounty hunters and purist werewolves to deal with.

Still, she wasn't sorry for what they'd done. She'd needed it. Needed the connection to Isaiah, even if it was just a physical one. He was here to fight with them. What happened after that, only time would tell.

One problem at a time.

And right now, she felt sticky. She padded to her desk and grabbed a handful of tissues from the package sitting on one corner, cleaning herself up as much as possible.

It took her a minute to find all her clothing. Isaiah had tossed it everywhere. Her bra was still wound around her torso with the straps hanging down. Her jeans were in a heap in a corner and one of her shoes had found its way under her desk.

He, on the other hand, only had to yank on his T-shirt and zip and button his jeans and he looked fine.

Very fine.

She couldn't help staring at the way he filled out his clothing. Very nice indeed.

Then she noticed he was staring at her. She shrugged and pulled up the straps of her bra and pulled on her panties. Isaiah leaned against the door, his flannel shirt bunched in his hands, and watched her every move.

Knowing that, she made a production of sliding her jeans over her thighs and wiggling her butt to make sure her panties weren't bunched. His eyes narrowed and he licked his lips.

She tugged her sweater on, smoothing the clingy fabric over her breasts and torso. Raising her arms, she eased her braid free from the neck of the sweater. The bulge in Isaiah's jeans wasn't getting any smaller.

"Tease."

"You better believe it." After the way she'd melted under his touch, it felt good to know she wasn't the only one so deeply affected by the physical connection that pulsed between them.

Taking her hair down, she smoothed it with her fingers and then swiftly braided it again. Isaiah muttered a curse, turned away and yanked on his shirt.

They both knew time had run out and their interlude was over. Meredith yanked on her shoes and pulled up the documents on her computer, hitting several more keys before sending the email she'd been working on when he'd come in.

Satisfied she'd done all she could to protect their financial assets in the event they had to move fast, she shut down the computer.

Isaiah waited as she worked. There was no sense of impatience from him. Only a rock-solid certainty that he would do whatever needed to be done.

She had the same resolve. She'd protect her children and Isaiah, no matter the cost.

She came out from behind her desk and paused in front of him. "Let's go."

He inclined his head, opened the door and followed her out to the bar where the rest of her pack waited.

Adams was a patient hunter, but he found even his patience was being tested. There were two females in that club according to the information they'd received. Whether or not they were pure werewolf remained to be seen. He wanted a female of his own. If she had a mate, he'd simply kill him and take the female for himself. Providing of course she wasn't a half-breed. No kid of his was going to be born with weak human blood in his veins.

Beside him Briggs and Spencer stirred. The three of them were hunkered down on a rooftop watching the bar just up the street. He shot them a glare and they settled back down to wait.

Haven looked like a popular spot. Adams only hoped they weren't wasting their time. Like most werewolves, he hated being in the city. It was too noisy, too crowded and stank of humans. He much preferred running free in the woods or the mountains.

Briggs sighed and glanced at his watch. "Not much longer now."

Adams kept his gaze on the building he was watching. Too much was at stake. He didn't trust bounty hunters any further than he could throw them. Okay, maybe not a good comparison. He could probably heave a human quite a distance if he chose to.

This would either be a trap, in which case the hunters were dead men. Or they would find others of their kind. Those who were pure blood could live. Those who weren't...

Adams rolled his shoulders and flexed the muscles in his arms. He was more than ready for a fight. Whatever they found, they would come out the winners. He'd never lost a fight and had no intentions of starting now. Especially not with a bunch of hunters or half-breeds. His lips peeled back and he snarled. Half-breeds were a fucking insult to his species. The only good one was a dead one.

He couldn't wait for the club to close for the night.

Chapter Sixteen

Meredith heaved a sigh of relief when the doors to the club finally closed for the night. All of them were on edge and the anxious mood had permeated the place. Even the patrons had sensed something was wrong. People had talked in hushed voices and even the band had been subdued. Haven was almost empty long before the last call for the bar usually went out, so they'd closed a half hour early. No one had complained and no one had lingered.

She'd taken all of her pack aside, one by one, during the course of the night, filling them in on their latest problem. None of them were happy.

Isaiah had sat in the back of the club. Watchful. Like a knight at the gate of the castle, not willing to relinquish his post until the threat had passed. They'd have to talk eventually. But there was no time for that now.

A sound near the back caught her attention and she turned, sucking in a breath. Benjamin leaned against the wall, Neema at his side. He looked pale, but surprisingly good for a male who'd been shot with a silver bullet less than twenty-four hours before.

"You shouldn't be up yet." She hurried toward her son and opened her arms wide. He might be thirty-five years old and almost six inches taller than her, but he was still her baby.

His arms closed around her. "Neema told me what was going on. We need all of us ready to fight."

Everything inside her protested even though she knew he was right. Three highly trained werewolves against her young, inexperienced pack weren't great odds. Hank was the only one of them who had real combat training, but that was in the human army, and she was pretty sure they didn't teach fighting techniques to use against werewolves. The rest of them relied on their preternatural speed and strength to get them out of sticky situations. That wasn't going to be an advantage this time. Not against mature, battle-scared males.

The only one who truly seemed to know what they were up against was Isaiah. She released her son, giving him a peck on the cheek and a final worried look before turning to her lover. "What do we do?"

The rest of the pack had gathered around them. Teague and Hank appeared stunned by her question. The last thing they'd expected was for her to defer to Isaiah. But she was smart enough to know she didn't have the experience he had when it came to fighting.

She'd mostly run. And any fighting had been against bounty hunters. Ruthless killers, for sure, but human nonetheless.

Michael appeared thoughtful, and Kevin was his usual laidback self.

Isaiah pushed out of his chair and stood, his massive body and sheer presence dominating the room. He prowled forward in a deceptively lazy lope. She knew the wolf in him was watching and listening for any sign of trouble. He could easily erupt into motion at any given second, attacking without warning.

She licked her lips as memories of their earlier encounter

threatened to swamp her. He was also sneaky as hell and a walking, talking advertisement for sex. The male oozed sex appeal without even trying.

He stopped in front of her, his body barely touching hers. She swayed closer as his scent, his heat, surrounded her. "You should all pack up and leave. I can handle this." The low rumble of his voice made her skin tingle.

God, she didn't know whether to kiss him or slap him. He was so macho, so much the lone wolf. Yet he was incredibly protective. He'd barely known them all a week and he was ready to put his life on the line for them. For her.

"You know I can't do that. This is my pack."

His nostrils flared and she knew he could feel her nipples puckering, pressing against his chest. They both tried to ignore it. One corner of his mouth quirked up. "I figured that, but it was worth a try."

"What do we do?" Michael stepped forward, diffusing some of the sexual tension swirling between her and Isaiah.

The heat pulsing through her was replaced by sheer icy terror. Once again, her pack was under attack. This time the threat was being brought straight to their front door.

"Neema needs to be protected," Isaiah began. "From what I saw at the park the other night, I assume she doesn't have much, if any, fighting experience."

"I can take care of my mate." Teague stepped forward, arms crossed over his chest, his green eyes flat and cold.

"How much fighting experience do you have?" Isaiah asked the group as a whole.

Hank stepped forward, his arms and legs loose, his right hand resting on the handle of a knife he had strapped to his upper thigh. Meredith knew the blade was coated with silver. "I was in the army for several years. I can hold my own."

"I can fight." Teague strode to Neema's side and pulled her into the curve of his body. Neema snuggled closer to her mate.

In many ways, they'd sheltered her and she was still so young and immature. Meredith only hoped Neema had the time to grow and mature into the strong woman she knew the younger female could be. Beneath the shy exterior was a female with a core of steel. She'd seen glimpses of it over the years. Neema hadn't had an easy upbringing, moving from one foster home to another, always different, never fitting in until she'd stumbled across Meredith and her pack.

"This isn't simply street fighting." Isaiah let his gaze wander over all of them, assessing strengths and weaknesses. "These wolves will kill any half-breed they find. Period. You do not reason with them. If they attack, you kill them."

The brutality of it all washed over her. Isaiah was so matter-of-fact, so okay with the idea of simply killing these males.

"It's kill or be killed. Beneath the human exterior, we're wolves," he reminded them.

Maybe she'd been in the city for too long. Maybe she wanted to block out the violence of her early years. Meredith wished that she could somehow make this problem disappear. She'd wanted a different life for her children.

But that was not to be. You played the cards that fate dealt you. They'd survive this and come out all the stronger for it.

She rubbed her hands up and down her arms. "Do we shift or fight in human form?"

Isaiah narrowed his gaze, his eyes watching the up-and-down strokes of her hands. The motion slowed until it finally stopped, her hands resting just above her elbows.

"At this point, there's no time to do anything fancy. Do whatever feels best. Hank and Michael will take the point with me. The rest of you hang back and wait. Let's see if we can get out of this with minimum casualties."

Isaiah's head swiveled around to the front door. "They're here."

He strode across the room and yanked the door open, facing the three males who stood there. Tall and strong, he braced his legs apart, his wide shoulders practically filling the wide doorway.

Meredith didn't have time to protest that he wasn't alpha of this pack, that she was. He'd taken over. For now.

She tensed as Isaiah faced the threat. "You need to leave. You're not welcome here." She nearly smiled as his words almost echoed the first ones she'd said to him.

"Are you alpha here?"

"Who wants to know?" Isaiah countered.

The male raised an eyebrow at the challenge, but Meredith glimpsed respect there as well. "Adams from the Black Ridge Pack. Who are you?"

"Isaiah Striker."

Meredith saw the man jerk back slightly. "Long way from home, aren't you, Striker?"

"So are you. I'm here to see the sights. You?" Isaiah shrugged, rolling his massive shoulders as if he didn't have a care in the world.

"Can we discuss this inside or do you want to risk someone hearing our business?"

Isaiah stepped back and allowed the three males to enter. Their gaze went immediately to her and then to Neema. The fine hairs on the back of her neck rose and fury straightened her spine. They were looking for brood mares to bear their young, but they were also here to threaten her pack.

Meredith stepped forward. "I am alpha here. Why have you come?"

The man called Adams raised an eyebrow and glanced at Isaiah. "You let your woman speak for you?"

The male chauvinist ass. Meredith wanted to kick him in the balls on principle. She forced herself to remain calm and composed when what she really wanted to do was attack him.

Isaiah looked totally unconcerned. "She is alpha of this pack."

Meredith bristled at the assumption that she was only alpha because Isaiah allowed it. She knew he didn't mean his confirmation in that way, but that was how it sounded.

Another of the men stepped forward. "Then she needs a mate. I'm Spencer and this is Briggs," he indicated the other man. Meredith's skin crawled at the way these men watched her. She knew their type. They were like Maxwell, her dead husband. They would take whatever they wanted, the hell with what she or any other woman wanted.

A low rumble came from deep in Teague's chest as he shoved Neema behind him. Kevin and Benjamin took up posts on either side of her. Hank and Michael spread out slightly to surround the males.

"We received some distressing information," Adams continued. His gaze flicked to Hank and Michael, but he dismissed them, focusing on Isaiah.

"Can't believe everything you hear." Isaiah appeared totally relaxed, without a care in the world.

Adams inclined his head. "True. But this news was very distressing. Seems as though there's a small pack in Chicago with several half-breeds." He all but growled the last word.

Again, Isaiah shrugged. "And your point would be?"

He was baiting the other men, she realized. She rolled her shoulders and softened her knees, readying herself to fight.

"Half-breeds don't deserve to live," Spencer growled.

"That's your opinion."

Adams eyed all the werewolves in the room, his gaze hovering on Meredith. "It's the only opinion that matters. After I kill your lover and your half-breed mutants, I'm going to claim you and fuck you until you remember what a real male is." His smile sent a shiver down Meredith's spine. This was a male who would enjoy subjugating her, hurting her, breaking her to his will.

"After I kill you, I'm going to make your tough hide into a purse." She paused for effect. "Or maybe a pair of boots."

Isaiah chuckled, drawing the attention of the three males.

"You find this amusing?" Adams eyes began to glow and his voice deepened. He was close to changing.

"I find the fact that you'd kill one of your own an abomination." Isaiah didn't move, but he seemed to grow larger somehow. His long hair brushed his shoulders and his face could have been hewn from pure granite. He was tough and mean and all male. And he was her heart. Meredith couldn't drag her eyes from him.

"I find the fact that you'd work with bounty hunters a crime against all werewolves. A crime for which you have to pay."

"Oh, and who's going to make me pay?"

"Me." Isaiah sprang without warning, but Adams was ready and met him halfway. The two gigantic men collided in midair.

The other two men took advantage of the confusion and attacked. Hank and Michael were suddenly engaged. It only took a moment for her to realize they were severely outclassed. They had the heart for fighting, for protecting their pack, but not the skills.

Briggs tossed Michael back against the bar. Glasses slid off the edge, smashing to the floor as her son rolled over the top of the bar and off the other side. He took out an entire shelf of liquor as he crashed to the floor.

No one hurt her children. No one.

Meredith yanked at her clothes, shifting on the fly. Her bones shifted and reformed, her jaw cracked and elongated. Teeth bared, claws raised, she jumped on Briggs's back.

He reached over his shoulder and dragged her off, throwing her aside. Meredith flew through the air, twisting her body so that her side and not her head took the brunt of the fall. The wall came up fast and she struck it hard. She slipped to the floor, momentarily stunned.

Hank and Teague were fighting Spencer. He was stockier than the other two, but thick with muscles. Both her adopted sons were strong, but they didn't have the strength of a purebred werewolf. Spencer tossed a chair at Hank. He batted it aside. Teague slid a table at his opponent, momentarily distracting him.

Blood flowed down Hank's arm and chest. Teague's face was bloody and he was favoring his left leg.

Meredith shoved herself up, nails clicking against the floor as she launched herself forward. She started to go for Briggs, but saw Isaiah falter. Blood ran down his shoulder. Without a thought to her own safety, she launched herself at Adams.

Isaiah was in the fight of his life. If he'd only had time to convince Meredith and her pack to leave. Having them here split his attention and made him handle the situation in a much different manner. Hell, he'd actually tried talking to the other werewolves, even though he'd told the others not to bother. Diplomacy wasn't his strong suit, but he'd tried. Anything to protect Meredith.

But they had killing on their minds. He'd seen it in their eyes. At the very least they planned to steal the women for themselves. Meredith would survive, but if they ever found out that Neema was a half-breed, they'd make her suffer long before they killed her.

Adams was a worthy opponent, a dirty fighter. But he wasn't fighting for his mate, his pack. Isaiah was.

He tossed the large man into a table and went after him. The two of them grappled, knocking aside several chairs and another table. Adams had partially shifted, his fangs had elongated and his fingernails had lengthened into talons. He growled and slashed at Isaiah with his claws. Isaiah jumped back but he wasn't quick enough. Sharp claws dug a short furrow across his shoulder, drawing blood. Isaiah pretended to falter, wanting to draw his prey into a false sense of victory. He waited for his chance to attack.

A low growl sounded off to his right. He caught a flash of black fur. Saw Meredith jump toward Adams, teeth bared and ready to tear at the man's flesh. Adams caught her in his strong grip before she reached him and he flung her aside.

Isaiah howled as he watched Meredith fly through the air, her body hitting the wall with a deadly force. Adams took advantage of his inattention, drew a knife and took a swipe at him. The blade cut into Isaiah's chest. Blood spurted from the wound.

Fury, the likes of which he'd never felt in his life, burst through him. Anger replaced the blood in his body. Determination filled his bones. He ripped his bloody shirt away as he kicked off his shoes and shifted.

Fabric shredded as his body changed. Bones reformed. Deadly claws replaced fingernails. Fangs dropped down from his elongated jaw. He wasn't completely changed when he vaulted toward Adams. His opponent swung the knife, but Isaiah clamped his heavy jaw down on the male's wrist and bit clear through the bone. The cracking sound and the resulting scream echoed around the room.

He heard another howl and whirled around in time to see Meredith with her jaw clamped around Briggs's neck. The male dug his fingers into her mouth, trying to pry it apart. Meredith used her strong legs to push against Briggs's body, launching herself away from him before he could break her jaw.

Isaiah growled and jumped at Briggs. He hit the other man with his huge wolf body and sent him sprawling on the floor. Isaiah sensed movement behind him and flung himself to the side just as a silver blade went flying past him. The knife hit the hardwood floor with a heavy thunk, the handle vibrating.

Michael was nowhere to be seen. Teague and Hank were doing their best with Spencer, but both of them were injured. Benjamin was injured, but he and Kevin were protecting Neema.

This had to end before one of them was killed.

Blood dripped from Meredith's jaws. Hers or Briggs, he didn't know. She was moving slowly, limping slightly.

"Give it up, Striker." Briggs rolled to his feet, his hand clamped to his neck. "You can still walk away. All we want is the women. Hell, we'll even kill the male pups quick and easy."

Isaiah didn't rise to the taunt. He kept his gaze on Adams who was slinking in behind him. The other male pulled out a gun and aimed it at him.

"Silver bullets." Adams smiled as he pointed the barrel of

the semiautomatic, not at Isaiah, but at Meredith.

Isaiah stilled, waiting for his chance to attack.

The door burst open and a huge black wolf flew at Briggs. Isaiah moved without thinking, launching himself forward and hitting Adams full force.

The gun went off. His leg burned, but he ignored it. He was on top of his victim now and there was no mercy left anywhere in his soul. This male had threatened his woman.

Adams shifted, but Isaiah already had his strong jaws clamped around his opponent's neck. He used his powerful body to hold Adams down as he tore at his flesh. Blood flowed over his muzzle and down his throat. He didn't let go.

When the male was weakened, Isaiah shifted back to human form, wrapped his arm around Adam's neck and twisted, breaking it with a loud crack.

He dropped the body and whirled around, ready to fight. But it was already over. Briggs lay on the floor, his eyes wide open, his neck at an unnatural angle.

Spencer was still alive, but Teague, Hank and Michael were subduing him. All of them looked the worse for wear, but at least they were alive.

Where was Meredith?

Panic filled him. Was she hurt?

The female black wolf was in front of him, teeth flashing, hackles raised as she stared down the massive black male wolf facing him.

Isaiah felt his heart turn over. Meredith was protecting him.

He stumbled slightly as he made his way to her side. His left leg was bleeding and he knew the silver bullet had hit him. He had no idea how bad the injury was yet and didn't care.

Isaiah's Haven

Meredith was safe.

Naked, he crouched beside Meredith and placed his hand on her back. Her thick, black fur was soft and glossy. He wanted to bury his face in it and just breathe in her essence. Instead, he swiped the back of his arm over his mouth. It came away bloody.

A massive male wolf sat across from them, waiting patiently, his head cocked to one side. The tension in the room grew. In spite of the gravity of the situation, Isaiah felt the corners of his mouth turning up in a grin. "Hey, brother. Nice of you to drop by."

Isaiah hunkered down beside her. Meredith felt his hand on her back, caressing her fur. She could smell his blood and her panic increased. How badly was he hurt? They needed to figure out who this strange wolf was and now.

Then Isaiah spoke, and it took her a moment to make sense of his words. *Brother.* The wolf was his brother.

The large black wolf began to shift. In seconds, the wolf was gone and a man remained. He was tall and broad. His rough-hewn face was familiar. It was easy to see the family resemblance.

Meredith shifted. Her body ached, but she knew she'd be fine in a day or so. That might not have been the case if Isaiah and his brother weren't here. She owed him. Both of them.

Normally, nudity didn't bother her. She was a werewolf after all. Still, it was disconcerting to meet Isaiah's brother wearing nothing but her skin.

Isaiah swore. "Ben, give me your damn shirt."

Her son didn't hesitate. Before she could protest, Isaiah was slipping Benjamin's shirt around her shoulders. He stood in front of her, blocking everyone else's view of her as he tucked her arms down the sleeves and did up the buttons. The tail of the shirt came down to the top of her thighs, covering everything important.

She drank in the sight of him. There was a wound on his shoulder and several gashes on his chest. But it was the blood flowing down his leg that worried her the most. Isaiah acted as though nothing was wrong. His hands were steady, his eyes clear and calm as he finished fastening the last button.

A male throat cleared. "You want to introduce us?"

Meredith peeked around Isaiah's shoulder at the very large, naked male standing in the middle of her wrecked club. He was a fine specimen of a werewolf, but he didn't make her blood pump hard and hot, not like Isaiah did.

She held out her hand. "Meredith Cross."

He took it, enfolding her fingers in his much larger ones. "Joshua Striker."

Isaiah reached around and gently disengaged their hands before dragging her beneath his arm. Joshua raised an eyebrow, but said nothing.

"Thank you for helping." Meredith couldn't quite manage a smile but her gratitude was genuine.

"My pleasure," Joshua said. "I would have been here sooner, but I stopped for some backup."

"What the hell are you doing here? Not that I'm not glad to see you," Isaiah added.

Joshua shook his head. "I got a strange phone call telling me you were in trouble and giving this address. I was already on my way to Chicago when I got it or I might not have made it in time." His gaze flicked to Meredith. "You didn't sound like yourself during our last call."

Meredith wasn't sure how she should take that. Thankfully, she didn't have to speak.

"You Strikers are more trouble than you're worth." A surge of dark power encompassed the room. Meredith gasped as a tall, dark male strode into the place like he owned it. Deadly menace poured off the stranger in waves. This was no werewolf. If she wasn't mistaken, this was a vampire. She'd seen one once, years before in New Orleans, and she'd hoped never to repeat the experience.

"Damek." Isaiah inclined his head.

"Is that him?" Damek motioned to the werewolf currently being held down by Hank, Michael and Teague.

"That's the only one left alive," Joshua informed him.

"Hmm." Damek strode forward and everyone took a step back. Everyone except Joshua and Isaiah. "There was one of those nasty bounty hunters outside. I imagine his job was to watch the carnage and report back to his masters."

He stared at Spencer, and for the briefest of seconds, Meredith felt sorry for the wolf. Damek swiveled his head around and stared at her. Isaiah growled and tightened his hold on her.

Damek ignored Isaiah and motioned to her sons. "Let him go."

They glanced at her. Or rather at Isaiah. When he nodded, they stepped out of the way, releasing the wounded werewolf. Damek struck with the speed of a cobra. One moment he was standing chatting with them, the next his fangs were in Spencer's neck.

Meredith cringed, but she wouldn't look away. Her sons took several more steps back. Although, she didn't think that would save them, any of them, if Damek decided he wanted to hurt them.

Vampires were far and few between, but those who did exist were incredibly old and powerful. No one knew the extent of their powers. They were a secretive lot, rarely having contact with other paranormal beings.

The room darkened. Shadows seemed to creep forward, reaching for Damek. He quickly withdrew his teeth and stood, swiping at the back of his mouth with his hand. His eyes were glowing.

"Stand up, my new pet." Spencer stood, his eyes vacant. "What were your orders and who else knew about this attack?"

"We were to kill the half-breeds and take the women. Only we knew about this attack. Adams didn't want to have to share the women."

"Good." Damek gently stroked the side of Spencer's jaw. Meredith shivered as she noticed that Spencer's wounds were healed. There seemed to be no end to Damek's powers.

"How did the bounty hunters contact you?"

Spencer rattled off an email account. "Very good," Damek continued. "You will return home, saddened by the death of your comrades. The bounty hunters tricked you. You found nothing here. You will tell this to your superiors and you will seek out and attack the hunters." Damek captured the male's head in his hands, staring deep into his eyes.

"Yes," Spencer replied.

"Go," Damek ordered. Spencer left and no one stopped him. Damek dusted off his hands. "That's done. I did much the same with the hunter. I told him that his information was wrong and that there were no werewolves here. Whoever their leader is, he'll have his hands full fighting off a group of pissed-off wolves. You and your little pack should be safe."

"I don't understand," Meredith blurted out. "Why are you doing this?"

Damek seemed to glide across the floor, coming to a halt in front of her. He reached out and touched a finger to her jaw. Beside her, Isaiah tensed.

"For some unknown reason, I seem to like these unruly Striker brothers. There is no doubting their exquisite taste in females." He inclined his head to Isaiah. "And it amuses me. Not much does these days.

"Then there is the added bonus of having them owe me." He smiled and his fangs gleamed. "I find that I like that idea best of all." He glanced at Joshua. "You'll be happy to know I took care of a few humans who were wandering the street. Really, Striker, you need to shut the door behind you when you enter a building."

Took care of? Meredith swallowed hard. Had the vampire killed innocent humans?

Damek continued on, seemingly oblivious to the growing tension swirling around the room. "They won't remember a thing when they wake in the morning. They'll just think they had too much to drink." He licked his lips. "They made for a tasty late-night snack."

Joshua strode up to stand beside his brother. Both men were stark naked. Next to the vampire, who was clothed in what looked to be a designer suit, they appeared primitive and feral.

"You and your pack should be safe if you choose to stay in Chicago." Damek pulled a card from his pocket and handed it to her. "If you ever need my help."

Her fingers closed around the heavy vellum card even though she knew she'd never use it. Anything this male did came with strings attached. Lots and lots of strings.

As though he could read her mind, Damek smiled and bowed. "I'll leave you now to clean up the mess."

The shadows deepened, seeming to swallow Damek whole.

They all breathed a sigh of relief when he disappeared.

"Bastard makes a hell of an entrance and exit." Isaiah gave her a gentle squeeze before yanking his brother into his arms. "It's good to see you."

"You too." Joshua surveyed the mess. "We gotta dump these two." He motioned to the bodies of Briggs and Adams.

Neema started crying softly in the background, pulling Meredith's attention back to her pack. They were all shocked. Teague, Hank and Michael all had injuries. They were all bruised, battered and bleeding, but they were alive. Neema was pale and looked as though she was barely holding it together.

"Neema, we need water and bandages. We can use Benjamin and Michael's apartment." She knew the younger female would recover faster if she had something to do. Sure enough, Neema quickly took charge, ordering Benjamin and Kevin to help Hank and Michael while she went to Teague.

Her little pack disappeared upstairs. Meredith sighed, knowing her job was just beginning. She dug deep for strength. Every bone, every muscle of her body hurt and her heart ached.

The threat was over. There was no reason for Isaiah to stay any longer. His brother was here to bring him home to his pack. Whatever responsibility he might have felt for her and her pack was gone. He'd more than done his duty toward them.

She straightened her shoulders and stiffened her spine. She'd had him for a short time, and she would have no regrets. What she needed was advice.

"What's the best way to handle the bodies?" She'd never had to dump bodies before. She swallowed hard as bile swirled in her belly and left a sour taste in her throat.

Joshua was staring at her like she had two heads. Isaiah put his hands on her shoulders, turned her and aimed her toward the stairs. His lips brushed the top of her head. "Go upstairs and see to the pack. I'll take care of this."

"You're injured." With everything, she'd forgotten he'd taken a bullet in his thigh. He was so big, so tough. He acted like being shot was no big deal. And maybe it wasn't to him. She really had no idea what his life had been like before he met her.

As she watched, he ripped a piece off his shredded shirt. He wrapped it around the wound, stopping the flow of blood. Thankfully, it seemed to have slowed to little more than a trickle. "I'll take care of it. It's not serious."

She really shouldn't let him take the burden of this on his shoulders. He'd already done enough. She was alpha. It was her job to clean up this mess.

He gave her a slight shove. "Go." His tone was soft, but there was no mistaking the steel command behind it.

Maybe this was his final job, to fulfill whatever sense of responsibility he felt toward her and her pack. Whatever it was, she was too tired to argue.

"Thank you." She didn't turn to face either male. Meredith had no idea if she'd even see Isaiah again or if he'd leave with his brother. She heard them moving around the club, righting tables and chairs as well as dragging the bodies closer to the back entrance.

Heart aching, tears pricking her eyes, she climbed the stairs to her sons' apartment.

Quinn ducked into a dark doorway and held his breath. He'd seen the purist werewolves head into Haven. Damn Macmillan for that anyway. Why he had to bring them into the mix, Quinn didn't know.

What the hell should he do?

He heard the first crash and winced. His fingers flexed around the stock of his rifle. He had to stay out of this. This wasn't his business. Yet it was. There were women and half-breed werewolves in there. They wouldn't stand a chance against three seasoned purebloods.

"Shit." He closed his eyes and banged the back of his head against the brick wall behind him. He was going to blow a year of hard work. He couldn't just stand here.

He started to move, but pulled back when a black SUV came to a squealing halt outside Haven. *What now?*

A huge man climbed out, stripping his clothing as he went. He kicked open the door and changed in one swoop. *Holy crap.*

Quinn blinked and the second man seemed to disappear. He heard a low cry and glanced to his left. He could see another bounty hunter there in the shadows. Mitch, he thought the guy's name was. Obviously, Macmillan hadn't trusted Quinn and had sent another man to watch the street. Right now, it looked as though Mitch was under attack. By a frigging vampire. Quinn had only seen a vampire once before, from a safe distance. And he'd never had the desire to repeat the experience. They were dangerous bastards. The situation was deteriorating rapidly.

Quinn melted back into the shadows as the vampire emerged, licking his lips. His gaze passed over Quinn but quickly moved on, focusing on a group of young men wandering down the street. The vampire quickly enthralled them, taking the time to help himself to some of their blood.

When he was done, he turned to the club and walked inside, closing the door behind him. Quinn eased out of his hiding spot and hurried over to Mitch.

The man seemed dazed. "You okay?"

Mitch nodded. "Yeah. I got a headache." He rubbed his

head. "We might as well head home. No werewolves here."

Quinn glanced back at Haven and then gripped Mitch by the arm, leading him down the street to his car. "Right. No werewolves here." Damn, the vampire was good. Saved Quinn the trouble of having to figure out what the hell to do. He couldn't lose his place with the hunters, not until he was sure they didn't have the information he needed. But he sure as hell wasn't killing women or half-breeds. Or any full breeds who weren't purists for that matter.

He opened the door to Mitch's car. "You okay to drive? I've got my truck parked a couple streets over."

Mitch winced as he eased into the driver's seat. "I'm good, man. I'm just gonna call Macmillan, then I'm hitting the bed."

Quinn shut the door and watched Mitch drive off. Shaking his head, he headed toward his truck. He had some serious thinking to do. Tonight a vampire had almost caught him. That would have ended badly. As it was, he couldn't quite believe the creature hadn't seen him.

Maybe he had. Maybe the vampire had been able to see into his head and knew exactly what he was and what he was doing.

Shivering, he pulled his long trench coat around him, hid his rifle beneath the folds and picked up his pace. He needed to be careful in the days ahead. He couldn't afford to die. Not until he'd done what he'd set out to do.

Chapter Seventeen

Isaiah's thigh stung like a sonofabitch. When he'd taken a good look at the wound, he'd noted the bullet had only skimmed him. Thankfully, the bullet hadn't lodged in his leg, allowing the silver coating to poison his system. It made for a bloody wound, but not a serious one.

"You okay?" Joshua had asked him that question several times as they'd loaded up the bodies in the back of Joshua's truck and driven to a secluded area well beyond the city to bury the bodies. They wanted no trace of either male found and linked to them in any way.

"I'm fine." They were now sitting in Joshua's truck outside Haven. They'd snuck up the back stairs to Isaiah's apartment building and used his shower. They'd both needed to wash away all the blood, sweat and grime, and Isaiah had needed to get some clean clothes since most of his had been bloodied or shredded during the fight.

Joshua hadn't commented on the fact that Isaiah was no longer staying at a motel, but had moved in just down the street from Meredith. He could sense his brother wanted to say something more to him but was choosing his words carefully.

"You're really staying?"

Isaiah didn't even need to think about it. "Yeah." Whether Meredith eventually accepted him fully into her life or not, he loved her and wanted to be with her. More than that, he needed to protect her. "She's the one for me."

Joshua tapped his fingers against the steering wheel. "You sure don't do things the easy way."

A rough laugh broke from Isaiah at his brother's dry tone. "I guess I don't."

"You deserve this, man." Joshua turned, resting his back against the truck door. "You were always meant to be alpha of your own pack."

His brother had struck the nail on the head. That was what terrified him the most. What if he let them down as he had his sister? He rubbed his hands over his face, feeling the heavy scrape of stubble against his palm. "I don't know."

Joshua snorted. "What's to know? I've never seen you look at a female like this before. And she looks right back. Love her and protect her. You'll figure the rest out."

"When the hell did you get so smart?"

His brother grinned, white teeth flashing. "I always told you I was the smart one of the bunch."

Isaiah punched Joshua on the shoulder. "You told James?" He hadn't had time to contact his alpha yet.

"Yeah, James is good. If anyone understands needing to find your own way, it's him. He wishes you well."

"I'll call him in a day or two when things settle down." He glanced up at the second floor. The lights were on even though the sun was starting to lighten the sky. Meredith was up there with her sons, her family.

"Is there anything I can do?"

Isaiah closed his eyes and swallowed hard as a wave of love rose up inside him. He could always count on his brother. Always. He was going to miss Joshua. Not that he'd ever tell him to his face. His younger brother had a swelled enough head as it was. Ever since he'd married Alexandra, he'd been strutting around like a peacock, more than pleased with himself.

He opened his eyes. "No. I'm good."

"Hey, it's not the end. You'll come to visit. And you know Alex is going to want to meet Meredith and the rest of your pack."

Your pack.

Isaiah liked the sound of that. But they weren't his. Not yet.

"I've got work to do before too many people wake up and start their day. The club is wrecked inside. It's going to take a while to make repairs." He opened the door and slid out. "Thanks again. For everything."

Joshua's gaze was somber, his dark eyes a mirror of Isaiah's. "Call me if you need anything. I mean it," he added. "I'll be in the city a few more days. I'll leave my truck at Riley's Garage and drive the moving truck back to Wolf Creek."

"Be careful, brother." Isaiah couldn't shake the nagging feeling they hadn't seen the last of the bounty hunters in spite of Damek's mind-meld vampire trick.

"You too."

Isaiah stepped away from the truck and gave the roof a thump. Joshua pulled away from the curb and the vehicle disappeared down the street.

He made his way to the front entrance of the club. He had no idea how he was going to get inside. He shrugged. He could always go up the fire escape around the side and enter through Meredith's apartment. Wouldn't be the first time.

The door opened and Michael stood poised in the entrance.

Every muscle in Isaiah's body tightened. Would Michael let him in or turn him away?

Not that it would matter. He wasn't going anywhere until he talked with Meredith. "I came to help clean up the place." That was true too. The club was important to Meredith. Therefore, it was important to him.

"That's funny, I thought you'd come to see my mother." Michael stared at him, as though he was trying to see into Isaiah's soul. He could have told Michael it was a dark, desolate place and, whatever he was searching for, he wouldn't find it there.

Michael suddenly stepped back. "Come on in."

Isaiah strode through the door, shutting and locking it behind him. Glass and shards of wood crunched beneath his feet as he walked across the floor. The stench of liquor and blood permeated the place. Glass glittered everywhere. Shelves of glassware and booze had been shattered when Michael had been thrown over the bar. Tables and chairs were smashed. There were several large gouges in the bar.

Isaiah winced. "You okay?" The younger male was moving surprisingly well, all things considered.

"Yeah. I'm a bit stiff, but nothing is broken." He paused. "You?"

Isaiah nodded. "I'm fine." He didn't want to talk about himself. "Do you have anything we can use to put over the windows to block the destruction from the outside? We also need to post a note on the door saying we're closed for renovations. Then we need to contact the human staff and give them all a week's vacation." He looked around, studying the damage. It wasn't too bad on second inspection. "We should be able to handle the bulk of the repairs in that time and it will give the rest of the pack time to recover."

"*We* should be able to do a lot of things, according to you." Meredith's voice was soft and thoughtful. Isaiah froze as she walked into view. Dark circles gave her eyes a slightly bruised look. Her face was pale, her lips compressed in a thin line.

He refused to apologize for wanting to make things easier for her, for taking on some of the burdens. She had enough to deal with. Most of her pack had minor injuries and those who didn't had to be shocked by what they'd just gone through.

She glanced over his shoulder. "Your brother didn't return with you?"

"He's gone to complete the business I came to Chicago to handle."

Meredith wrapped her arms around her upper body. "I see."

Frustration filled him. He was glad that she seemed to understand something because he was totally lost.

"Umm, I'll just get some brown paper to cover the windows." Michael left without a backward glance, stopping only to place a kiss on his mother's cheek.

Meredith meandered farther into the room, checking out the damage.

"I'm sorry about wrecking the joint."

"Not your fault," she countered.

Her leather loafers weren't very sturdy and Isaiah worried about her cutting her feet. "Maybe we should talk in your office."

Her cheeks flushed a flattering rosy shade and her hand shook slightly as she pushed a lock of hair over her shoulder. "Not a good idea."

Memories of what had happened the only other time they'd been in her office slammed into him. His muscles rippled, his dick springing to attention. His need for her was always simmering just below the surface, taking little to send it surging to life.

He shifted slightly, trying to find a way to stand comfortably with a huge erection. An impossible task.

"Why are you here?" Meredith tugged on the hem of her top, not meeting his gaze.

Isaiah narrowed his eyes, studying her. He could skate around the issue or he could be totally honest with her. He went for the second option. There was no reason to hold anything back. Whether he stayed with her and her pack or lived down the street, he wasn't leaving.

"Because I have to be." He took a step closer. Meredith's head jerked up but she stood her ground. Pride filled him. She'd fought alongside him to protect the pack, to protect him. "Because whether you ever accept my claim or not, you're my mate, the only female I'll ever want."

She tilted up her chin and swallowed hard, the slender column of her neck rippling. He wanted to put his lips against her fluttering pulse and feel her life's blood pumping through her. He wanted to taste her soft skin.

"Why do you want to claim me?"

Isaiah raked his fingers through his hair. The motion tugged at his shoulder wound, reminding him he wasn't at a hundred percent yet. Still, the pain in his body was nothing compared to the ache in his chest.

"Why? After everything you need to ask me why?"

Her chin went even higher and her stormy blue eyes flashed. "Do you want a brood mare as those other men wanted? A female at your beck and call? A pack of your own? The financial stability of the club? What?"

He rubbed his hand across his chest, surprised his

damaged heart wasn't bleeding through his shirt. The red furrow from where Adam's knife had ripped through him stung, reminding him of how much he was willing to sacrifice for this woman.

"What do I want?" He prowled forward, cupping her chin in his hands. He lowered his face until their noses were practically touching. He could smell her spicy fragrance and knew she was aroused. But he could also smell the slightly sour bite of fear mixed with the coppery flavor of spilled blood.

"I want you in my bed every night. I want to take you once, twice, three times a day. I want to shoulder some of the burdens you've carried. I want to protect all your kids and teach them. But most of all, I want you to love me."

She blinked and her eyes filled with tears.

He wanted to pull her into his arms and soothe her, but resisted the urge. She needed to know what she was getting herself into if she accepted him. He did, however, give in to her lure and rub his thumbs over her cheeks. She was so soft, so beautiful.

"Do you think I want to live in the city? I hate the crush of people, the stench and the lack of fresh air to breathe. I live for the woods, the wide-open spaces. Freedom.

"My younger brother, Joshua, is in charge of pack security when the job should have been mine. Want to know why?"

She slowly nodded.

"I had a sister," he began.

Meredith gave a small cry.

Isaiah nodded. "Hunters got her. Rachel was only fifteen. She was in the woods alone." He gave a bitter laugh. "I was going for a run and she wanted to go with me. I told her no. I never knew she followed me and got lost. By the time I returned that night the pack was in an uproar. She was gone. That was thirty-five years ago, but I've never given up looking for the hunters that took her." He heaved a sigh of frustration. "For all I know, I've killed the sonofabitch who took her. I'll never know for sure."

"It wasn't your fault," Meredith whispered. She slid her arms around his waist, hugging him to her.

He closed his eyes and savored her touch and the caring behind it even though he didn't deserve it. Opening his eyes, he pinned her with his dark gaze. "It was my fault and I've had to live with that. It's why I refused to take over as protector of the pack after my father was killed. My family is everything to me. There's nothing I wouldn't do to keep them safe. I couldn't put the pack ahead of them."

He buried the relentless feelings of helplessness and fury that filled him whenever he thought of his baby sister. "But your safety comes ahead of all of them. There is nothing I wouldn't do to protect you. And since your children are an extension of you, that protection extends to them.

"You asked me what I wanted." He placed a kiss on her forehead and took a step back. "I want you as my mate. Forever. But even if you say no, I'll be watching out for you." The corners of his mouth quirked up. "We're neighbors. I rented an apartment down the road."

Meredith didn't know whether to laugh or cry. Isaiah was so brash, so male, so everything. She couldn't believe he'd rented an apartment in her neighborhood. She'd figured for sure he'd leave the city as soon as his pack business was done, and now he was telling her he was moving in, had already moved in.

The story of his sister tore at her heart. It had happened

many years ago, but the anguish tearing at him was as raw as if it had occurred only the day before.

She pulled him closer, unable to let him bear such pain alone. Meredith had a feeling he'd spent too much of his life alone. And for a wolf, that was the worst punishment of all. Pack life was everything.

Her heart was pounding, her blood racing. She hadn't expected Isaiah to put everything on the line—his heart, his pride, himself. He'd held nothing back. She could only do the same, praying she could be as honest and brave as him.

"I was mated once," she began. Isaiah tensed, every muscle in his big body rippling. She told him the story of her mating, the way Maxwell had taken her when she was in heat and too weak to refuse him.

His jaw tensed and a nerve pulsed beneath his eye. "I would never do such a thing to you, Meredith. It is your choice."

She swallowed the lump in her throat and asked the final question she needed an answer to. "What about Hank, Teague, Kevin and Neema? They'll always be half-breeds." As much as she loved Isaiah and wanted to be with him, she wouldn't do anything to put her kids at risk.

Isaiah snorted. "So what? My sister-in-law is a half-breed. All wolf pups are to be protected."

A huge weight slipped off her shoulders and she laughed. "Just don't let any of them hear you calling them pups."

He shrugged. "That's what they are. They might be a few years past adulthood, but they have a lot to learn."

She sobered. "That's my fault. Maybe I've protected them too much. Living in the city certainly hasn't allowed them to explore their werewolf side as much as they should."

"You have nothing to apologize for." Isaiah's expression was fierce as he curled his hands into fists by his sides. "You've protected them and loved them. You're a hell of a female, Meredith."

Her decision was so easy to make she knew it was the right one. Smiling, she held out her hand to him. "Come with me."

Chapter Eighteen

Isaiah took her hand and allowed her to lead him away from the bar area toward the back stairs.

Michael passed them on the way, a roll of tape and some butcher paper in his hand.

"Don't worry about the club. I'll handle things and start the cleanup."

"Thank you." She was so proud of her son. His acceptance of Isaiah and her choice warmed her. She was under no misconception that things would be easy. Isaiah was definitely an alpha male. But her sons needed a male to look up to, to teach them, and Neema needed to see that there were werewolves who would accept and embrace half-breeds.

She still couldn't believe his sister-in-law was a half-breed. If only she'd known earlier. It would have helped ease some of her fears. No matter. He was here with her now. The threat was behind them and the future loomed before them, more positive than it had been in a long time.

Isaiah's fingers squeezed hers, the heat of his hand seeping into her skin as she led him up the stairs to her apartment. She could hear the voices of the others, muted as they talked. They all knew Isaiah was here. Michael would have told them.

Meredith pushed open the door of her apartment, pulled Isaiah inside and closed it behind them. The silence was deafening. The refrigerator hummed. A garbage truck rumbled down the street. Isaiah's breathing was deep and slow.

She started toward the bedroom, but he dug in his heels, stopping her. Turning, she raised her eyebrow in question.

"Give me the words," he commanded.

He was so big, so tough. His battle-scarred body was a testament to his strength and determination. His dark hair framed his face—the broad forehead, slightly crooked nose and stubborn jaw. His lips were full and sinful and very talented.

A shiver skated down her spine and she licked her lips. His deep brown eyes followed the motion of her tongue, his chest expanding with each breath he took.

He braced his legs slightly apart. The denim of his jeans hugged the thick muscles and curved lovingly around his erection. She wanted to touch him, taste him.

"The words, Meredith," he growled.

She realized he'd meant what he'd said. It was her choice. Unless she asked him to mate with her, he would walk away.

She felt lighter than she had in years. Like a young female tempting and enticing her chosen mate. And he was her choice. Unlike her first mating, this was about what she wanted.

Isaiah was a male with honor. He was stubborn and possessed a deep streak of protectiveness, which would probably drive her crazy on occasion. But she wouldn't change anything about him. He was perfect for her just as he was.

"I love you, Isaiah. Mate with me. Share my pack."

He didn't move, didn't twitch. His eyes narrowed and his nostrils flared. Then he pounced. He moved so fast she had no time to react. She was in his arms and he was barreling toward the bedroom.

The door slammed shut and the bed was in front of her. He

lowered her, starting to strip off her clothing before her feet had barely hit the floor.

"I've got to have you naked," he gritted out from between clenched teeth. His desperation was infectious, and she jerked at his shirt. She needed to see his bare flesh.

They both tugged and pulled. Fabric ripped and then the cool air hit her skin. They were both naked from the waist up. Isaiah gave a low growl, dipped his head and captured one of her straining nipples between his lips. His tongue curled around the bud before he suckled.

Meredith moaned, sliding her fingers through his hair, her nails digging into his scalp. The heat from his mouth migrated from her breast to the rest of her body. Her slick inner channel pulsed and cream slid over the folds of her sex, coating her, readying her for his penetration.

It was all happening so fast, yet not fast enough. She trailed her hands down his shoulders, feeling the strength that resided in him. And she knew without a doubt that he'd always use that strength to protect her. It was a heady feeling.

Isaiah scraped his teeth lightly over her nipple before pulling away and blowing on the damp tip. She gasped and shivered. Her body felt alive, sensitized like never before.

If she wasn't careful, he'd have her facedown on the bed and be mounting her before she got her chance to touch him. Not happening. Not this time.

She stepped back and reached for the waistband of his jeans. Somehow the button had already come undone. She reached for the zipper. The rasp of the metal being lowered seemed unusually loud. Isaiah didn't stop her, but every muscle in his body tensed as his erection popped free into her waiting hand.

He was thick and large and quintessentially male. Bluish

veins ran up and down the length of his shaft, pulsing like a heartbeat. The flared plum-shaped head was much darker, almost reddish in color. A pearly bead of fluid seeped from the tip.

Meredith licked her lips. She had to taste him. She went to her knees in front of him. He growled her name, his fingers tangling in her long hair. He tugged until she was looking up at him.

His penis was mere inches from her mouth.

"You don't have to do this." His tone was harsh, but his eyes were gleaming with lust.

She flicked out her tongue and lapped at the liquid leaking from the slit. He was salty and musky and warm. "I know."

Isaiah groaned as she shoved his jeans down his hips and thighs. He toed off his sneakers and kicked his pants away. Naked, he towered over her.

God, she loved his body. She ran her gaze over him, stopping when she hit the stitches on his thigh. She'd forgotten he'd been shot. How had she forgotten that? Then there was the cut on his chest and the slashes on his shoulder. They were already starting to heal, but were still red and raw.

She must have made a small sound of distress because he took her face in his hands and gently caressed it. "Hey. It's okay. Just a graze." He dropped his hands, wrapping one of them around his cock. "This hurts more."

She laughed and shook her head. He wouldn't admit if he were hurting or not. "I'll be gentle," she promised.

"Not too gentle, I hope." He smiled at her and her heart almost stopped. He looked relaxed. More than that, he looked happy. She'd given him that.

"Meredith." She could hear a tinge of frustration in his tone and smiled.

"In a hurry, are you?" She closed her fingers around the base of his shaft and squeezed. The veins pulsed against her palm.

In reply, he tugged her mouth closer to the head of his cock. Meredith teased the tip with her tongue. She lapped and twirled and flicked. He grew larger, his shaft throbbing now.

He swore and brushed the top of his penis against her lips, urging her to hurry. Without warning, she opened her mouth and took him as deep as she could. He groaned, his hips jerking, driving his erection deeper.

She gagged slightly and he eased back immediately. He started to pull away, but she dug her nails into his butt, keeping him where she wanted him. Pulling back, she released him. "I'm okay. Just took me by surprise. It's been a very long time since I did this."

His eyes glowed, but he still looked concerned. He smoothed her hair away from her face. "If you're sure."

Even now, he was concerned for her. Love burst inside her, shimmering around her like a rainbow, painting the world in a beautiful light.

She leaned forward and took him into her mouth once again. She used her tongue and teeth to tease his shaft as she moved her mouth up and down his hard length.

The skin covering his shaft was so soft. But what was underneath was pure steel. She savored the taste of him. The way the thick hair of his groin tickled her nose and fingers. She kept one hand twined around the base of his penis, pumping in rhythm to the action of her mouth.

Using her free hand, she gently raked her fingernails over his balls. He groaned and tugged on her. "Stop. Meredith," he gasped. "You have to stop. I want to be inside you when I come."

She wanted that too. She didn't want to waste another minute without being mated to Isaiah.

Releasing his shaft with a wet pop, she sat back on her heels. He reached down and dragged her to her feet, all but tossing her onto the bed. She laughed as happiness bubbled over inside her.

Isaiah grinned as he flicked open her jeans and dragged them down her legs. Her right shoe went flying but her left one tangled in the fabric of her pants. He swore and tugged until it came free. She didn't wait for him, but pulled her panties over her thighs and tossed them away.

"Let me look at you." The reverence in his voice brought tears to her eyes. He crawled on the bed beside her. His eyes flowed over her, pausing at her breasts and the juncture of her thighs. Her breasts swelled, nipples puckering. Her slick channel spasmed.

"I can smell you. So sweet and hot."

He cupped her breasts in his hands. His thumbs flicked over the swollen tips sending a flash of heat down between her thighs. She moaned and arched her hips.

His cock stood out proudly in front of him, eagerly proclaiming how much he wanted her. It was a heady feeling.

Isaiah smoothed his hands over her ribcage and around her waist. "You're so tall, sometimes I forget how much smaller you are than me." He shifted lower so he could cup her hips. He raked his teeth over her hipbones. Goose bumps broke out all over her body, skating over her legs and arms.

"Isaiah," she moaned as he knelt between her legs and used his broad shoulders to push them wide.

"Hmm," he answered. He settled on the mattress, his

mouth mere inches from her core. "You have such a sweet pussy." He lapped at one side of her labia. "So hot." He licked the other side. "So juicy." His tongue flicked against her clit.

Her hips rose up to meet him, but he continued to tease her mercilessly. She dug one heel into the mattress, pushing upward. The other foot thumped against his back, urging him to hurry.

As if sensing how close she was, he eased two thick fingers past the opening to her channel and pushed. He stretched her sheath in such a delicious way. Her inner muscles rippled around him as his fingers withdrew and then advanced.

Her scalp tingled and her toes curled. Sweat coated her skin and she panted hard, trying to catch her breath. "Isaiah," she gasped. She loved saying his name, knowing he would soon belong to her forever.

"Come for me, Meredith." It was part command, part plea. She couldn't deny either. Her sheath rippled. Then she exploded with a strangled cry.

Hips bucking, she clung to him. He rode the storm out with her, keeping her safe, bringing her down slowly. When it was over, she sighed and relaxed, letting her body sink into the mattress.

Isaiah, however, had other ideas.

He moved swiftly, flipping her onto her stomach and pulling her hips back toward him. In spite of her resolve, she tensed. Her blood pounded in her ears and her heart raced.

Isaiah stilled. "Meredith?"

This was what she wanted, what she needed. Finding renewed strength with the adrenaline coursing through her veins, she pushed up on her hands and thrust her bottom toward him. "Claim me. Make me yours."

His hands were gentle as he held her hips. She knew he was letting her know she could move away at any time. Love for him swelled up within her. Isaiah was a male like no other. Willing to forgo his own pleasure, to give up what he wanted, for her.

The broad head of his penis nudged at her opening. She sucked in a breath as he pushed past the constricted muscles, nestling just inside.

"Please," she moaned. She had to get him inside her. Her body was crying out for him. Her channel was wet and aching.

His fingers dug into her hips and he surged inward, not stopping until he was buried to the hilt. He stilled and she could hear his heavy breathing. It matched her own.

Her inner muscles gripped his cock, squeezing and releasing it over and over.

He swore. "I'm going to come without even moving."

Pride filled her. She affected him as deeply as he did her. In this, they were equals. This time she squeezed him on purpose. He leaned down, his large body curling around hers, and nipped the curve of her neck. The slight sting was an erotic caress. She leaned forward, rubbing her swollen nipples against the sheets.

Breathing was getting harder with each passing second, and she didn't care. Breathing was overrated. The pleasure coursing through her was more necessary, more vital to her.

Isaiah reached around her and cupped her breasts in his hands. Then he began to move. Short, hard jabs that stimulated all the nerve endings in her slick channel.

He seemed to grow larger inside her and she knew he was close. She arched against him, bucking her hips, trying to get closer.

He tugged lightly on her nipples one final time. He banded one arm around her waist and slid the other hand between her thighs, teasing the nub of nerves at the apex.

Meredith whimpered and moaned, crying out as he thrust into her over and over. His fingers stroked her clit. His arm tightened around her, holding her steady while he pounded into her.

She felt him swell, felt the rush of heat. His shaft pulsed. He filled her, stretching her sheath. Throwing back her head, she came in a burst of pleasure. Light flashed behind her eyelids. She splintered apart, her body no longer her own.

Isaiah's shaft locked inside her and she knew it would be a while before he would be able to pull away from her. It was done. He was her mate. His bonding scent would be on her now. She sniffed, smelling the slightly musky, woodsy scent. Isaiah.

Slumping forward, she let her face fall into her pillow. Her back end was held up by Isaiah. Eventually, he collapsed, his body half on, half off hers, his cock still buried deep within her.

Exhaustion pulled at her. She shivered, the sweat from her body beginning to cool. Isaiah reached out one long arm and managed to snag one end of the comforter, tugging it over them.

She must have dozed for a moment or two, but woke as Isaiah withdrew from her. She bit her bottom lip to keep from protesting. He threw his thick, muscled arm around her waist and pulled her into the curve of his large body. "Sleep," he whispered.

Content in a way she'd never felt in her life, she did.

Isaiah lay awake watching Meredith sleep. She was on her back and he was propped up on one arm beside her. She was so beautiful. Her long, black hair flowed over the light green sheets. Her skin was soft and pale, except where it had been rubbed red by the stubble of his beard. It would fade in a matter of an hour or so due to the fast healing that was part of her werewolf heritage. Still, he'd have to watch that in the future. For now, it represented another way he'd marked her as his.

Meredith was much more than just a stunning woman. She was smart and strong and stubborn. The fact that she'd kept her small pack safe all these years was a testament to her ability to adapt and to strategize.

Now she was his. And he was hers.

For the first time in years, maybe even in his life, he felt as though he belonged.

She'd given him that.

Meredith shifted slightly in her sleep, her lips parting on a sigh. His body tensed, his cock swelling. The claiming should have drained him, but he was more than ready to take her again. He didn't think he'd ever get enough of her.

Thankfully, he had about four hundred years to sate himself.

He smiled as she snuggled her butt against his erection, seeking him out even in sleep. The only thing keeping him from waking her to make love again was the fact that she was exhausted. Her health and well-being came ahead of everything, even his wants.

He could wait now that he'd claimed her.

Isaiah closed his eyes and breathed deep. The scent of sex permeated the room. The mixture of her sweetness was now tinged with his more earthy scents. The two had become one.

He opened his eyes to find her staring up at him. Her gaze softened and her lips parted on a smile. "Hey."

He leaned down and kissed her, a slow, leisurely caress that went on for long minutes. He traced his tongue over her bottom lip, then the top, before sliding in to reclaim his territory.

They were both breathless when he pulled back.

Her eyes were sultry and inviting. "Now that's a morning greeting I could get used to."

"Get used to it," he told her. He wasn't going anywhere.

He hated to do anything to ruin the closeness of the moment, but there were things they needed to discuss. "We need to talk."

She frowned and dragged the comforter closer to her chin. "Okay."

Isaiah swore and sat up, leaning against the headboard. He reached out and dragged Meredith into his arms, needing to feel her skin against his.

She gave a slight squeak of surprise before settling in his arms. "What is it?" She paused and her voice became small. "Regrets?"

Shock filled him. "Hell, no." He shook her slightly as he stared down at her. "You're everything to me. Everything. My heart and soul. Don't ever doubt that."

She nodded. "Okay." She moved her hands over his chest, soothing him. "What is it then?"

"Thanks to Damek, you should be safe from the hunters and rogue werewolves. Should being the operative word. Do you want to stay here?"

"Do you think it's safe?"

It warmed his heart that she wanted his opinion before making a decision. She'd been alpha of this pack for years and now she had to share that position with him. In time, he knew the members would look to him first and her second. It was simply the way of things. She knew it too, but still she'd accepted him.

"I think there's a risk. But there's a risk anywhere today. Hunters are everywhere, especially with technology to help link them. The only good thing is those bastards are not very trusting, not even with each other. We'll have to keep a watch for a while to make certain that Damek's plan worked. Hopefully the purist group and the bounty hunters are too busy fighting one another to be a problem for us."

"I want to stay. Chicago is home. Haven is home."

"You know you can't stay here forever," he added gently. They'd already been here over a decade. People would soon start to wonder, to ask questions about why none of them seemed to age.

She nodded, her cheek brushing against his shoulder. "I know. People will start talking. Asking why we don't seem to change. I figure we have another five to ten years before that time comes."

"I want to take you to meet my family." He ran his fingers up and down her arm from shoulder to wrist, loving how soft it felt.

She tensed and then relaxed. "I think I'd like that." She glanced up at him, her expression tense. "Your alpha will welcome my children? All of them?"

Isaiah grinned and nodded. "Oh, yeah. Considering his daughter is a half-breed and she's married to my brother." At her incredulous look, he continued. "Alexandra Riley, now Striker, is married to Joshua. Her father, James LeVeau Riley is the alpha of the Wolf Creek Pack. Not everyone will welcome you with open arms, but most will. And those who won't will keep their mouths shut or face the wrath of the alpha and the Striker family."

Meredith's eyes twinkled with laughter. "I guess that's a definite yes then. I'd love to meet your family."

"Maybe you might even think about building a home on pack land. Something we can get away to every now and again. The kids can use it too."

Meredith stared up at Isaiah, hearing the hope in his voice. He was giving up so much for her. She wanted to meet him halfway. "If things work out okay with your alpha and the pack, we could think about building a vacation home there."

"What about your former pack?" he questioned.

She took a deep breath and laid everything out for him. They were mated now. There could be no secrets between them. "You know about my marriage." He nodded and she continued, letting out the entire story of how her alpha had wanted to force another mating on her and how she'd taken her children and run, picking up more children along the way. "They are an extreme pack who won't accept half-breeds. They'd accept Benjamin and Michael easily, but they'll kill me for taking them and running, and the others simply for not being pure werewolves."

"Over my dead body," he growled. "No one touches my family and lives."

She shivered over the certainty in his voice and knew that he would protect them with everything that he was. "If they find us here we'll have to run."

He nodded. "If they find us, we'll seek refuge with the Wolf Creek Pack. They won't risk all-out war." He shrugged. "And if they do, they'll regret it."

Meredith was beginning to understand the enormity of what Isaiah offered her and her small pack. He came with some powerful allies, including that very scary vampire.

"Don't worry about Damek. He a mean, tough bastard, but he's got a code of honor. Not one that I've ever figured out, but it's there. And he considers us, not exactly friends, but certainly not enemies."

It took her a second to realize that Isaiah had tapped into her thoughts, using the unique communication that existed between mated pairs. It had been so long since she'd experienced it, she'd forgotten how intimate it could be.

She'd built walls between her and her first husband. Ones he hadn't even known existed. But she didn't want to do that between her and Isaiah.

I love you.

His arms tightened around her.

I love you too.

Isaiah lowered her to the bed and rolled until he covered her. His erection pressed against her stomach.

"Again?" She rubbed her hands over his wide chest, teasing his flat nipples with her fingers.

"Again," he growled, burying his face in the curve of her shoulder and biting down gently. Her core clenched and her breasts swelled. She wanted him. Now.

He nuzzled and licked away the slight sting as he worked his way to her ear, his voice a hot whisper that left her breathless. "Again and again and again."

Epilogue

Life had been a whirlwind of activity the past ten days. The damage to the club had been repaired and they'd done some needed renovations to the place as well since they were closed anyway.

Isaiah had integrated himself easily into the pack, taking control without ruffling too much fur. Both her sons looked to him for direction. It had taken the other four a little longer to trust him fully. But he was endlessly patient with all of them.

Now they were in North Carolina at Wolf Creek and she was about to meet his alpha and his family. Her children stood behind them and she could sense their tension. They'd never been around so many pureblooded werewolves before. At least not ones who didn't want to kill them.

The compound was situated in the midst of a dense forest, accessible only by truck, and that's only if you knew where you were going. The road was well hidden for the protection of the pack. A large wooden fence surrounded the small cluster of homes. With the rough mountain terrain behind them, they were well fortified.

Isaiah had told her that most of the pack was spread out over their land. Many were artisans and craftspeople. Others grew organic produce, selling it to local restaurants. They lived simply, keeping a low profile and protecting the pack from the outside world.

A shiver went down her spine and she glanced over her shoulder, not only to check on the rest of her pack, but to make certain the gates to the compound were still wide open in case they needed to make a run for it. Not that she expected to have to, but it was better to be safe than sorry.

"Everything will be fine."

She realized she'd almost come to a complete stop. Meredith peered up at Isaiah and smiled. "I trust you."

A look of pure male satisfaction crossed his face and he turned to watch a tall man exit the largest home. This must be the alpha, James Riley. He was a few inches shorter than Isaiah but that in no way diminished the aura of pure power rolling off him in waves. His hair was brown, but was silvering at the sides. It was a sign of his maturity. His golden-brown eyes were piercing as he studied all of them.

Meredith straightened, throwing her shoulders back and meeting his gaze. Maybe it wasn't the right thing to do, but it was what she had to do. He was an alpha, but so was she. His pack was larger than hers, but that didn't mean the responsibilities weren't the same.

James sauntered down the steps and walked toward them, his gait measured and steady. She sensed other wolves around them, but knew none of them would acknowledge them until the alpha did.

Several large males hovered off to the side. Waiting. Watching.

The tension grew as James stopped about five feet in front of them. "Welcome home, Isaiah."

Isaiah nodded, acknowledging the greeting. "I bring greetings from the Haven pack out of Chicago."

Meredith jerked slightly, but kept her composure. She'd never given her pack a formal name. Really hadn't considered it. But it sounded right. And it gave them more status.

Isaiah's arm came around her as he pulled her close to his side. "This is my mate, Meredith Striker."

She could feel heat creeping up her cheeks. In spite of the fact that she'd willingly mated with Isaiah, it was still weird getting used to being called Striker instead of Cross. She could have kept her own name, but knew that her taking Isaiah's name meant so much to him. In spite of his stalwart outward appearance, he had insecurities just as she did.

She held out her hand. "It's a pleasure to meet you, Mr. Riley."

His hand engulfed hers as he shook it. "Please, call me James. Welcome to Wolf Creek."

Meredith turned to her pack. "I'd like to introduce you to my children."

They stepped forward as she called their names, inclining their heads slightly as James acknowledged them. She watched for any indication that he would treat Kevin, Teague, Neema or Hank differently from the rest of them, but he greeted them all the same.

When the formal introduction was done, four males stepped from the shadows and a female stepped out from the open doorway of one of the smaller homes. She recognized the male who went to greet the female. It was Joshua, Isaiah's brother. The woman must be his mate, Alexandra. She was a tall female with short, glossy brown hair and silvery gray eyes. Her lanky build and coloring was similar to her father.

The other three men looked incredibly familiar. Isaiah was an older, more rugged version. These males had to be his brothers.

They came toward them as a group, stopping just behind James. Alexandra broke rank and hurried toward her. "You must be Meredith. I'm so glad to meet you." The younger woman opened her arms and hugged Meredith, taking her off-guard.

She returned the hug, truly touched by the warm welcome.

"Call me Alex. I know we're going to be good friends. After all, we have a lot in common." She glanced over her shoulder and grinned at her mate, who smiled indulgently at her.

Alex continued to greet the rest of the pack, putting them at ease. Before long, Meredith found herself ensconced in a comfortable chair in a fairly large living room. Food and drink were abundant as the two families chatted and got to know one another.

She could put names to all his brothers now. Micah was tall with medium brown hair and chocolate colored eyes. Levi looked exactly like him, except he was the somber one of the twins. Simon was the youngest of the Striker brothers. His hair was black and he was a serious soul. He was chatting with Hank and his voice had almost a musical quality about it.

"How are you doing?" Isaiah perched on the arm of her chair and touched his hand to her head, smoothing down her hair. He hadn't been more than five feet from her side since they arrived.

"I'm good."

"Simon is bunking with the twins tonight and giving up his house for us. Michael and Benjamin are going to stay with them at Levi and Micah's place, but I thought you'd feel more comfortable having the other four with us."

Isaiah was so thoughtful, always thinking about what she wanted or needed. "Thank you."

"You're welcome." His gaze heated and she felt a familiar

warmth fill her. He only had to look at her and she wanted him. It had been that way from the beginning and she didn't expect it to change any time soon, if ever.

"In fact, I think you're tired after the long drive."

"But we stopped at a motel last night and finished the drive this morning." She knew what he wanted, but couldn't resist teasing him.

His eyes darkened and he slid his arm over her back. "I insist. As your mate it's my job to look after your health."

She forced a fake yawn, hiding her smile behind her hand. "Well, I am a little tired. A nap might be just what I need."

Isaiah stood and held out his hand. "Meredith needs her rest," he announced to the rest of the room. With that, he scooped her into his arms and strode from the place.

Laughter followed them. Meredith couldn't bring herself to care as he carried her out the door and across the compound to his brother's home. He headed straight for the bedroom, kicking the door closed behind him.

He dropped down on the bed with her in his arms and rolled until she was beneath him. Meredith hooked her arms around his neck and her legs around his waist. Batting her eyelashes, she played with the hair at his nape. "Suddenly I'm not so sleepy anymore."

Isaiah laughed and kissed her. Soon neither of them was laughing. The shadows lengthened in the room as the afternoon waned and they loved one another.

Later that night, Isaiah stood at the edge of the woods. He'd already shifted into his wolf form. Now he was waiting for his pack to join him. One by one they appeared, also in their lupine forms. Michael and Ben. Teague and Neema. Kevin and Hank.

Still, he waited for the one who mattered most.

Meredith.

She emerged from the darkness, a female wolf, her coat shiny and black. He waited as she padded to his side. *Ready?*

Yes.

He loved being able to communicate like this with her, loved the sensation of belonging with someone, to someone. He hadn't realized how lonely he'd been until Meredith had come into his life.

Tipping back his head, he howled long and loud, announcing the presence of his pack and promising swift retribution to any who might think to threaten them.

An answering howl rose from the woods. He recognized his brother. Soon Joshua's voice was joined by others until every Striker brother could be heard. He might have left the Wolf Creek pack, but the bond he shared with his family was unbreakable.

They'd be returning to Chicago in two days. The club had already been closed for far too long. Not that money was an issue. As he'd told Meredith, he had more than enough in investments to keep them all. But he understood and respected the fact that they all wanted to earn their own way. Now that he was there, the others could choose different careers if they wanted, or they could remain at Haven. Either way was fine with him. They would always be a part of the pack.

He nudged the sleek black wolf with his muzzle, whirled around and began to run fast and hard through the woods. She followed him and the rest of the pack joined in. He matched his stride to hers, while keeping an eye on the others.

They ran freely, romping and playing like puppies and Isaiah loved every minute of it. He was proud of his pack and of his mate.

There was a short howl and then his brothers joined them, along with James and Alexandra. Isaiah and James took the lead. Meredith stayed close by his side. He didn't worry about his pack. Not with his brothers here to add their protection.

He glanced over at Meredith. She gave him a wolf grin and let go a little yip. He caught a glimpse of what was in her mind. Naked limbs entwined. Hard thrusts as he took her. He stumbled. Recovering quickly, he began to herd her back toward the compound. He was suddenly in the mood to make love to his mate.

Happiness flowed through Meredith. She hadn't felt this free, this alive since she was a pup. Isaiah ran beside her. Her mate. Her companion. Her lover.

They'd spent the afternoon heating up the sheets, their naked bodies sliding over one another as they'd made love again and again. And still, she wanted him.

She purposely planted some images in her mind and sent them to him. He stumbled and she gave a yip of laughter. Isaiah immediately began edging her toward home. And she knew what was in store when he got her there. She picked up the pace and raced him all the way back.

Back in Chicago, Steve Macmillan swore as he tossed his cell phone down on the table. "We've got werewolves after us. Those mangy mutts were supposed to find and eliminate those stinking half-breeds, not come after us."

"You can't trust a dog not to turn on you." Red Coulter, an old buddy of his father's tapped his pipe against an ashtray. "You ought to know that, boy. Your daddy taught you better than that."

Steve raked his fingers through his blond hair. "I know,

Red. I don't mind taking 'em out if they're easy pickings, but I've got better things to do with my time than chase down some crazy purist wolves hell-bent on revenge. Mitch said that he and Bob must have misunderstood what they'd seen at that club, that there were no werewolves there, half-breed or otherwise. He thinks that what they saw was nothing more than a big fucking dog. Now I've got some powerful werewolves pissed off at us." His fingers clenched into fists. If he had Mitch or Bob close to him, he'd gladly choke them for the mess they were in.

"I've already wasted time and manpower I couldn't afford to lose." The death of several good men in the park raid, men he trusted, still angered him.

"I know." Red gave him an understanding nod. "I know you want that bitch that done killed your pa."

That was an understatement. Steve would kill her when he found her, but not before he made her pay for what she'd done. There were a lot of hunters out there who'd pay good money to fuck a she-wolf. He'd use her to fatten his wallet until there was nothing left to use. Then he'd kill her.

"What did that new guy Quinn say?"

Steve focused on Red. "I'd set him to watching the park. He didn't see a damn thing. It's been quiet at Riley's Garage for weeks too. I think that might be a dead end.

"The wolf pack the boys fought must have just been passing through the city. I've never known a wolf that could stand living in a crowd. Those bloodsucking vampires are another thing altogether." Steve sure as hell didn't want to fight those creatures and left them to the crazy-assed hunters who specialized in vampires.

"Sure enough," Red agreed. "What about those purist werewolves who are on our tail?"

Steve picked up his rifle and loaded it with silver bullets. "I need a new winter coat."

Red laughed at the joke and rose from the table. "Let's get Quinn and my boys and do us some hunting."

He grabbed his gear and followed Red out to the truck. He shut the door of the dingy motel room behind him, eager for the chase. Steve knew it was time to leave Chicago behind and start searching the surrounding states. He had a female to find.

And when he did there would be hell to pay.

He smiled as he tossed his belongings behind the seat, stowed his rifle in the gun rack and climbed into his truck.

Quinn lay on his back, arms stacked behind his head, staring at the ceiling. The mattress sagged and several springs dug into his back. The room stank of stale cigarette smoke. The faucet in the bathroom dripped—a never-ending torture.

He closed his eyes, shutting out the sight of water stains. Unfortunately, there was nothing he could do about the smell or the dripping faucet. It was simply another crappy room in an equally crappy motel.

He didn't have a book to read. Nor did he have his wood carving tools. Nothing to pass the time. Like the rest of his life, everything was packed away. Waiting.

All he could do was lie here and think. Remember.

He'd been doing this for a year and it was starting to eat at his soul.

Was it worth it?

His pale blue eyes snapped open and he rolled over and sat on the side of the bed. "Hell, yes," he muttered. If it took another year or ten, he wasn't stopping. Not until he found—

The ringing of his phone rudely interrupted his thoughts. He glanced at the call display. He thumbed the talk button and held the phone to his ear. "Yeah?"

"We're moving out." Macmillan didn't bother to identify himself. He rarely did. "We're heading to Kentucky." He rattled off the meeting point and hung up.

Quinn stared at his phone. It would be so easy just to walk away from all of this. His duffle bag contained a few changes of clothing and weapons. He had no ID, nothing that could trace him to his old life.

He raked his hand through his shoulder-length hair and stood. "Not today."

He shouldered his duffle and left the room, closing the door softly behind him. He would find out what happened to his twin if it was the last thing he did.

About the Author

To learn more about N.J. Walters, please visit www.njwalters.com. Send an email to N.J. Walters at nj@njwalters.com or join her Yahoo! group to join in the fun with other readers as well as N.J. http://groups.yahoo.com/group/awakeningdesires

The truth will set her free...or get her killed.

Alexandra's Legacy
© 2009 N.J. Walters

Alexandra Riley's day starts out like any other in her normal, predictable world. Then a tall, dark stranger bursts into her father's garage and shatters the illusion. In one shocking moment, she discovers why she's been feeling hot, restless—she's the half-breed daughter of a legendary werewolf and is a much-sought-after prize.

Joshua Striker, enforcer in charge of protecting the alphas of the Wolf Creek pack, has come to take Alex home. Nothing more, nothing less. From the first moment he sees her, she becomes the one thing he can't afford—a distraction from his duty. A weakness he doesn't want—but can't resist needing.

If only keeping her safe was as simple as fending off males on the hunt for a mate. Through city streets to the mountains of North Carolina, Alex and Joshua have to evade those who don't want their pure bloodlines tainted with human DNA, as well as bounty hunters who think the only good werewolf is a dead one.

What Joshua and Alex can't outrun is the passion that flares between them—or the choice Alex must eventually face. Whether to claim her inner wolf, or forfeit her chance to claim Joshua as her own.

Warning: This book contains sexy werewolves, rogue werewolves, nasty bounty hunters, a mysterious vampire and plenty of hot sexual interludes that will raise your blood pressure.

Available now in ebook and print from Samhain Publishing.

This second chance at love could get them both killed.

Cry Wolf
© *2010 Donica Covey*

Fifteen years ago, denied the only woman he ever wanted as a mate, Remington Aldrich packed his few belongings and left home without a backward glance. Now the pack leader who ripped his world apart is on the other end of the phone, asking for his help.

Angela Martin, Remy's first love, is missing and the trail has gone cold. She may have refused to defy the alpha and run away with him all those years ago, but Remy can't stop himself from coming to her rescue.

Abducted by two men—one for his ghastly scientific experiments, and the other for his driving need for revenge against all Lycans—Angela despairs that no one will find her. Then she senses Remy nearby.

Together again and on the run from a killer bent on hunting them down, Remy vows to never again let Angela out of his arms. But first they have to survive—and fight against history's tendency to repeat itself…

Warning: Hot shape shifters, mad scientists and vengeful hunters, and steamy alpha marking his mate may induce a massive adrenaline rush.

Available now in ebook print from Samhain Publishing.

HOT STUFF

Discover Samhain!

THE HOTTEST NEW PUBLISHER ON THE PLANET

Romance, fantasy, mystery, thriller, mainstream and more—Samhain has more selection, hotter authors, and everything's available in ebook.

Pick your favorite, sit back, and enjoy the ride! Hot stuff indeed.

WWW.SAMHAINPUBLISHING.COM

GREAT CHEAP FUN

Discover eBooks!

THE FASTEST WAY TO GET THE HOTTEST NAMES

Get your favorite authors on your favorite reader, long before they're out in print! Ebooks from Samhain go wherever you go, and work with whatever you carry—Palm, PDF, Mobi, Kindle, nook, and more.

WWW.SAMHAINPUBLISHING.COM

CPSIA information can be obtained at www.ICGtesting.com
Printed in the USA
LVOW122032020112
262082LV00001B/118/P